THE TWO BROTHERS KNIGHTS OF THE RUSHING WIND

Battle at Rose Shar'On

L. Meurell Ball

Copyright © 2018 L. Meurell Ball
All rights reserved.

FOREWARD

*To all those who face real adversaries and challenges (dragons)
in their lives...*

*"Be strong and of good courage; do not be afraid, nor be dismayed for
the Lord your God is with you wherever you go."
Joshua 1:9 NKJV*

*Let not your nightmares deter you from dreaming...
Let not the dragons deter you from winning...*

*"Put on the whole armor of God that you may be able to stand against
the enemy." Ephesians 6:11-12 NKJV*

*"...and trample the dragon underfoot."
Psalm 91:13 NKJV
Romans 16:20 NKJV*

*Be Courageous!
Trumpet the Adventure!*

With Love, LaTasha

PREFACE

Saint Maurice, also known as "Mauritius", was an African leader of the legendary Roman Theban Legion of Emperor Maximian Herculius' army in the 3rd century. This legion was comprised mostly of African soldiers who came to Christ. Maurice is referenced in the story a few times because of a personal sacrifice that he made because of his faith. The remembrance of that sacrifice was the catalyst for the creation of the Codes of Chivalry during the Middle Ages. These practices dedicated to honoring the memory of Maurice and the Theban Legion, are traditionally known as the Knight's Codes. Today, we applaud the chivalry of a respectful man who is generous, not selfish and instinctively helpful. These values reflect back to an age when Knights lived for the specific code of honor, bravery, loyalty, and protection of the weak.

"Learn to do what is right! Promote justice! Give the oppressed reason to celebrate! Take up the cause of the orphan! Defend the rights of the widow!"

Isaiah 1:17

I dedicate this novel to my two sons, Letete and Lucas. Both of you listened to this story with anticipation as children. Years ago, as homeschooled children, stories and classical literature were a key part of your experience. I am thankful to the Lord that you have grown into Godly young men. You challenged me once as little ones with the declaration, "Daddy, tell us a story!" You were the inspiration for this tale that began the evening of that declaration, taking two years every bedtime to tell. I thank my beautiful wife LaTasha for inspiring me to write it down after years of telling a bedtime story that I hoped would teach our young men to trust God, never be afraid and never run from a challenge. I love you all dearly.

You have nothing to fear from the enemy of this world for greater is He that is within you than he that is in this world.

"...for the weapons of our warfare are not human weapons, but are made powerful by God for tearing down strongholds."
2 Corinthians 10:4

You are His Knights!
Trumpet the Adventure!

ONE

The Wishing Well

A lonely grey van appears at the top of a hill at the open end of La Verde Valley. The south end of the valley is where the town of Johnson Parish sits. The vehicle drives steadily toward a small obscure office at the hill's base. The van, dusty and a little worn for wear, slowly begins to turn off the main State Highway. It is reflecting an image as a heat mirage cast at the bottom of the hill. The brakes of the van, as it comes to a stop, protest with squeaks and squeals. The vehicle creates a dust cloud as it comes to a pause in front of a small flamingo pink building. Inside the van, four weary travelers begin to move and bustle about, stretching their stiff limbs. The band of four starts releasing sighs and moans as they prepare to exit.

"Well everyone, this is it! We are almost at our place of new beginnings!" The father says with great enthusiasm.

"Once we meet with the realtor, she'll give us the keys, and we can start settling into our new place." The mother stirs and stretches as she fixes her vision on the building.

"I hope that this office is not a sign of how the house will look? Who paints a building pink anyway?" She says with an edge of sarcasm.

The youngest son, who was asleep, sits up and places his face on the window. He responds to his mother's comment in his unique way.

"It's the culoor of that stumach medicine that you give me when it huurtz. I hate that stuff! Where are we anyway? I hope that this isn't our new house Dawddy!" He says.

The youngest son has a slight lisp that eventually will disappear with time, or that's what his doctor says. This "lisp" adds a particular color to his comments that's endearing. The oldest son, now awake and listening to this banter, responds to his younger brother's question.

"Are you kidding me? Of course, this isn't the new house, dufus! Do you think Dad is stupid? It's pink for crying out loud!"

Lucas looks at his brother and scowls at him, pursing his lower lip.

"I'm not a doofuz!"

"You are a dufus!"

"No, I am not!"

Back and forth the two siblings hurl sharp insults at each other.

"Enough!!" the father intervenes as he speaks with a stern voice.

"Your mother and I are not going to put up with this type of behavior today!"

He takes a deep breath to compose himself. He understands that this has been a difficult transition for his family, so he focuses on being patient with them during the process.

"Look, guys, I know that this is all new and different. I know it is a little scary moving to a new town, a new house. But don't worry. Just think of it as an adventure, okay? Now everyone, let's go inside to find the realtor so that we can get the keys to our castle, our new adventure!"

The mom with her face in her palm looks at the building with stretched eyes. She shakes her head and ponders a thought to herself as she looks on.

"Sure, a new adventure, though I never really liked pink."

The father exits the van, runs to the passenger side and opens the door for his wife. He pushes the remote button for the rear doors of the cab which in response slide open to free its occupants in the back.

The day is bright and sunny. Hot and dry would be an excellent way to describe it. There is a haze that appears to mingle with everything within view causing the eye to squint, as they adjust to the sun's hot drenching rays.

It is a short jaunt across the gravel driveway to the front door of the Realty office. The father walks behind the boys to keep an eye on any vehicle that might pull into the parking lot. The mother is in front leading the family parade. As she draws near to the front door, she pauses anticipating the usual chivalry of her husband as he steps past her and the boys to open the door. He places his hand slightly on the small of her back in a gesture for her to enter first, then he motions for the boys to follow. As the father opens the second door just beyond a smaller vestibule, there is a little hanging door chime that jangles, and clanks more than it chimes as they enter the second door. As the door closes behind them, they continue into a small waiting area. The walls are pale white and yellow with pictures of houses. There is a gallery of cheap paintings, which appear to have survived a neighborhood garage sale. In the room are four small desks with personal items, pictures and the clutter of paperwork.

Seated in the far corner of the office is an older woman in a pink dress with a white pearl necklace draping her neck. She is fair-skinned and appears very tall. Her height is given away even seated. Her hair is long and white with a silver hue. That hints at her advanced years, but her face is youthful. In years past, she must have been striking to view. She is wearing white horned rimmed glasses with pink cords dangling behind each ear. Her hair, almost entirely white, extends to her shoulder. She has a name tag that bears the title "Walk Good Reality."

She looks up from a magazine that she is reading with a smile and says, "I will be right whit you in a moment dear, pleeze ave a seat right over there." she says with a strong Caribbean accent.

She is heard speaking to herself softly.

She exclaims, "Now there! De last word in de puzzle. Query? What is a six let' er word fer conflict between two op'osing groups in a wawr?" The older woman chimes.

"Battle!" the father exclaims!

The old woman peers over her horned rimmed glasses staring at the father and winks.

"Cor'ect, Sir! Well done! E'en though me knew de ans'er.

Ow may I 'elp you today Gov'nah?"

The father looks at the old woman with a smile.

"I am here about our house. I'm Mr. Richardson. My family and I relocated here from Florida. I spoke with a Mrs. Bailey and scheduled a time to meet with her this morning. I would assume that would be you, ma'am?"

The older woman replies, "Yes Sir you would assume cor'ect Gov'nah! Hmm, Deh Rich'ardson fam'lee? Pastor Rich'ardson?"

The Pastor, smiling expectantly, replies to the question.

"Yes! The one and only!"

"Meeezz Bailey" but that is a noda stor'ee and yes sir I am she. Welc 'ome to Johnson Paar'ish" she exclaims.

She stands to extend her hand, first to Pastor Richardson, the mother and lastly the two sons. She pauses for a moment and holds her head sideways to get a good look at the boys. She pinches each cheek of the duo who fidget and fuss in response as any boy would do.

"Such fiiine look'eng child'reen!" She rubs them both on the tops of their heads.

"Ow would ya bowt like ah piece of coconut cawndy, if dat is okay wit ya paarentz? I made it me self. Ow bowt a cup of cawf'ee for de paarentz?"

Their mother says that it would be okay, but they had to wait until later to eat them. Both parents decline the offer of coffee. They are too excited and are anxious to see the new place.

"It's a fortuitous hap'ning thawt you, and dis fine look'eng fam'lee should purchase dis prop'er tee, dis house, to turn it into a 'ohm. It's a fine piece of prime re'al estate and has man'ee a "smiling place" located on deh prop'er tee."

The four travelers look on in bewilderment in response to the statement of the old woman.

"Smiling place?" The father asks.

"Naw'tur-e-lee, you will find dem and dem will find you. No need to seek dem, dem will find you sur'lee."

Ms. Bailey turns towards a file cabinet in the corner, topped with a coffee pot and a stack of paper cups. She pulls the top file open and reaches in to pull out a folder with papers inside. She sits back down and begins to talk with the parents.

The father motions to Ms. Bailey and says, "Pardon me Ms. Bailey, boys, could you excuse us for a moment? Can you go to the other side of the office until we finish?"

The father motions with his hand for the boys to move towards the corner of the office.

"Don't go outside!" Their mother exclaims.

"Okay, Mom."

The boys quickly move to the corner of the office. Located in front of a set of four folding chairs is a small, weathered looking, coffee table with old magazines no better looking for ware. The boys begin to shuffle through the pages of the old magazines to see if there is any content that may hold their attention.

About thirty minutes or so has passed. Ms. Bailey, once she has reviewed all of the paperwork expresses a great sigh with a broad smile.

"Okay Pastor Richardson, before ya sign yer fin-awl pay'pers to take oh'ner-ship of yer new 'ohm, do you 'ave any questions?" Ms. Bailey asks.

"No, I don't, but maybe my wife does? Honey, do you have any questions?" He asks softly.

"Well," she says with concern, "I hope that it's not a bother to at least see the property first? I know that this is a gift from the Church, and I am very grateful for such a great gesture, but it's just a little unsettling to move to a new town, into a new house that I have only seen via the internet." The pastor, now looking a little uncomfortable, turns to face his wife and says

"Now honey, we discussed this before, it's a part of the benefits package. It's a chance to have what we've always wanted, our very own home."

Ms. Bailey looks at the pastor's wife with a smile and chuckles loudly.

"Dear, it is not a problem; we're own'lee a min'eets drive to de house. I am sure dat you will 'ave no problem wit signing de pay'pers once ya see dis 'ohm."

"I'm sorry for the inconvenience honey, is it ok?" She asks her husband.

"Of course, it is. If that will make you feel comfortable, no problem at all".

At that moment, someone screams out brashly, "Stop It!"

The Pastor can see that it is the youngest child Lucas.

"No, you stop it!" exclaims Letete, the oldest brother.

The father stands up and quickly walks over to the where the children are sitting and says firmly "Stop it!! What is wrong with you two? You know that you are not supposed to behave this way. Let's go!"

He pauses for a moment and gives the boys a stern scowl that melts into a smile. The father motions to the boys to follow him.

"Okay guys; let's head to the van before you declare war! We're going to see the new house."

He walks the two combatants towards the door and through the vestibule. He tells the boys to wait one second as he reaches into his pocket to get the keys to open the sliding doors to the van.

"Once the doors are open, on my signal quickly get inside."

The father looks to see if any vehicles are pulling in.

"Go!" He says.

The two brothers' dart towards the open side doors, kicking gravel in every direction, making loud crunchy sounds with each step. The father stands at the door holding it open for the two women to exit.

"Boys are always full of fie'are. I love dat about dem two." Ms. Bailey says with her accented flair.

"Fire, that's what they call it these days huh?" Pastor Richardson says with a chuckle.

Ms. Bailey responds." Yes, fie'are dear'ee. Now let us go ta see your new ohm."

The expanded caravan begins to form as the two cars head towards the church parsonage.

"I don't see another car; Ms. Bailey would you like to ride with us in the van?" Asks the father.

"No, that's not necessary, meh car iz parked en da bawk of da office 'ere. I will pull it ar'ound da front, and yuh can follow meh to da 'ouse."

The father nods in agreement and loads everyone into the van. As the father backs out to position the vehicle towards the highway, he notices a faded, pink convertible pulling from around the back of the building.

"Wow!" the father says.

"She is consistent with that pink theme, isn't she?"

The mother looks on as the four-wheeled pink ornament pulls out in front of them.

"Honey, maybe we can ask Ms. Bailey if she can set us up with her car contact so that you can have your very own pink convertible."

The Pastor asks his wife. She instantly begins shaking her head in response.

"Nooo, Nooo, uh aaah. Not going to happen. She looks like a birthday cake or should I say a "bert" day cake mon."

Everyone in the van laughs out loud in response to the mother's "mock" accent.

"That was pretty good mom," Lucas says.

"Pink is not my color of choice."

"From a business standpoint, it really stands out." The father says as he pulls the van out to follow Ms. Bailey towards the house.

They travel northward on the state highway, then turn west off the main onto a smaller road that has curves and dips along the way. They pass a moderately sized church en route to the house. It is well manicured, white with a tall steeple and a brass cross positioned at the top that seems to glisten just ever so slightly in the noonday sun. Near the front of the church at the beginning of a stone path that leads from the road, the church signage is located.

The name on the signage reads "The Rose of Sharon Community Church."

The signage, surrounded by varieties of flowers, roses, gardenias others, stands like an adorned herald.

"Rose of Sharon, honey isn't that the name of the church that you will pastor?" The wife asks.

"Yes, it sure is. Nice looking edifice and grounds. To my understanding, the house is not that far away from the church. We should be there soon."

The boys, with their faces pressed against the window of the van, look on as they view new places where they will be spending Sunday mornings and afternoons together as a family. The pink car signals to turn right onto a smaller road that seems to wind and roll under a green canopy covering. The van follows as the car in front disappears over the hill. When the vehicle clears the top of the range, the pink car can be seen turning into a driveway on the right. The father pulls in and parks just to the left Ms. Bailey's vehicle. The father says with anticipation "Okay everyone, here we are, our new home."

He opens the sliding doors to the rear of the van, and the occupants spill out.

"Woooow! The two boys say in unison.

"It has two floors!" They exclaim!

"Dad! Dad! Can we look around the yard?"

He looks at Ms. Bailey who is already near the front door searching for the keys to open it. She nods and says "Itz perf'ectlee safe mon, let dem run ar'ound and make dis place their ohm."

He looks to the kids and nods; they take off like a shot, shouting in excitement. The pastor looks at his wife and says "honey, what do you think?" She stares and looks around in amazement.

"It's not exactly what I thought it would be."

The pastor sighs rubbing one hand on his head, as he looks on with concern.

"It's better than I imagined!" She tells him with a big smile. He grabs her and spins her around.

"Let's go inside!"

They walk up the sidewalk to the front door where Ms. Bailey is standing.

"Come on boys, let's see inside."

The boys scamper up the sidewalk, up the steps and dart past their father. Ms. Bailey takes the family on a full tour of the house. It's an older Victorian style home. Very warm and inviting. It has a study downstairs with bookshelves and a sitting parlor on the opposite side. The kitchen is large and in the eastern corner, there is a breakfast nook with a booth. There is also a dining area adjacent to a great room with a small fireplace. Upstairs are three bedrooms that could comfortably accommodate their needs.

"Okay deerz, ar we red' ee ta sign yer fin-awl pay'pers to take oh'ner-ship of yer new 'ohm?"

Both the pastor and his wife respond in unison, "Yes, yes we are."

After signing the papers, the family walks Ms. Bailey to her car. She gives the pastor and his wife a hug and a smile. She then looks to the boys and says, "Such fiine young men, full of fie'are. Remember deerz to always listen to yer par'entz. Your father will instruct you on ow to become great cedars o Lebonan. Our God en 'eaven sayz dat "de righteous shall floureesh like the palm tree eevon like de Cedars o Lebanon." Be great cedars young men o God." The two boys look at her curiously.

"Cedars? Isn't that a tree?" The older brother says.

"Dawddy, why does she want us to be a tree?" The younger son asks.

"I'll explain it later son."

"Thank you, Ms. Bailey, for all of your help. Maybe you could come to visit us at The Rose of Sharon one Sunday." Ms. Bailey smiles and says, "I would love dat, but de invitation is not needed. I'm already a member der. See you on Sunday Pastor." The father smiles as the pink car pulls out of the driveway.

"Come on everyone, let's go inside and get settled, the movers will be here in a couple of hours."

A few days have passed since the movers arrived. The movers brought a truckload of the past into the Richardson's bright and shiny present. Things are looking up at this moment in their lives. They have seen their share of rough times, but it seems that there is a break in the storm, at least for now.

"Honey," The wife says soothingly to her husband.

"Can you come here in the kitchen for a moment? I need help with this heavy box on the counter."

"Sure! Be right there." He quickly moves to the corner of the kitchen where the box sits flush against the counter wall.

"Whoa! This box is heavier than it looks! What's in here?"

"Oh, it's just some of the dishes from the old place. I'm really excited about the house LB," A term of endearment that she uses for her husband.

"I think that this is just what we needed."

"I agree. I know that things have not been the best between us, but this move to a new place, a new town, a new congregation... I just believe that God will continue to bless us. We just have to continue work on us."

The wife motions to her husband to open the refrigerator door.

"Grab that carafe of orange juice in the fridge."

She reaches into the cabinet and pulls out two glasses. Her husband pours juice into each.

"Here's to us!"

"To us! What's the game plan for today LB?"

"Well, I plan on getting some small supplies for the yard. There's minor work to do, and I want to give you something that you always wanted."

"Wow, a new Mercedes maybe?" She says with a sarcastic grin.

"No baby not quite that, I want to plant a rose garden for you."

"A rose garden? Wow! I have always envisioned myself sitting outside, on my favorite bench and just spending time reading and praying. I guess that it is real. We have our very own house." She says endearingly, like that of a little girl whose playtime game of house now became real.

"More importantly babe is that we have a home."

At that moment, the boys were upstairs unpacking and getting settled into their room. The boy's mother ran up the stairs to inquire about Letete. He has allergies, dust, and peanut to name some, that makes her sometimes overly concerned.

"Letete, are you O.K.? Are you feeling a little tight in your chest? Don't forget that your inhaler is in your coat pocket if you need it."

"Mom, I'm fine! You worry too much."

"I know, I know. It's just that the house is a little dusty that's all."

"I'm fine."

She looks in on the two boys just to make sure.

"O. K.," she says and heads back downstairs.

The room is large and very "boy like" in its appearance. It even had a lived-in boy smell, not anything offensive, just that lived in smell. One wall had paper with prints of footballs, baseballs, and puppies. The other walls were painted a pale blue color with white trim and shelves for enshrining boy things.

"This room is cuuol, isn't it 'Tete?" The younger brother asked the older.

"It sure is. But I wonder why we can't have separate rooms? There's another room just across the hallway that's just as big as this one?" The older brother replied.

"I don't know; maybe Dad is planning to use it for an office or somethin." Says Lucas.

Letete continues saying," Dad has a study downstairs remember, and Mom has a sitting room as well. When I asked Dad about the room, he just said that your Mom and I have plans for it. I think that it's strange. They even locked the door after we moved in. What's that all about?" Lucas just shrugged his shoulders.

"Maybe there's some reeallee cuuol secret thing inside like maybe a cuuol treasure. Do you think Mommy and Daddy could be seecretlee pirates!!! Avast ya lawnd lubbers, aargh!" Letete looks at his brother with a big smirk and replies, "You are such a dufus! Mom and Dad are not pirates; Dad doesn't even have a hook for a hand."

"I'm not a dufus, you take that back or, or...I"

"Or what?!" replies Letete.

"What are you going to do, Captain Dufus of the Pirate ship Dufus!"

The younger brother screams and immediately lunges at his older sibling and in classic NFL linebacker style, He locks and rolls with his brother, off the bed to the floor.

"Knock it off you dufus! Get off me!"

Letete, the larger of the two but not as aggressive pushes his younger brother off of him.

"Take it back now! If you don't take it back, I'll smack ya!"

Letete, after righting himself now standing replies,

"Oooh reeally! I won't take it back! Captain Dufus, Capitan El Dufus! Captaaaainnnn Duuuuufussss!" He laughs and giggles at his mockings.

"That's it! Enufs anuufff!" Shouts Lucas.

He runs across the large room to a plastic footlocker in the corner and kicks it open. Inside are plastic shields and helmets. Their Dad would often read different scriptures to the boys and act out certain aspects related to "putting on God's Armor." The locker is a veritable full armory of swords and play things that tiny spiritual warriors may use. It even has several light swords, red, blue and green, used by the boys and their father to play "Space Knight Wars" during impromptu battles. Lucas reaches in and pulls out two of the sabers.

He tosses a green saber to his brother and pushes the release button on a red saber that he is holding.

"Waaaulllmmmmshhisssh!" The sound the blade makes as it extends telescoping outward from the stocky, short, figure holding the hilt in both hands.

"Pick up yuur weapon! yuung warrior! Let us seee whooo is the true Maawster." Lucas dramatically exclaims.

"I'm not picking up nothin! Don't even think about it."

"Whack!" Lucas delivers a sharp blow to the head in answer to his brother's retort.

"Are you nuts!!!!"

Letete immediately grabs the other saber laying on the bed in front of him. "Waaaulllmmmmshhisssh!" Letete's saber now extended.

"Whack!"

Letete blocks the second blow of the stocky, saber-wielding assailant.

"I'll teach you a lesson you'll never forget! Hit me on the head will you."

"Blah, Blah, Blah!" replies Lucas.

"Talk is cheap, especially yours," Lucas says as he swings wildly and intently at his brother who is frantically blocking each blow.

"Let's take this fight outside."   Shouts Lucas.

Both brothers bound the stairs and scamper out the back door into the backyard.

The father jumps into his old white pickup driven to his new home by a close friend later that week. He heads into town to buy some materials for the yard. He plans on picking up some plants, flowers and other items to finally give his wife something that she always wanted which is a flower garden with a reading bench to sit on. After picking up most of the items from a local garden supply store, the father turns down a narrow, cobblestone road. He figures it's a shortcut back to the main highway. On the way, he notices a wishing well in front of a small shop with a for sale sign taped to the front of the well. The father thinks that the well might be an excellent centerpiece for the flowers he intends to plant. He quickly pulls into the parking space in front of the store. He immediately gets out of his pick-up and walks over to the wooden well sitting in the grass.

"This would be great to set up in the yard. Just don't know exactly where to put it. I don't have much money left." The father thinks out loud.

An older woman opens the door and walks outside to greet the father out front.

"Hello, kind sir. Welcome to my humble establishment. I noticed that you're looking at my well here. Do you think that you may want it?"

"It's available for a great price."

"Well, it would be a great centerpiece for a flower garden I want to plant for my wife. How much are you willing to take to part with it?"

"You want to plant a garden for your wife? That's really nice of you young man. Do you have any children?" The old woman asks.

"Yes, two boys, 8 and 6. Very rambunctious kids but they are great." The old woman smiles brightly and says to the father,

"You know that this is no ordinary well, it's a "wishing well. It would be a great addition to your yard, especially for the boys."

"How much?"

"Well, why don't you take it on consignment? I overheard your conversation with yourself. I understand your concerns. You can take it home and pay me later only if you decide to keep it. If your family likes it, then just pay when you can. Deal?"

The father looks at the well and then the old woman and asks,

"Are you sure that you would trust me to do that? You don't really know me."

The old woman points to a sticker in the back window of the pickup that reads "Pastor."

"You're the new Pastor at the Rose, aren't you?"

The father smiles and replies. "You could be a good detective. Yes, I am. I'm Pastor Richardson."

The old woman starts toward the open door of the store and exclaims, "Then it's settled! Jimmy, come outside and help the Pastor with the well here." She turns back to the Pastor who is now looking again at the well smiling.

"One thing to know about the well Pastor, make sure to place it in a "smiling place" in your yard."

"A smiling place? That's the second time this week that I have heard that phrase. How do I know a smiling place, as you put it, when I see it?" She turns towards the door speaking as she is walking and says,

"It's the place that makes your heart smile when you see it. You will know."

Shortly after Jimmy, a young man that helps the old woman from time to time at the shop, helps the father to secure the well on his truck. The father gives a gentle wave and nod to the shop owner as he heads back toward the main highway on his way home with the wishing well. Pleased with himself, he begins to wonder where a "smiling place" might be in his yard.

The father arrives at the house.

Shortly after backing the truck into the driveway, a car pulls in just as he is getting out. He looks on curiously only to see a tall, freckled face young man walking towards him.

"Jimmy?" The father says.

"Did I forget something at the store?"

"No Pastor, the store owner, Ms. Smith, sent me. She figured you would probably need help getting the well situated and all."

"Oh Jimmy, that wasn't necessary. I could have managed on my own."

"Oh Sir, it's no bother. I brought a small pull-sled and cart. We can make quick work of it. I don't mind helping the "new" Pastor at my church."

"You a member Jimmy?"

"I sure am. So's my family. You just tell me where you want it. Oh, Ms. Smith told me to wait until you find some kinda "smilin' place" o sorts."

"Oh yeah, she did mention that didn't she. Well, I guess I better find that "smilin' place." They both chuckle a little at the statement.

The father begins to walk towards the backyard. He thinks to himself and a thought to pray about the "smiling place" enters his mind.

"Dear Lord in Heaven, give me direction. Show me the place that smiles. A place where prayers will ascend and intimacy with you will take place, In Jesus name. Amen!"

The father opens his eyes and begins to stroll through the backyard. He pauses for a moment as a great breeze picks up. He hears the wind "whistling" through the pines on the back line of the property. He sees a spot just towards the rear of the property with a large tree that is providing a canopy of shade in a certain area. Just at one angle, a patch of light shines through the branch covering, and a beam of light gathers on the ground below. He looks at the spot and smiles.

He hears this verse in his mind, "Blessed are the people that know the joyful sound: they shall walk, O LORD, in the light of your countenance."

"That's it." He says softly.

"That's the "smiling place, Jimmy. Let's get the well and get started."

The two sibling combatants, swords swinging and clacking, run down the stairs and rush through the hallway past their father's study out the back door. They jump from the top landing of the stairs at the back door. Lucas shouts a playful threat,

"I have you nooow! Take thawt!" He swings wildly.

"No, you don't! I have you, Sir Doofus Knight!"

"Heeeey!! That's not fuuuny! Replies Lucas. The two swing, counter, block and perry then suddenly..."Whhooaa! Look at that!" Says Letete. "Whack!" A blow to the head again of the older brother by Lucas.

"Owww! Stop It! I said wait a minute! Look over there!" They both stop to stare at the wishing well in the "smiling place" in the backyard.

TWO

Knights of the Backyard

Pastor Richardson, after setting up the well in the backyard with the flowers, thanks Jimmy for helping him.

"Jimmy thanks for all of your help. I'm looking forward to seeing you and your family on Sunday." The Pastor reaches into his pocket to offer Jimmy a little token for his help.

"No Pastor, that's not necessary. Just pray a blessing for me and the fam'. That's all I need. If you need anything else, just let me know." Jimmy says with a smile and a tip of his weathered baseball hat.

"I will do just that Jimmy. Thanks again."

The Pastor walks up the steps into the house. He can smell the sweet aroma of dinner.

"Mmmm, something smells great!!" He says to his wife who is out of view in the kitchen.

As he walks into the kitchen, He sees his wife cutting and mixing items in preparation for dinner.

"I'm baking a hen in the oven and preparing some veggies to go alongside. It was nice of the church to stock the kitchen with groceries for us fully."

"Yes indeed. The few members that I have met are extremely nice. I can't wait to meet the congregation on Sunday."

He asks his wife if there is anything that he could do to help her. She insists that he takes a seat and relax. She pours him a cold glass of freshly squeezed lemonade as he sits at the booth in the corner of the kitchen.

"How do you think the boys are adjusting to their new surroundings?" Asks the Pastor.

"They seem fine. I know that the boys love the house and the large backyard. I happened to notice them a minute ago playing out back."

"Have you gone out back yet?"

"No. Not yet. Why do you ask?"

The husband smiles at her and says, "The garden is almost finished. I want you to wait to see the finished product before going out back, O.K.?"

"Sure!"

The husband looks at his wife as she is preparing the meal for the evening. He watches her mixing cornbread batter in a bowl as she is softly humming to herself. She smiles at him as she glances and makes eye contact. He can smell the aromas of spices and roasting meat in the air. His mind goes to another scripture from Psalm 34:7-9,

"The angel of the Lord encampeth round about them that fear him, and delivereth them. O taste and see that the Lord is good: blessed is the man that trusteth in him. O fear the Lord, ye his saints: for there is no want to them that fear him."

He says a simple prayer to himself. "Thank you, Lord, for your tremendous blessing. I don't deserve it, but you bless me in spite of that fact. I trust in you o Lord, the one who protects my family and me. With love, Amen."

The two brothers call a temporary truce to investigate the new addition to the backyard.

"This is neat." The older brother says.

"Dad did a good job with the flowers and all. There's a crank on the side connected to this rope hanging in the middle. I think that it's a well." Letete exclaims.

The younger brother climbs the side of the well and leans over the edge to look inside.

"A well? Cuuool. Ya think there's any watawr in it." Lucas asks, his voice echoing slightly, as he leans and looks over the edge.

"I don't think so. I think that it's decoration or somethin," The younger brother sees something in the bottom of the well, something shiny and rectangular.

"I see somethin' in the bottom. I can't reach it."

He stretches to try to reach the shiny mystery item in the bottom of the well.

"Just leave it, for now, let's finish playing. We will have to go inside soon. I have a great idea, let's pretend that this is a rook on a castle that we have to protect from invaders."

Lucas jumps down from the side of the well and replies, "Awesome, let's pretend thawt we are Knights fighting drawgons and other creechuures who are attacking the castle. What are we going to call it?

"I got an idea; let's name it after Dad's Church. I heard him and Mom talking about it in the van on the way here the other day. Let's call it "Castle Rose Sharon." Lucas shakes his head in agreement.

"I like thawt big brother; we'll call ourselves Knights of Shawron." Exclaims Lucas.

"Knights of Sharon, good deal. Knights of Sharon, a call to arms!!" Letete shouts his edict. The two boys raise their swords high in the air.

"To arwms!" cries Lucas. "To awrms!" The two Knights run, dodge and perry with imaginary foes as they race around the wishing well, now christened "The Rose Sharon" by young rulers of the backyard. They run and leap, swinging at low hanging limbs that double for dragon's heads and wings. They imagine the roar of the beasts, the fluttering of leathery wings and fiery flumes of dragon's breath as they raise their shields in mock defense of invisible foes.

"Take that you file beeasts!! And thawt!! And anowther!" Lucas exclaims as only he can in his endearing fashion.

"It's not "file beast" Lucas, its "vile" beast!"

"Thawt's what I said, "file beasts!"

"Still not right!"

"Thawt's it! I hawve hawd it! You must be on the drawgons side! Take thawt!" Lucas swings wildly and lunges at his brother who just barely manages to block the attack with his shield.

"Are you nuts!!!? You almost hit me in the head! Come here!" Lucas takes off in a flash around the well, fleeing his pursuing brother who is closely chasing him swinging his plastic sword just inches from the back of his brother's retreating vestige.

"Drawgon minion! Drawgon minion!" Lucas screams at his brother as he runs the perimeter of the wishing well.

"Who are you calling a Dragon Minion? I'm one of the good guys! Daddy says that Dragons aren't considered as good in the Bible."

"What about Barney?"

"He's a dinosaur! You are such a dufus!" The older brother snaps back.

"Ooh yeaah! Heeeyy, I told you I don't like being called thawt." Lucas stops in his tracks, sliding on the grassy covering around the well. Lucas who began as the pursued has quickly now become the pursuer. He swings wildly at his brother with one hand and throws his plastic shield at him with the other in a Frisbee-like manner. Letete manages to duck the sword lunge of his brother and block the flying projectile with his shield.

"Hahh!! You dropped your shield!! I have you now!! Letete shouts. At that moment as the older brother began to descend on the younger, a loud familiar call was heard from the steps of the back door.

"Booooys!!! Come inside; dinner is ready. Come in so that you can get cleaned up."

Letete looks at his brother, who is frozen in a defensive posture with one knee on the ground, and says, "Boy are you lucky! You better be glad that Mom saved you by calling us in." At that moment Lucas lunges forward from his crouching position and whacks his brother on the right shin with his sword soundly and cleanly.

"OWWWWWW! Heeeyy!!! That wasn't fair!!" Lucas takes off in a dash like a blue and red blur, laughing and giggling, as he bounds the steps leading up to the back door.

"Boy, I am going to let you have it!! A beat down is definitely in your near future."

Letete limps slightly towards the back door murmuring as he climbs the steps.

"Dufus!"

The next morning Pastor Richardson rises early in the morning to make sure that all of the final touches are complete on the well. Just on the east side of the well, in a shaded area in the clearing, he places a wooden bench facing the well. The Pastor plants fragrant flowers around the base making sure to pay attention to every detail. He then reaches into his pocket and pulls out a gold metallic permanent paint pen that he picked up at the art supply store and writes something on the back of the bench. He steps back to survey his handiwork and says softly to himself," That's nice, I think that should do it."

He picks up all of his tools, makes all of the final touches and heads towards the tool shed. After placing everything back in the shed, he bounds towards the back door. He leaps the first two steps and quickly enters the house. He hurries quietly up the stairs to the master bedroom to see if his wife was still asleep. He notices as he opens the door slowly that she is already stirring and beginning to wake. He walks in slowly, the older wooden floors announcing his every step. A squeak here and a creak there. His wife hearing the chorus of footsteps and creeks rolls over to see her husband looking down at her.

"Wow, aren't we an early riser today." She says.

"Good morning sleepy head. Did you sleep well?"

"I slept great! I haven't slept like that in a long time. I like the new house babe. I believe the boys like it as well. I feel that this is a place of new beginnings as you put it. I am thankful to God for this blessing."

"I know that we have had our trials, Lord knows we have, but I believe that this will be a good place for us as a family and as a couple. I am looking forward to meeting the congregation on tomorrow. So far, the few that I have met seem to be very nice. Say, why don't you get freshened up, I will go downstairs and get breakfast started for everyone."

The wife sits up and looks at her husband with a big smile and says, "Wow honey, to what do I owe the pleasure? You're going to cook breakfast for us?" She gives him a gentle kiss on the cheek.

"Yes. I just want to show my appreciation to you and the boys for being so understanding with the move and all. That's the least that I can do. I think that the boys may be stirring, so I better get started on that breakfast. Honey, I want to show you what I have been working on out back. We can look at it after breakfast."

After breakfast, the Pastor and his wife take the time to head out back to see what he has set up for her. He tells her to close her eyes and to lean on him as he holds her arm, walking her safely down the back doorsteps. He guides her to the place where the wishing well sits. Holding her hand gently, he tells her to stop in place.

"Now honey, on the count of three I want you to open your eyes. One, Two, Three!"

She opens her eyes to see the wishing well now flocked with flowers at its base. The sun seems to shine through the clearing of trees illuminating only that spot.

"It's beautiful Honey. So this is what you were working on so diligently. Oooh, look a bench to sit on. It's delightful." She says kindly with a smile.

She notices the golden words scripted on the back of the bench.
"Proverbs 31:10, I see you remember your words from your proposal." She says.

"Of course I do." Who can find a virtuous wife, her value is above rubies." He says with a broad smile.

"Here, honey, sit down. I want you to understand that this is your secret place to commune with God." They both slide closer to one another on the bench. The Pastor places his arms around her and gives her a gentle kiss on the cheek.

"Anything that is in my power through Christ to make you happy. I love you, honey."

"I love you too and thanks." They both sit for a moment on the bench in the clearing; the only sound is the wind whistling through the trees and the songs of birds.

"So honey, are you excited about tomorrow, meeting the new church members?" The wife breaks the silence.

"Yes, yes I am. It's all new and exhilarating to see what God has planned to unfold for us as we meet our new extended family in Christ. I believe that the potential for great things is boundless." The Pastor, as he is holding his wife and discussing the coming day, happens to see something on the side of the well, just behind one of the rose bushes.

"What's this?" He exclaims. He stands and walks to the strange item only to see that it's a plastic shield that belongs to one of his sons.

"I see that our would-be-knights have left a memento of their adventures." He says to his wife as she chuckles and smiles. He turns it over to see emblazoned on the front of the shield one word, "Faith."

"Faith indeed Lord, Faith indeed." He says to himself. His wife, now standing, takes her husband's hand and says "Let's go inside dear, it looks like we may get some rain. We can finish talking inside."

"Yes, it does. I better take this inside. I would not want one of the Knights of the well to be lacking in any part of his armor." They Both chuckle and laugh at his statement. He reaches for the hand of his wife sitting on the bench, just as drops of rain begin to fall. They both start to laugh and giggle like children as the rain falls. They sprint hand in hand towards the steps of the back door. They quickly scale each stair as they clear the landing and close the door behind them.

THREE

A Reason Not to Fear

Later that night after dinner, Latasha is in the kitchen cleaning up. The boys are taking a bath upstairs and getting prepared for bed. LaTasha asks her husband, "Honey, can you run upstairs to check on the boys and make sure that they are not goofing off. I want to make sure that they have a good night's sleep. Tomorrow is the big day and I want everyone to be rested." The Pastor acknowledges her request and quickly ascends the stairs. As he steps on the last landing on the second floor, he sees a brown blur that rushes by him screaming. It was Lucas running in his full glory, his birthday suit and a large red towel dragging behind him.

"What in the world are you doing Lucas?" The Pastor exclaims! Just then another blur rushes by the Pastor. This blur did have some modicum of clothing. It was Letete running behind his younger brother shouting all manors of threats.

"You know that I hate it when you pop me with a towel! I'm going to give you a taste of your own medicine!" Exclaims Letete, holding a white towel by the tips in each hand.

"Letete and Lucas, front and center now! The Pastor says firmly.

"Guys, what are you doing? I came up here because your mother wanted me to check on you because she feared that you two just might be goofing off and not taking a bath. What is going on here?"

"Lucas popped me with a towel when I had my back turned getting ready to take a bath. Ooooohh!!! I don't like it when he does that!" Letete explained to his father.

"Lucas, did you pop your brother with a towel?"

Lucas, now struggling to keep the towel wrapped around him, looking up at his father with a mischievous grin answers, "weeeellll, yes, I guess so. I was just playing. I didn't reeeally mean to pop him so hawwwrd."

The father looked at the two brothers and said, "Look, guys, I don't mind you playing around, that's what kids do. But I need you to be serious sometimes, especially when we tell you to do something or to finish a task. Lucas, apologize to your brother." Lucas, awkwardly attempting to position his towel, turns to his older brother and musters a response.

"Sowrry Letete." He says, with a telltale grin.

"Once you have finished, come on down for dinner. Mom and I will have set the table. We have a big day tomorrow. We will be meeting our new church family.

"Daddy," Lucas says, "I'm a little nervouuus about tomorrow. I haven't been able to sleep thawt well. Can you read a stowry to us? Letete hasn't been sleeping thawt well either, even though he probably won't admit it." Letete looks up at the dad and says, "Dad, I have been sleeping just fine."

The pastor replies, "Letete, Lucas does not fib about things. Are you sure he isn't correct? Is there something that you need to tell me?" Letete looks at his brother then again at his dad.

"Well, Ooo Kaaayy! I haven't been able to sleep that well either. It's just that; you know living in a strange place and all. Everything is different than what we are used to." The father places an arm around the shoulder of each of his sons with concern.

He says, "I thought you guys loved this place? You seem so excited about the new house. I saw the both of you playing in the backyard; you seemed to be having a great deal of fun."

Letete replies," Dad, it's not that we do not have fun, and we do love the house. It's just that it's all new and we have to meet all of those new people. This church is bigger than the last church that we left. I know that it's silly." Their father bends down on one knee and looks at both of his sons.

"Guys, that's not silly at all. You should have said something earlier. How about I spend some time with you guys before I start working on my sermon for tomorrow. I want to remind you of something. I think that this will help you with your sleeping.

Deal!" The father extends his hand to both boys in a gesture to shake in agreement. "Deal!" Both boys say in unison. I'll meet you both downstairs guys for dinner.

After dinner, the father tells the boys that he will meet them upstairs in a minute after he helps their mom with the dishes. She tells him to go ahead and take care of the boys. She can handle the kitchen. "I know that you have to prepare for tomorrow. Go ahead and tuck the boys in." After the kids brush their teeth and prepare for bed, the father tucks them in and begins to talk to them about their concerns.

"Now guys, tell me, what's the matter? Why can't you sleep?" The boys look at each other and then look back at their father. Lucas replies, "Well Daddy, I have had nightmaarez. I can't explain them. It's just that I don't like them." Their father scratches his chin then focuses his gaze on the elder son.

"What about you Letete?"

"I haven't been able to sleep either. It's kinda scary too. I think about the new house and getting used to new things. This house actually creeks at night."

Their father looks at them with concern and compassion.

"I'm sorry to hear that boys. It sounds like you are fearful of some things. I'm quite sure moving to a new city, a new house and shortly a new church home, has to be a little scary. I'm sorry that I didn't get a chance to speak to you earlier. I want you to know and believe that you never have to be afraid, ever. You remember the bible verses that I would read to you?" The boys nod in unison to answer yes to their Dad's question.

"Great!" He replies.

"God does not want you to fear. Remember that His Son, Jesus Christ, tells us in the Bible that He is always with us. Also fellas, in II Timothy 1:7 It says that God has not given us a spirit of fear, but power and of love and a sound mind. He says not to be afraid because He gives you the power not to be. He also gives you a sound mind. What do you think that means?" He asks his two sons.

"That in our minds, we should not worry about things?"

"Yes, that is right. You don't have to worry. This house, your room, the great backyard, all of these things God gave us as a family because He loves us. He also gave us these things so that we can tell others that He loves them as well. I also want to read something for you. You're familiar with it, but I want to start back to reading it to you again. It's from Psalm 91."

Lucas replies, "I like that boook of the Bible Dawddy. It makes me feel good about sleeping at night."

Letete also nods in agreement.

"I like it too! I agree with Lucas; it does help me to sleep too!" Their father pulls his large Bible from under his arm, weathered and tattered from years of reading; he carefully opens the book.

He opens it to Psalm 91 and begins to read the first verse;

*He who dwells in the secret place of the Most High
shall abide under the shadow of the Almighty.
I will say of the Lord, "He is my refuge and my fortress;
My God, in Him I will trust."*

*Surely He shall deliver you from the snare of the fowler
and from the perilous pestilence.*

*He shall cover you with His feathers,
And under His wings you shall take refuge;
His truth shall be your shield and buckler.*

*You shall not be afraid of the terror by night,
Nor of the arrow that flies by day,*

*Nor of the pestilence that walks in darkness,
Nor of the destruction that lays waste at noonday.*

*A thousand may fall at your side,
And ten thousand at your right hand;
But it shall not come near you.*

*Only with your eyes shall you look,
And see the reward of the wicked.*

*Because you have made the Lord, who is my refuge,
Even the Most High, your dwelling place,*

*No evil shall befall you,
Nor shall any plague come near your dwelling;*

*For He shall give His angels charge over you,
To keep you in all your ways.*

In their hands, they shall bear you up,
Lest you dash your foot against a stone.

You shall tread upon the lion and adder:
the young lion and the dragon You shall trample under
feet.

"Because he has set his love upon Me, therefore I will
deliver him; I will set him on high, because he has known
My name.

He shall call upon Me, and I will answer him;
I will be with him in trouble;
I will deliver him and honor him.

With long life, I will satisfy him,
And show him My salvation."

Their father gently closes the Bible, careful not to catch the leaves in a folded position as he closes the book. He looks at the boys sitting up in their beds and says, "Now boys, do you see why you don't have to be afraid? God covers you. He says that he will place you both in a secret place and He will abide or stay with you. He even will give angels assignments to watch over you as you rest. They will keep you safe. He says that he will even give you power over scary things and even give you the strength to trample dragons under your feet."

At that statement, the boys to stare at each other and then back at their father.

"You mean that we could even defeat an actual dragon?" Letete looks on with eyes wide in anticipation of his dad's reply.

His father chuckles as he replies, "with God, son, all things are possible. Usually, in the Bible, a dragon is a symbol of some other threat to men. A dragon is also a symbol of our greatest enemy." Lucas looks at his father and says, "Like the devil? He is our greeaatest enemy, right Daddy?" Nodding again in agreement.

"You are absolutely right Lucas. The good news is that Jesus already gave us the victory through his death and resurrection."

Letete replies, "I will be sure to remember that the next time that we are defending Castle Rose Sharon from dragons."

The father looks at them curiously.

"Castle Rose Sharon? Is that what you call the well in the back? I saw you guys playing in the back the other day."

Lucas replies," We were playing Knights Dawddy. We were fighting dragons and protecting the castle."

Their father replies, "Good, good. I also like the name as well. Now, are you guys convinced as to why you don't have to be afraid?"

The boys respond in unison, "Yes Daddy, we are convinced."

"O.K. let's get you tucked in. We all have a big day tomorrow. And remember, God gave you the power to trample the enemy and angels to keep you. He also gives His love. Good night fellas, I love you both."

"We love you too Daddy, good night."

He kisses both boys on the forehead and walks out the room. He is thinking about his sermon tomorrow and how he has a good head start with an address.

"What better way to address fears." He thinks to himself.

"I can begin with the scriptures that I mentioned to my sons."

He thanks God for His presence. After preparing in his study downstairs, he heads up the stairs to go to sleep. He first looks in on the boys. They are both sound asleep, showing no signs of bad dreams. He closes the door and heads back towards his room. As he enters, he sees his wife sleeping peacefully. She even seems to have a smile on her face. It brings a smile to his face.

He looks down at her and simply says to himself, "Lord I thank you for the gift of family, your love for me gives me no reason to be afraid. With love, Amen."

The next day, the Richardson Family arrives at the church. There is a welcoming committee to greet them. The Deacon board also welcomes them, each Deacon addressing them individually.

They escort the Pastor to his study and give him a set of keys to his new office. Later, that day, he preaches from the subject "A Reason Not to Fear."

Their father talks about how the map makers of ancient times would write a certain phrase on the map that would mark the edges of their known world.

Written on the ancient maps was the phrase "hic sunt dracones!" He says, which translates, "there be dragons here."

He tells the congregation of how men would write this phrase as an expression of fear of the unknown.

"But in Christ, we have no reason to fear; we have the victory! Even if we face a tremendous challenge that grips us in fear, move forward anyway and take courage. Courage is fear that has said its prayers!"

The congregation is receptive to his sermon. They thank him later after the service. After the Benediction, the Pastor greets several people and shakes their hand. He laughs with some of the members and is cordial to most.

"That was a fine sermon Pastor, a mighty fine sermon indeed!" An older woman exclaims.

He thanks her for the affirmation and continues to shake her hand as she begins to head towards the side exit. After the last member has left, the Pastor begins to gather his things with the assistance of his two sons. The Deacon Board attends to the Pastor, assisting him as he prepares to leave. As the Pastor and his family are set to go, one of the Deacons, Deacon Johnson, motions to him to speak for a moment. He is a descendant of the namesake of the town. He wants to invite the family to his home for Sunday dinner. The Pastor and his wife accept and begin to head to the van.

After leaving Deacon Johnson's home and thanking him for such a generous spread, they head home, full of natural food but also spiritual food as well. The boys are quiet and reflective. Lucas, who loves chocolate cake or anything sweet, is thinking about how the taste of chocolate is still lingering in his mouth. He anticipates eating another piece of the delicious chocolate pastry later. The Deacon's wife made a second cake for them to take home.

"That was a stroke of shear chocolaty genius!" He thinks to himself.

His brother, with his face leaning on the window in the rear, watches the trees zip past. He is thinking about his father's sermon, and the words that he told him and his brother the night before. He sees images of dragons and castles with other strange and interesting creatures. As Letete begins to ponder his musings, he begins to repeat a refrain of the verses" quietly...

"...the young lion and the dragon you shall trample under feet. Because he has set his love upon Me, therefore, will deliver him."

Lucas in his mind declares the battle cry, "Knights to arms, knights to arms!"

FOUR

Trumpet the Adventure!

Later that day, during the early evening, the Pastor calls his sons into the study where he is reviewing what he preached to the church earlier that day.

"Boys, I want to thank you for your assistance last night with my sermon." He says to his sons. They look at him bright-eyed and reply, "Dad, when did we help you with your sermon?"

"Well boys, did you notice that the sermon was very close to our conversation from last night? You were my inspiration, or should I say that the Spirit used you to inspire me. I just want to thank you both."

"You are welcome Daddy." Both of the boys reply.

"Fellas, I want to show you something that I made for you. It's a neat little game that will help you with learning scriptures that you can use as weapons against the enemy. Just think of the scriptures as your armor."

The boys look with anticipation, "Armor? Weapons?" They respond.

"That sounds pretty cool. Is it like the armor that we play with Daddy?" Lucas asks.

"Yes, the armor that we bought for you represents different types of protection against our enemy the devil. I thought that this would be a powerful way to learn about scripture and commit them to memory." Letete stands and leans on his Dad's shoulder, seated in front of his desk.

"Are we going to fight with armor and weapons?" Letete asks his father.

"I like to fight!" Lucas says energetically.

"No, guys, you are not going to fight. I have something else in mind."

"Well Daddy, how does the game work?"

The father stands up and walks over to a credenza. From the side of it, he pulls out two long sticks with a string attached at one end on each. Their Dad reaches with the other hand and removes a stack of cardboard fish. He looks at his sons with a large smile and says, "Guys, how would you like to go fishin'?"

The boy's father begins to explain to them how the game works. They smile in anticipation as they listen intently to their father's instructions. It does not take much for them to be amused. They can find joy in the simplest of situations. That is what makes them both so endearing. They can of course sometimes be a little rambunctious, but they are, for the most part, very well-mannered young men, a commodity in today's youth. The father explains the fishin' game to the boys as he calls it.

"Now boys, each fish that I have placed on the floor has a number or point value assigned to it. I placed a paper clip in the mouth of each fish. You will simply toss or cast your hook, or should I say magnet just in front of the fish's mouth. For each fish that you catch, you will add the points to your tally sheet to keep score. There is also a written bible verse on the other side of your fish that is face down on the floor. You will read out loud what the verse says. You will also find a special fish that will have a coin on the back of it. This coined fish will have an extra point. I will show you how it's done by going first."

The father takes the magnet in his hand and tosses it towards the fish that is farthest away from his standing position. He gently nudges and pulls the line with the magnetic bait towards him. The fish slides across ever so slightly and connects itself to the magnet bait.

"Got one!" the father exclaims.

He pulls the paper catch up by the string and flips it over to reveal words on the other side.

"What have we here? Words? I wonder what it says. *Philippians 4:4 Rejoice in the Lord always. Again I say rejoice! Wow, God's word on the back of fish*," the father says.

"That looks like fun Dad, can we try it?" Letete replies.

"Sure! That's the plan. I thought of this for the both of you. I figured that it would be a nice way to make scripture memorizing more fun versus just reading them from the page. Let's see what you can do." Their father gives both boys a stick each. Letete try's first. "Got one Dad, I got one!" he says, very happy with himself.

He flips it over to read its content.

"*Psalm 150:6 Let everything that hath breath praise the Lord.* Coool! I like this game."

"Can I try, huh Dad?" Lucas asks.

His father nods and says, "Of course! Cast out ye line ye land lubber, arrggh!"

The father says in a convincing pirate's drone. The boys laugh in response.

"I got one too Dad!" Lucas reads his words on the back of his fish. Psalm 91:11 *He wiiill give hiis angels chawrge over you...*"

"Great job Lucas!! Guys, I have to head into town for a while and then to the Church. I'll speak to your Mom on my way out. Good fishin' guys!"

After a few tosses, Lucas starts picking up some of the cardboard fish from the floor of their Dad's study.

Letete asks his brother, "Hey, what are you doing? I'm not finished playing. I like this game, and we just got started." Lucas, still picking up cardboard fish, replies "I like the game too! I have an idea, leet'z take the fiiish out to the well and pretend to go fiiishing from the well. It could be like we are fiiishing from our castle or a lake or somethin."

Letete looks at his brother and nods in agreement.

"I think that I would like that. Good idea shrimp!"

Lucas turns and stops abruptly and retorts, "Hey, who are you calling a shwrimp!"

Letete begins to chuckle and tells his brother, "Pump your breaks, I was just kidding. Let me help you pick up some of the fish."

The two would be fisherman both dart through the backdoor and trod down the back stairs. They run and skip their way towards the well. Once at the base of the well, the two look inside to ensure that the way is clear and dry. Lucas has to tip-toe to get a clear view of the inside of the well. The boys begin to drop the cardboard fish intermittently inside of the well. "Let's make sure to spread the fish around to make sure that they are not piled up on each other," Letete says.

"All done!" Lucas says. The two fishermen begin to cast their magnetic baits into the well. Lucas first pulls out a cardboard fish from the well.

"Got anoother one!"

"What does it say, Lucas?"

"Let's see. Well "*For I know the plaans I have for you, saays the Lourd. They are plans for good and not to haarm you, to give you a fuuuture and a hope.*"

Letete replies, "That's good stuff."

The two fishermen both cast their lines into the faux well again in hopes of landing another catch. Lucas hears an odd sound, sort of like a metallic tap or thud. He pulls on his pole, and it does not give.

"Hey! I think a got a big one heeerrre."

Letete quickly runs to the other side of the well.

"Here, I'll throw in my line next to yours to see if I can attach it to whatever you have caught. This way we can both pull it up together."

Letete takes his bait and strategically drops it next to the taut line of his brother.

"Thud!"

The sound it makes as it hits something. The two brothers both pull on their strings to see what great catch they have had the good fortune of snagging from their make-believe castle rook. They each pull on their lines and can hear what seems to sound like metal scrapping on the side of the well wall.

Letete reaches in, "I can see something kinda shiny. Wait, here; I got it!"

He also sees one of his father's fish connected to his magnet bait and the shiny metal object that he and his brother caught.

"What is it?" Lucas asks his brother.

"Let's see here; it's some sort of sign with words. "Trumpet the Adventure" what does that mean?" With a contorted face Lucas replies.

"I don't know, but it's written on this thing three times."

The sign, a shiny copper-brass colored metal that appears to look hand beaten. The words seem to be impressed into the metal, thick and uneven, seemingly pounded into the metal with a rounded blunt instrument. The sign is about a foot in length and approximately six or seven inches in height. It also seems curved as if it was fashioned to fit a rounded surface, maybe even the outer surface of the well which is definitely round in its construction.

"I wonder where this came from?" Letete asks.

He begins to read the impressed words as written, "Trumpet the Adventure, Trumpet the Adventure, Trumpet..."

"Hey!!!" Lucas interrupts.

"I see a faded spooot on the siidde of the weell over heaar. See, its lighter thaan the woood surrounding the spot."

Letete takes the sign and holds it up to the light patch of wood on the side of the well.

"It seems to fit. This sign must have fallen off or somethin' when the well was dropped off."

"I woonduur who made the siiign?"

"I don't know. It's a mystery. Maybe we can try to find some clues like detectives."

"We coould ask Dawddy. I'm suure thawt he would knoow."

"Let's try to figure this out on our own for now. Just to have some fun, let's start looking for clues today."

At that moment, the back door creeks open and a stern but pleasant voice cascades over the backyard.

"Boys, it's time to come inside, it's getting late."

"Okay, Mom!"

Before the boys begin to gather their things, Lucas asks his brother to read the fish card that was attached to their metallic catch.

Letete pulls the card from between his magnet bait and the metal sign and begins to read it.

"*Psalm 91:13, Thou shalt tread upon the lion and adder: the young lion and the dragon shalt thou trample under feet.* Cool, that's perfect for our castle! Daddy is always reading to us from this bible verse. Let's go inside; we can try to catch the other fish on tomorrow. We'll just leave the rest in the well until later."

Letete takes the metal sign and wedges it between planks of wood on the top face of the well. The two fishermen quickly exit the well and run up the steps that lead to the back door.

"What do yoou think the sign meeans Letete?"

"I don't know. I think that it could be cool to consider the idea of adventure. Just like pirates or even as knights!"

"Cuool indeed, cuool indeed!"

Later that night after the boys enjoy a bowl of ice cream with their parents, their Dad tucks them in and reads some Bible verses from Psalm 91. Letete tells his Dad about the fish card that had one of the verses from that Psalm.

"Hey Dad, I caught a fish that had one of the verses you read. It talked about trampling and treading lions, adders and dragons under our feet. Can we honestly do that?"

The father replies, "With Christ, all things are possible. That verse tells us that we do not have to fear anything because He gives us power over what we fear. Just remember, when you guys ever get scared, just put it under your feet."

The boys reply to their father, "Yes Daddy." The father places his hand on their heads and gruffly rubs their hair.

"Good night guys, love you."

"Love you too Daddy. Goodnight."

The next morning, the boys start back on their routine from before the move to the new house. They sit attentively to listen to the lessons of their mother. The boys are both homeschooled by their mother and father. The move sort of interrupted their usual schedule but now they are starting to get back on track. They finish their lessons for the day, and after a quick afternoon snack, the two brothers gather their armor and head out the back door.

The boys, jumping over the steps, dart quickly towards the well.

"I know that we were supposed to continue fishing, but I want to play knights of Rose Sharon again. We can pretend to catch fish after we conquer some more dragons." Letete says.

"Plus, that verse that Daddy read to us last night started me to thinkin' about fighting some dragons."

Lucas shakes his head in agreement.

"To awrms! Hey, we can use the wourds on the siign as a battle cry. I like that better thaan the one we use." Lucas states to his brother.

"That's a good idea, Lucas. I'll grab the sign."

The boys both look at the sign and begin to read aloud the embossed words on the metal.

"Let the battle cwry go fowrth!!" Lucas exclaims!

Both boys take the sign, Letete on one end and Lucas on the other. They begin to read and exclaim the words loudly on the shiny placard.

> "TRUMPET THE ADVENTURE!"
> "TRUMPET THE ADVENTURE!"
> "TRUMPET THE ADVENTURE!"

With the speaking of the last line on the shiny placard, the boys notice that something is happening around them. They feel a wind come up from nowhere. The leaves on the ground begin to swirl in a circular motion around them, and the make-believe castle. They hear a loud strange sound that seems to emanate from inside the well. As they stare wide-eyed at the well, they see the sides of the outside of it seem to transform. The outer surface seems to move and ebb as if a thing that breathes. Tiny little points of light begin to run through and around every nook and crevice. Then suddenly, what appears to be water of sorts, begins to overflow the boundary of the well and flow in every direction. Beginning first from within then overflowing from without. The strange water runs swiftly and quickly envelops their shoes covering the bottom of their pants. It's cold and tingly, but strangely not like water but more like water than any they have ever known. The boys look at each other in amazement, "What is going on?" Letete exclaims.

"I don't know, buut this freaking me ouut!" Lucas states with a panicked voice. Suddenly, the side of the well nearest to them splits, like the opening of a large volume book. As the walls of the well part and separate, more water rushes out and overtakes the boys in a small crystal wave, knocking them to the ground. At that moment, instinctively, the boys reach out and grab each other. The wave that roles over them, now seems to roll back, the current of the wave pulling them towards the well. In an instant, the boys are pulled past the open walls of the well and pushed by the current towards the center. They instantly began to scream, "AAAAAAHHHHHH!!!", and in that instant, the walls slam close, and the boys screaming voices stop. The water disappears, and there is complete silence. The ground is arid, and the only thing that remains is the shiny metal sign lying in the grass next to the rose bushes. The boys play armor can be seen lying in the flower beds around the well. One can only imagine what adventures the boys are about to experience.

FIVE

A Cloud in the Woods

For what seems like an eternity of falling into or maybe a better description being swallowed by the well, for the boys, time seems to have disappeared. The boys feel the sensation of falling and being propelled at the same instance. It was as if they were at the beginning of a drop on a roller coaster and never realizing the sensation of slowing down at the base. It was not dark as one would think that it would, falling into a well as it were. Quite the contrary, it was bright and colorful. The light itself seemed almost to take on a hard form as if one could almost feel the light wrapping around you. There are colors of all sorts. There are reds, oranges, yellows, greens, blues, and hues of violets and purple all swirling about them. They are afraid, and yet their senses are overwhelmed by the cascades of colors that seem to cancel out their fear. Below them is a bright light, almost like a star becoming closer and larger with each passing second. They watch as the light, bright and ebbing, begins to grow as the two boys like satellites come within the orbit of the star-like body. And suddenly, as instantly as their descent starts, it appears to lessen. It culminates in a "flashbulb-like" burst of light that paints everything a brilliant white that can be seen even through tightly closed eyes.

The boys have a new cacophony of emotions that give way to a harmony of senses. As they feel some foundation under their bodies, finally terra firma is sensed under them. Letete, with his eyes tightly closed, feels like his senses are overwhelmed. He smells different fragrances, like expensive perfumes and wildflowers of a kind. He feels the warmth of the sun on his face. He can hear birds singing a song that seems very foreign to him. Not like the bird's songs that he is familiar with back home. He also can sense another fragrance that is familiar to him as well. It seems like vanilla and a very familiar scent.

"I think I smell chocolate?" Letete says to himself quietly. He opens his eyes to find himself laying in what seems to be a meadow of grass and wildflowers everywhere around him. He immediately sits up in the clearing to make a quick assessment of his situation.

"AAAAAAHHHHH!!!" Lucas screams wildly. Letete turns quickly to his right to see his younger brother dart past him like a red blur, which is the color of his t-shirt, screaming and whaling frantically.

"Whaat happened? Where are we? The well ate us; it ate us! Why did the well eat us?"

Lucas begins to run toward a clearing in the meadow. Letete takes off behind him and tackles him in mid-stride.

"Stop it, stop panicking! Screaming and yelling is not going to help the situation!" Lucas pushes his brother aside and sits up alongside his brother.

"What is going on here? Can you tell me that, big brother?"

Letete looks at his younger brother, wide-eyed and just merely shrugs his shoulders.

"I don't know Luc; I'm just as freaked out as you are. But in the same breath, everything is so; I just can't put in into words."

"Yea, I know, the colors and the lights, and the smells. I must be crazy, but I know that I smell chocolate in the air and other stuff."

"No, you're not crazy, I smell it too! Hey!"

"What's up with the way you're speaking? You're speaking just as clear as I am."

Lucas looks at his brother and stands up to reply dusting himself off.

"Yeah, I noticed that. I can speak clearly. How's that possible?" "Lucas, maybe you hit your head during the fall or somethin', knocking a loose screw back into place."

Lucas smirks at his older brother, "Ha, Ha, very funny. This place is not like back home; it is so strange, almost like a dream. Heeyy! Letete look at the grass all around us. It's blue and kinda purple. Now it's a kinda reddish color. Oh no! Are we dead? Is this Heaven?"

"No dufus, we're not dead! If we were dead, could I do this?"

Letete reaches over and pinches his brother on the arm.

"Owwww!! That hurts, knock it off. O.K. so if we are not dead, where are we? "
Letete looks at his brother and says, "I don't know."

The boys stand up in the clearing and begin to look around in every direction. They look at the alien grass that seems to change color randomly. The grass is tall and sways in the wind. A gentle breeze whisks the grass appearing as a brush passing through a woman's hair. In one direction, changing color in unison and then in another direction with the same effect. There are strange flowers with sweet fragrances that fill the air. They see strange trees just at the edge of the meadow that have leaves that are even more colorful than the grass. The barks of the trees are brown, with a strange, waxy appearance.

"Chocolate, the trees look like chocolate. I think that's where the smell of chocolate is coming from." Letete says.

"I looove chocolate! I am kinda hungry; maybe we should walk over and see if it really is chocolate?"

Letete reaches out and grabs the back of his brother's shirt.

"Wait, Luc! I don't think that we should run off investigating strange stuff. It might not be safe."

Lucas pulls away from his brother and replies.

"Strange! Strange! This whole thing is strange. We were swallowed by a wishing well and end up in this weird, real life, oil painting and you talk about strange? Speaking of strange, what is that over there? It looks like a river of diamonds or somethin'."

The boys walk to the top of a small hill only to see something beyond belief. A river, and not just any river, but a river that looks like it is running uphill instead of down. The water appears to be like the water that burst out of the well, but even more sparkly like a precious gem. The current seems gentle and even sounds like water in a stream. Lucas takes off toward the river.

"Wait, Luc, remember to be..."

"Yeah, Yeah Letete, I know, be careful. But maybe since that's the stuff that brought us here, maybe it can take us back."

Letete starts jog behind his strong-willed brother who is pacing quickly towards the crystal river. They stop at the river's edge and look both downstream and up.

"It looks like it's the same stuff that brought us here alright," Lucas says.

"It's running up this hill and seems to narrow that way just several yards there at the top of that point. Look there at the top; it's a beam of light that looks like it goes straight up into the sky, straight into space."

Lucas begins to bend down at the water's edge in complete awe of the strange liquid. Up close it looks like individual droplets of water that appear as crystals. So drawn is Lucas to the spring, he begins to salivate and lick his lips.

"I am really thirsty. Do you think that it's safe to drink Letete?" Letete shakes his head and says emphatically,

"No! No! I don't think that is a good idea. What if it makes you sick or something. It looks like we are the only ones here and if you get sick, I won't know what to do."

Lucas quickly takes two hands and cups them together and scoops the sparkly water into his mouth. Letete tries to reach out and knock the water from Lucas' hands but is too late.

"Wow, Letete! This stuff is great!! I don't feel sick on the stomach at all. I have never felt like this before."

Letete stands up and grabs his brother's arm.

"Are you crazy? What if that stuff made you sick!"

"You're not listening. I feel great! Here, you should try it. I know that you're thirsty too."

Letete looks at the crystal stream and then his brother. He smirks at him and then bends down and scoops a hand full of the strange, beautiful, liquid.

"Woooow!! You're right. I feel great!! I am not even hungry anymore either."

Letete bends down again to scoop up another hand full of the liquid to examine it.

"It's soooo strange. When I role it around in my hand, it separates and comes back together. The drops look like little diamonds that sparkle and give off little rainbows in my hand. And it does not feel wet! How is this possible?"

Lucas smiles and says, "It doesn't matter. What matters is that it is here, now, right in front of us. You are always so serious; more than you were before we crash-landed."

Lucas reaches down and scoops up a hand full of water. He drenches his brother's face and laughs uncontrollably. The water runs down his face and some of it into his shirt. It's cool and tingly. Letete returns the gesture with two hands of the crystal liquid and pours it over his brother's head. They look on as the water runs down his brother's head, down his chest and legs then on the ground. It rolls and gathers, finding its way back to the rushing stream that is running up the hill. The brothers look at each other and say in unison, "Cooool!!"

Lucas looks at his brother and asks, "Do you think that there are fish in this weird river?"

Letete looks at his brother as he is sipping more of the crystal water.

"I don't know Lucas but let me ask you. How do you feel?"

Lucas looks at his brother strangely.

"Great! Just like I told you. You feel the same, don't you?"

Letete stands up, looking down at his brother.

"Yeaaah, I feel greaaaat, but I also feel something else. I feel strooonnng! For some strange reason, I feel like running too!"

Letete takes a step, then two, then seems to bound 5 feet, then 20 feet in a single stride.

"Whoooa!!" Lucas says excitedly, as he jumps to his feet.

"That was awesome!! I wonder if I can do that!"

Lucas takes one step then two and is an instant covers the remaining distance between him and his brother.

"Did you see that Letete!! I jumped as high and far as a gazelle! "What's that stuff!" Lucas says with wide eyes and a big faced grin.

"I don't know, but I'm going to drink some more!"

The two boys bound effortlessly to the edge of the gravity-defying spring that is running up the hill.

"Ha!" Lucas snorts at his brother.

"I beat ya! I'm the fastest here"

"No, you didn't, I beat you!"

Both boys are now laying almost chest length in the crystal brook, grabbing handfuls of the crystal water, drinking laughing and splashing each other with the gem-like droplets. Lucas jumps to his feet and begins looking at the running river.

"I bet ya I can jump across this river in a single leap!"

He says to his brother.

"Hey, don't be silly, what if you fall into the stream? The current looks a little fast, and I don't think that it's.... Hey!! Stooop!!" Letete in a motion leaps in the direction of his younger, headstrong, sibling. He misses him by mere inches as he takes off like a projectile. As Lucas launches himself, he accidentally slips on a large stone that is just at the river's edge, slightly submerged.

"Owwww!" Splash! Kabluunk! Lucas disappears below the surface of the crystalline torrent.

"Luuuuccccasssss! Noooo!!!"

Letete is screaming in horror. He wades out just at waist depth, cautious of the current; he begins yelling Lucas' name. He looks frantically in the direction of the current upstream and the middle of the river and does not see his brother anywhere. In a moment of despair, he looks on feeling utterly helpless.

"Oooh noo! Lucas, what have you done? I can't believe it. I just can't believe it."

He falls to his knees, now chest deep at the edge. His eyes begin to tear up. The only thing that he can hear is the rushing water and birds in the distance. Then suddenly, "Whhoosshh! Whoo Hooo!!"

A red blur bounds out of the river like a water rocket and lands on the other side on the opposite bank.

"That was sooooo coool!"

It is Lucas, laughing and dancing a silly jig on the opposite side of where his brother was now standing.

"Are you absolutely, nuuuts!!! You scared me silly!" Letete immediately shouts at his brother.

"Scared? Why would you be scared? The water felt great. I will admit that I was a little scared when I tripped and fell, but that ended when I looked up and could see thousands of tiny rainbows just under the water. It was amazing! Once my feet touched the bottom, I just bent my knees and jumped with all my might. That's when I landed on the other side right here. Sorry to scare you. I guess you do like me?" Lucas says with a mischievous smirk.

"Like you? When I catch you, I'm going to knock your block off!"

Lucas looks at the expression on his brother's face and says with concern, "Oh No!" and begins to run.

Lucas, on the cusp of his brother's threat, takes off in a bound following the current as it runs up the hill towards the bright beam of light. Letete takes off behind him in like fashion on the opposite side of the crystal stream. He is shouting threats at his younger sibling across the running torrent.

"Yeah, you better run, when I catch you, I'm going to bop you good! Letete shouts.

"Oooh, I'm so scaaaared, NOT! Ha! Ha! You have to catch me and that ain't happenin'!" Lucas replies sarcastically.

He begins to run even faster towards the top of the hill. His older brother easily matches his increased speed. The stream starts to narrow as the two brothers bound several feet effortlessly at a time, almost appearing to glide from bound to bound. Lucas slides dramatically to a stop, colored grass and gravel cascading into the air. He is closer to him as the stream is beginning to narrow.

"Wait, Letete Stop! Look up ahead at the beam of light. It looks like something is floating in it just above the top of the hill."

Letete slides to a stop, just a little past his brother's location across the stream.

"Yeah, I see it. It looks shiny, and it looks like its twinkling. I wonder what it could be."

The two, now move a little slower, not bounding as before, but with a little more caution. Both brothers begin to get a clearer picture of the twinkling item inside of the beam of light. Still not too sure as what the object is or its origin. Even though the boys both are cautious, their boyish curiosity still drives them closer to the strange, floating diadem. Lucas in a moment throws caution to the wind and bounds the final distance to the unknown object.

"I betcha I can get there first!" Lucas says to his brother.

"Wait!! Not again!" Letete says agitated at his brother's impatience and seeming disregard for caution.

He bounds just to the left of where his brother is standing at the top of the hill.

The stream of crystal water narrows to a point at the base of the beam of light and blends with it as one, apparently the source of the strange liquid. But even stranger is the object that is now clearly seen floating and spinning in mid-air, directly in the middle of the beam of light.

"It's, it's a sword! An actual spinning sword!! That is so cooool!" Lucas says excitedly.

"You're right! How is that possible? And why is it here? It looks like the water stops here at the beam and disappears. That is sooo strange."

"It's so pretty if you can call a sword pretty that is. And it seems like the blade is growing larger then smaller with each spin. Whooa! That is so cool! Much cooler than the play swords we have back home"

Both of the boys stare at the spinning weapon. Lucas is right about the sword. It was bright and shiny. The handle or "hilt" was grooved and very ornate with filigree all around it. At the very bottom of the "hilt" is a Pommel, shaped like a dove's head with the beak pointing downward. The eyes of the dove were two bright green emeralds that seemed to glow. The top of the "hilt" or the "Quillon," is shaped like wings, above the grip open to form the top branding that holds the blade in place. The filigree or decoration on the branding appears as fruit made from gems of different colors. Above the Quillon on the tang of the sword where the hilt holds are decoration as well. Some of the markings on the lower portion of the blade look like some unknown writing or letters. The fuller, a central channel of the sword runs from the hilt to the middle of the saber and begins as the shape of flames of fire before coming to a point in the middle of the weapon. The sword seems to glow and ebb what appears to be a fire of some sorts, swirling and cascading all about the metal of the sword. The sword is emitting a low fixed hum as a note struck on a xylophone that is constant.

Letete and Lucas stand gazing, fixated on the spinning spectacle, not speaking a word for a period. Lucas, as usual, is the first to break the silence.

"I'm going to touch it," Lucas says softly.

"What did you say, I didn't h..." Lucas interrupts,

"I'm going to touch it!" He says louder as if trying to convince himself to go through with the action.

"I don't think you should do that. Of course, I know that you are not going to listen to me. You haven't listened to me since we've been here. Don't you want to try to figure out how to get back home?" Lucas begins to look at his brother and for a moment stops his gaze at the spinning sword.

"Well, now that you mention it, I do want to go home. Although, as I think about it, I am having the time of my life. This blade is cool and all. I want to take a crack at those chocolate trees, but I don't want to stay here forever. Letete, how do you think we ended up here in the first place? Obviously, the well is magic or somethin, but what could have caused it to do what it did?"

Letete looks at his brother and squints his eyes as he is pondering the answer to his brother's question.

"I don't know. I remember we were playing at the well. We both had that shiny sign in our hands; while reading what was written on it aloud. Hey, Lucas, did you see the sign anywhere when you landed?" Lucas shrugs his shoulders and replies, "No, I was too busy screaming for my life when the well ate, I mean when we fell into the well. Do we need the sign to get back home you think? If so, we need to find it. The thought of staying here and not seeing Mom and Dad again makes me feel sad."

"It makes me sad as well.

"I wonder what all of this means? The grass, the flowers, the smells, the water that flows to this spot and this spinning, floating sword. Why is it here?"

Lucas begins to place his gaze back on the spinning sword.

"Hey, Letete. Do remember what we were saying when we were touching the sign? Maybe we should touch the sword and repeat it? It is made of metal just like the sign, well kinda."

"Again, I don't think that would be good I... Hey!!! Don't touch..."

Before Letete can finish speaking, Lucas has already lunged forward with both hands and grabs the grip of the hilt of the sword firmly with both hands tightly and instantly pulls back. To his surprise and his brother's, he is standing, holding the sword in his hand that is no longer spinning but is still growing larger and smaller in his grasp. But that is not the extent of their surprise. They turn, with their mouths agape, and stare at the blade in Lucas's hand, then each other, and back at the beam of light that has an identical spinning sword, floating as the first had been.

"Whoooa!!" Lucas exclaims.

"It almost feels like it's alive! Funny thing; it's not heavy at all. It's light as a feather. I can even hold it easily with one hand. I also feel a tingly feeling running through my hands down to my arms."

Lucas inverts the weapon and looks at the sword in his hand admiring the sheer beauty of it. He stares at the bird-shaped pommel, golden, ornate, with emerald gems for eyes. For a split second, Lucas in astonishment is startled. It almost seems like the bird's head bends to look at him, staring directly into his eyes.

"Whooa!" Lucas says, his brother not noticing his brother's response. Letete looks at the sword in his brother's hand. He does not chastise him because he is more amazed than angry. Instinctively he reaches out with both hands outstretched to the twin spinning blade that's floating in the beam. Just as the first encounter, the same outcome takes place. Letete now has a sword in his hands as well, with still another like sword spinning before them.

"It is light as a feather!! This sword is too, too, cool!!" Letete says excitedly.

"It is, it is! It is, it is!"

Letete and Lucas stand there for a moment staring at the three swords, all of the blades synchronized together, growing long, then short, then long again repeating the pattern. They both feel the tingling sensation in their hands and arms. Even the hilt of the blade, the pommel and the wing-shaped guards seem almost alive.

"Whoa!!" Letete and Lucas say in unison.

"What are we supposed to do now with these things?" Lucas queries.

"What do you mean? What are we supposed to do, we sure in Heaven's name can't fight each other with real swords!"

"No, that's not what I meant. Now that I'm holding the sword, it feels reeally great! It's like the feeling with the water after we drank some. Don't you feel it too Letete?"

"Yes, I do."

"This is so strange and awesome at the same time. Daddy always says that everything happens for a reason. What could the reason be for all of this?"

Letete looks at his brother with a smirk and a tilt of his head.

"Now you want to find a reason to everything! That's what I have been saying since we fell into the well and landed here. We were trying to figure out a way to get back home before you decided to turn junior Jedi and grab the sword. We figured out that it started when we were holding the sign and reading the words out loud."

Lucas looks at his brother with raised brows and replies.

" Well, we're holding metal now, maybe if we say the words three times, we can go back home."

Lucas begins to say the chant, "Trumpet the adventure, trumpet the adventure..."

"Stop!!!" Letete interrupts his brother.

"Don't say it yet! What if you say it and end up in not so nice a place like this one, plus we should say it together."

Lucas looks at his brother with concern.

"Oh yeah, I didn't think of that. Let's say it together."

At that moment a breeze begins to rise and increase. The tall, colored grass begins to swirl and shift directions quickly.

The leaves on the trees before them at the edge of the strangely clad forest begin to sway and creek with the increasing gust. The air starts to crackle and feels tingly with each passing second. Above the woods, in the distance, a cloud forms then seems to pour itself into it. At that moment the forest begins to glow. There are lightning flashes accompanied with thunder in the distance within the forest. The sound of the thunder and the flashes of lightning become louder and brighter with each passing interval even shaking the ground around them. Then suddenly the cloud seems to stand up just before the clearing at the edge of the woods. The trees in its path fall like twigs, almost resembling servants in a King's court bowing before their royal magistrate. The top of the cloud reaches into the sky. It clears the last row of trees at the edge of the forest. The two brothers in utter astonishment and awe now see the cloud in its full spectacle. It is a spiraling tornado of mist, smoke, and fire. It swells and ebbs as a cord of swirling smoke and lightning arcs all about and through it. With each flash of lightning, the cloud illuminates and undulates with power and strength. The top of the vortex, like the head of a man, seems to move and toss as if searching for something or maybe someone. Then great lightning arcs shatter the grassy clearing just before the base of the hill where the boys are standing. The three swords begin to glow brighter, and the blades elongate with each lightning arc emitted. The boys stand still, looking straight up at the swirling cloud of fire and smoke. The undulating fog starts to glow from inside. The glow swells at the top and cascades down the cloudy column and spreads out like a ripple in every direction covering the ground in cloud and smoke. There is a sound that seems like many voices softly speaking in a language not recognized by the brothers. Then suddenly it happens.

"Tidings Sojourners of the Well! I greet you warmly and extend my grace and hospitality unto you!"

A voice like none other the brothers have ever heard, speaks from the core of the fiery cloud. It shatters the air and shakes the ground like a microquake. The concussive syllables bristle the boy's clothing like successive breezes flowing across their bodies. In utter horror the boys instinctively grab each other in the process of dropping their swords which float back towards the beam of light, melding with the spinning sword suspended in the beam.

"AAAAAAAAHHHH!!!!!" The boys shriek out of terror.

"Trumpet the adventure! Trumpet the adventure! Trumpet the adventure!"

In unison, they shout the etched phrase on the shiny placard they found in the well back home. Instantly, the boys disappear from the base of the hill in a puff of smoke and light.

The boys find themselves in their bedrooms. Each of them in their respective beds, each wearing their favorite pair of pajamas. It is much later than the first time they entered into the well. Letete sits up in the bed to look at the time on the clock.

"Eleven fifteen PM? How is that possible? Lucas are your there? Are you O.K.?"

"Yes I'm here, I'm O. K., and I'm freaked out!!!" Lucas says to his brother, peaking from under a bed cover.

"What in the world was that, that talking cloud thing Letete? And how are we back home at a later time than when we left? We were wearing something different."

"I don't know the answer to any of those questions. I didn't think we were gone more than an hour, two tops. But it's obvious that we were gone longer than that, at least seven to eight hours. At least we are back home and not lost anymore. If we are here like this, then Mom and Dad must not have known that we were gone."

At that moment, a voice breaks up the boy's conversation. It is coming from outside of the boys closed room door. It's their father.

"Boys, make sure that you go to sleep. I can hear you talking to each other. Lay down because you need your rest for the morning."

"O. k. Daddy!"

They wait to listen to hear the footsteps of their Dad descending the stairs.

"I think he's gone," Letete says.

"I am glad to be home, that place was great but a little scary."

"What if we end up back in that place? What if I end up there by myself without you? I'm a little nervous about the thought of it." Lucas says with a concerned voice. At that moment, in that dark room, a glow appears in the corner. It glows brighter than the sun, then suddenly a flash of light and the sword appears, spinning in the boy's room.

"Tidings Sojourners! Don't be afraid; I mean you no harm. I seek your friendship and want to cover you in my glory."

The voice is so soft and comforting. Immediately the boys lay down and cover themselves.

"Sleep with an assurance that I am here, watching over you and will keep you. You never have to be afraid."

Then, just as suddenly as it appeared, the sword vanishes into thin air. The boys feel comfort at the words of the sword. Letete feels something under the bed cover. He reaches in and pulls out one of his Dad's paper fish. He flips it over to reveal a scripture on the other side. He begins to read it softly to himself, squinting to read it in the ambient light. It says,

Joshua 1:9

"Have I not commanded you? Be strong and courageous. Do not be discouraged, for the LORD your God will be with you wherever you go."

They lay their heads on their pillows and say nothing to each other and just drift off to sleep with confidence and no fear. They each ponder in their minds the events of the day, the smells, the flowers, the water, the sword and eventually that cloud that speaks. What does it all mean and what can they expect to happen next?

SIX

A Rushing Wind

The two brothers woke up the next morning refreshed and felt as if they have awakened from a literal dream. They question themselves whether what happened the previous day occurred. The well, the cloud that spoke to them and the sword that seemed to follow them back home and talk to them as well. Extraordinary enough, they slept better than they ever have since they moved to the new house. Both boys sit up in their beds and stare at each other. Then simultaneously they break out in laughter for about a minute, then they stare at each other again in silence. Lucas is the first to break the hush.

"Did that happen to us yesterday Letete? Did we fall into a well and visit that amazing place, another world?"

"Well, something happened. You're still speaking clearer and even better than me. Luc, I also think that the effects of the water have not worn off totally as of yet. I still feel almost like I did when I first drank some back in the other place."

Lucas's eyes widen.

"Funny you should mention that Letete, I feel it too!"

Letete rolls to the edge of his bed and slides to the floor. He looks back at his brother who is now kneeling at the foot of his bed looking back at him with curiosity.

"Luc watch this!"

Letete with little to no effort leaps as if almost levitating to touch the top of their ceiling in their room. The leap would not be such an accomplishment except that their ceiling is vaulted, at least 12 plus feet or more. Lucas looks up as his brother completes his astonishing jump.

"Hey, let's see if I can still do that!"

Lucas leaps from the foot of his bed and bounds like a sparrow to a cross beam in the ceiling and hangs for a moment, then swings and lands clear across on the other side of the room.

"Show off!!" Letete says in response.

"Yep, that's me!"

Suddenly two voices can be heard from downstairs. It's their parents shouting through the wooden floors below.

"What are you two boys doing up there?" The mother chimes.

"Are you swinging from the rafters or something? Stop it now and come down for breakfast after you wash up! Your food is getting cold."

The boys look at each other and begin to laugh hysterically.

"If only they knew!"

Letete says with a wide-face grin.

"Coming, mom and dad!"

The boys reply as they head towards the bathroom to freshen up before heading downstairs.

Letete and Lucas are downstairs in a flash as they head to the breakfast table to take part in the mini spread that's set before them by their mother. As they arrive in the kitchen, they see their dad, helping their mom set the table.

"Good morning sleepy heads."

The father says as the two siblings enter the kitchen.

"Go ahead and pull up a chair, breakfast is almost done." The boy's mother replies.

"How did you guys sleep last night? I have been praying that you both have a peaceful nights rest. I also have been praying that God's presence watches over you both while you are asleep."

The boys look at their father wide-eyed and then at each other.

"You have been praying that Dad?" Letete asks.

"Of course! You know that I always read the 91st Psalm to you, especially the parts about His covering wings, no sickness coming near you and God giving His angels charge to keep you from stumbling. I pray that for everyone here. After I had to tell two rambunctious little night owls to go to sleep, I went into my study and prayed after reading the Bible for a while."

"Well Honey," the wife responds, "it must have worked because I slept like a baby. There! The biscuits are done. Let's all sit down and enjoy a good meal before we start the day. Honey, will you do the honors?"

The father motions to everyone to hold hands and he begins to pray.

"Dear Father in Heaven, we thank you for the food that comes from the bounty of your creation. We thank you for family and fellowship. Bless others who may not have as we thank you for what you have given us, In Christ Name, Amen! Now, let's eat."

There are the usual sounds of glasses, china, and conversation that takes place as the family shares stories and dreams at the table while they break bread. The boys through it all cannot help but think of all the strange things that happened the prior day. Now and then they look at each other, wide-eyed, pondering what their discovery will mean. Letete is even considering the thought of sharing what happened with his father, but where would he begin? It's not every day that you end up in another world.

"Okay, guys," their Mom chimes in,

"go upstairs and get cleaned up. When you are finished brushing your teeth, come downstairs so that we can start class. If we can finish today's project early, I'll give you some additional time to play."

The boys reply to their mom's statement with a unified " Whooo Hooo!!"

They both run upstairs to quickly begin cleaning up so that they can get an early start on their play time.

As the boys prepare for a new day of classes with their mother, their father is in the kitchen helping their mother clean up after breakfast.

"Honey, how're things at the church? I know that it's been only a few weeks since we came here. I like it here and so do the boys. The people at the church seem nice as well."

"Well Honey, I'm glad that you and the boys like it here. I like it here too. But I must be careful not to let my spiritual guard down. I was just praying yesterday at the church. I prayed a blessing over every pew, every piece of furniture, hymnal, the entire building and the contents. I prayed that the Lord would bless the church and the congregation with an anointing and presence like they have never experienced. I want us to be open to His will and to show us his presence through His manifested Spirit."

At that moment, the boys were starting back down the stairs. They could hear their father speaking to their mother about his prayer.

"I prayed that we would even see a manifestation of the Spirit like that of Pentecost and even what was seen by the children of Israel, a pillar of fire and a cloud."

Letete looks at his brother whose mouth is wide open about to shriek a response to what he just heard.

"Whaaattt did Dad sa…"

"Shhhhhssssshhhhh!!!" Letete tells his brother as he places his hand over his brother's mouth.

"Are you nuts? Do you want dad and mom to hear us?" Letete whispers.

"Did you hear what dad said? A cloud of fire. That sounds like what we saw!! How is that possible?"

"I don't know at all how that is possible. But maybe we can find out by going back into the well." Lucas' eyes stretch as he responds.

"I was hoping that you wouldn't say that, Letete. I don't think that I want to go back to that place."

Letete turns to his brother with a puzzled look.

"I thought that you liked that place. When we were there, I couldn't get you to listen to anything that I said, you like the adventure of everything there, and now you don't want to go back?"

Lucas stands up on the stairs and points his short index finger into his brother's face, touching the tip of his brother's nose.

"Yeah, so what! That was before a cloud caught on fire, stood up and started talking saying "welcome to the Strange World Hotel!!""

Letete looks at his brother with his head tilted and replies.

"The cloud never said that!!"

Lucas begins to laugh simultaneously with his brother at his funny retort. At that moment, the boy's mother walks to the base of the stairs and eyes both boys sitting on the top landing.

"What are you guys doing up there? Come on down; it's time to start your lessons for the day."

The boys look at each other and smile a smirkish grin. Letete whispers to his brother again.

"I still think that we should go back. Remember what the Sword said to us. It said never to be afraid."

"Yeah, did you forget to consider that a talking sword said that? A sword for crying out loud!"

Both boys go to the kitchen area to begin their lessons, pondering over and over in their minds the things that happened at and in the well.

Just before the boy's lessons, their father tells them both to have a good day and learn as much as they can. LaTasha follows her husband outside to the front step of the house to give him a gentle kiss as he heads to the church to meet some of the Deacons to discuss a matter. She looks at him with a particular look that he had grown familiar with over the years. He did not necessarily always know what was going to follow that look, but he could count on something.

"Okay honey, what's wrong? I know that look."

She smiles at him with a big grin.

"Oh, you think you know me so well. I was wondering about what you said that you had been praying regarding a spiritual manifestation. You said that you prayed for a manifestation of the Spirit like that of the Israelites. Did you mean that you want to see "tongues of fire" on our heads in a literal sense?" She says with a hint of exaggeration in her tone.

"That would be great, who would not want to see those types of signs and wonders, but I was more referring to a manifestation in the lives of men and women. To have the Spirit to bear fruit in the heart of my people and my congregation. That would be the best sign of all."

LaTasha looks at her husband with a sweet smile and gently kisses him on the cheek.

"Have a good day sweetie, love you." She says softly, still in her husband's embrace.

"You have a good day as well, and I love you too."

The Pastor walks to his truck and pulls out of the driveway. The boy's mom enters back into the house and walks into the kitchen where the boys are waiting, seated at the kitchen table talking to each other.

"Okay, guys let's get started. Get your books; I have a reading assignment for you before I talk to you about the lesson. Start with the opening paragraphs of chapter two."

The boys, grabbing their books, begin reading quietly to themselves.

Later that day, after the boys finish their lessons early as planned, they head outside towards the well in the backyard. They both dart over to where the well is sitting in the clearing. It looked the same as if nothing ever happened. The flowers were not disturbed at all. This scene is very confusing to the two young boys.

"Look at it. It's just sitting there like nothing ever happened, not even a board missing or out of place." Letete says.

"Weird! Weird! Weird!" Exclaims Lucas.

"Strange. I wonder if the sign is still around. Let's see if we can find it Letete."

The boys circle the well, looking for the brazen metal placard. They don't see the sign initially, but on closer inspection, Letete finds it behind one of the larger rose bushes next to the well.

"Here it is! It must have been thrown here when we went into the well."

Letete picks it up and brushes off the loose dirt. Lucas begins to back away from his brother with a concerned look on his face.

"Hey man, don't come any closer to me with that thing in your hand!"

"What do you mean? Oh, you can't be afraid of this little sign. Not when you grabbed a spinning, talking sword that moved."

"It wasn't talking at the time, and that's not the point. I don't know if I want to go back to that place. Maybe we should trash that thing. That will be one way to make sure that it doesn't suck someone back into that other world."

Letete responds, a little agitated at this point, "It was the well that pulled us in, if you remember, not the sign. I think that we should go back. I don't think that the cloud would hurt us. Remember the voice from the cloud was the same as the voice of the sword. I'm going to say the words myself and go on my own."

"Nooo!!! You can't do that! O.K.! O.K.! I will go with you. You sure are pushy when you don't get your way."

The boys both take one end of the sign in their hand and look at each other with wide eyes. They take a deep breath.

"Are you ready?" Letete asks his brother.

"No, but I will be once we start."

"Okay, here we go!" Both boys begin to chant.

"Trumpet the adventure!"

"Trumpet the adventure!"

"Trumpet the adventure!"

Instantly they vanish into the well as it swells, glows and then swallows both boys in a crystalline wave that flows from it.

The boys appear back at the same spot at the top of the hill where the sword is still spinning suspended in the beam of light.

"I don't think that I will ever get used to that," Lucas exclaims.

"Yeah, you and me both!"

"I see that we are right back where we started, here on top of the hill. I remember the last time that we were here we reached out to grab the sword or swords, that's when we saw the cloud appear."

Lucas looks at his brother with concern and replies, "Do we honestly want that cloud thing to come back Tete? It was terrifying!"

Letete shrugging his shoulders says, "I don't think we have anything to fear. Remember what the sword told us in our room."

Lucas is still a little leery but gives in.

"Okay, Okay, let's do it!"

Both boys reach out to grab the sword but this time together. To their astonishment, they both draw the same sword simultaneously, producing the same effect. Like before there are three swords, each growing larger, then smaller with each complete revolution of the third sword still suspended in the beam of light.

"This is still so cool!" Letete resounds.

"Yeah, but here comes the scary part! Brace yourself!!"

The wind picks up and swirls. The air begins to crackle and feels tingly as before. Above the forest, in the distance, the cloud forms then pour itself into it. There are thunderings and lightning flashes just as before, shaking the ground around them. The cloud stands up just before the clearing at the edge of the woods. The top of the cloud, reaching into the sky, bends and turns looking as if scanning the area. It clears the last row of trees at the edge of the forest. The two brothers in no less awe brace themselves with their mouths open for a second encounter with the spiraling tornado of cloud, smoke, and fire. Lucas, wide-eyed and trembling begins to say a simple phrase,

"Oooh boy!"

"Glad tidings Sojourners of the well! Welcome! I extend my grace and hospitality unto you!"

The boys stand utterly motionless, except for trembling in place. They do not reply, frozen by fear.

"I see that fear grips you, do not be afraid. Remember that I told you that I mean you no harm and you have no reason to dread."

The boys try to become a little more comfortable with the spiraling, speaking, maelstrom. Letete tries to utter the first salutation, but the effort comes out like a squeak. He clears his voice and makes a more successful attempt.

"Hhhhhh Hi, Sir or Mr mrr Mr. Cloud." The spiraling entity laughs and seems to smile of sorts.

"Young one, you can refer to me as Neuma Ru." Lucas, now a little less tense in his stance, replies.

"New man who?"

"Neuma Ru young one, the covering for this realm as well as infinite others."

The boys, both with their mouths still agape in amazement, stand looking in awe .at the spectacle before them. Just as majestic as the cloud itself are the fragrances that are filling the air, seemingly emanating from the cloud, swirling all around them.

"What are you?" Lucas asks in a trembling, curious voice.

"I am no mere what. I am no more and no less than who I am, but more than what can be comprehended. I am the wind; I am the breeze, I am the storm, the smoke, and the fire. I am power, and I am a covering. I am the one who requested your presence. I am a friend."

The boys look up into the spiraling, glowing entity, still with no less amazement.

"You requested for us to come? I did hear that you said that, correct?" Letete, says as he is staring up at the entity.

"Yes, you did hear me correctly young one, I did send for you. I need you both. I have an assignment for you two. A task, a quest as you will."

The boys look at each other, removing their gaze from the spiraling cloud for the first time and focusing on each other in a bewildered expression.

Letete looks back at Neuma Ru and asks, "Why would you need us? We are only little kids. What could we do to help someone like you?"

The top of the cloud, like that of a man's head, begins to lower itself towards the two brothers. The two instinctively recoil and step back from the form.

"You underestimate yourself. The size of a man is not as important as the size and content of his heart. Your hearts are pure and can be used to achieve great things if I am with you. What will give you power is not your strength, but my power that I will endow you. My presence will be your strength. You will need only to trust me, and I will do the rest.

What is your answer to my offer Sojourners, will you accept going on a quest?"

The boy's eyes widened in response. Letete naturally asks the obvious question, "Well, what is the quest that you're referring to?"

The cloud begins to glow and swell even more in intensity.

"I will tell you only if you accept!"

The two look at each other and ponder what the outcome could be if they accept.

"Well Lucas, you have always wanted to go on an adventure. You can't get any more adventure than this can ya?"

"No, you can't. Let's do it!!" Lucas says excitedly.

"Are you sure?"

"If I were surer than I am now, I would be able to sprout wings and fly!"

"Whoa! O.k.?"

Letete looks at his brother with a sideways smirk. He turns to Neuma Ru and answers for them both, he and his brother.

"We accept your offer. We will go on a quest for you!"

"This is good news indeed. The quest will challenge you both, but you will be prepared and strengthened. I will be with you, always at your side and within you."

The boys anticipate as to what manner of adventure they have agreed to participate. They are excited and nervous at the same time.

The magnitude of it all and the sheer energy of the anticipation exhilarates them. A quest, this is what every kid dreams of, unbridled adventure!

"Excuse me sir, or I mean Mr. Neuma Ru, you said that if we accept the quest, you would tell us just what the actual quest may be?"

Letete asks. The cloud swells and glows and again bends towards both boys.

"Yes, yes indeed. I am one that keeps my word. Your quest will be a quest of deliverance, a quest to help others, a quest to bring freedom and a quest to bring a message of hope! You will also have to fight for others in this quest!"

The brothers look at each other and then back at the swirling cloud.

"Fight?" Lucas says, "With the swords? I like to fight!"

Letete looks at his brother with a smirk.

"Yeah, I know that you do, but you forgot to ask a crucial question. Neuma Ru, who will we be fighting?"

The cloud stands back up and begins to swell and glow even brighter. Neuma Ru, at that moment, utters a thunderous reply,

"It's not who young ones but what?"

The boys look at each other again and reply in unison,

"What? Just what is what?"

"In your world, tales and myths are written of these creatures. In your world they are known as Dragons young one!! Dragons!!"

Lucas begins to back up and, in an instant, places his hand with the sword in the beam of light, replacing it. It merges with the spinning sword still suspended in place.

"Well, it was nice meeting ya Sir, I'm out! Trumpet the adventure, Trumpet the..."

"Hey!! Whoa, Lucas!" Letete shouts as he places his hand over his brother's mouth.

"What are you doing? And where do you think you are going?"

"I am out, leavin', l-e-a-v-i-n! He said draaagons, and I think that he is talking about the real fire spittin' types. I don't want no part of that!" Lucas retorts.

"But we gave our word, and you know what Dad says about keeping your word. He says that if we give it, we keep it! It's a gift that we get to keep. It makes sense now."

"Yeah, I know, but I don't think Dad ever thought that we would be fightin' real dragons. I'm just a little freaked out about this. How can we do this? Just how?"

Lucas looks at his brother with concern, then looks at the spiraling cloud just behind his brother.

"Young one. Remember that I will be with you, you will not be alone. You will also have others that will aid and assist you at the proper time. And yes, there is the other matter of your protection that I will endow you with."

Letete and Lucas look up at the cloud with curiosity. Lucas replies first.

"Protection? What kind of protection?"

Neuma Ru begins to glow brighter in response to the question. Lightning arcs pepper the surrounding ground at the base of the cloud.

"Take the sword into your hand Lucas. Trust me in this."

"Okay."

He reaches in with one hand and just as previously, he is holding the sword once again.

"Good young one. Come closer young warriors; you do not need to fear. Now that is better. To answer your question Lucas, I will protect you with my armor. I will endow it and you with my strength."

Letete looks on with stretched eyes in amazement.

"Armor? Our very own armor? Will it be too heavy for us? We are of course just little boys."

"Remember, you are more than you think. If you believe that you are small then small, you shall be. If you believe that you are great, then you shall be great. You would only have to trust me, and I will give you gifts to accomplish anything. And you shall accomplish a great thing in this place. I will see to it."

The two brothers stand at the base of the cloud, as it ebbs and flows brighter then darker then lighter again, lightning and thunderings all about the scene that they are fixed in. Lucas asks the all-encompassing question that is burning in the boy's mind.

"Just how are we supposed to get this armor? How do we wear it?"

Neuma Ru glows and swells.

"The swords in your hands, take them and hold them in front of you. Good! Good! Now open your outstretched hand with the sword before you."

The boys, following the instruction of the cloud of fire and smoke, do just as they are told to by the storm. Just as they open their hands, their swords levitate in place, just like the third sword in the beam of light.

"Whoooa!" They both say in unison. Both swords begin to grow larger, then smaller, then more substantial again. Synchronized, they start to spin rapidly, levitating just above the outstretched palms of the two boys. At that moment, lightning arcs flash, and the cloud begins to grow brighter than before. Neuma Ru speaks a word that the boys can't understand. It sounds like a different language that is foreign to both boys. They feel the air tingle and swirl about them. They begin to feel their bodies float just above the ground. At that moment they see a massive arc of lightning light a few feet away, merely to the right of the cloud. It burns through the grass and turf, throwing dust, rocks, and sand into the air. It almost looks like a finger, drawing a line in the sand. It approaches the boys so quickly they do not have an opportunity to react. They are overtaken in an instance by the massive arc. They are bathed in a bright white wash of light, devoid of any color; It is so brilliant from within, that view is seen even with their eyes closed. And then just as quickly as the arcing appears, it vanishes.

The boys are now standing on the ground as before. But there is something different about them. Letete feels as if he is looking through a viewer or slit in a box. He looks down at his feet to steady himself because he feels a little dizzy. He notices that there is something different about his feet. Bright, shiny, polished metal now covers his feet. He sees it start from his feet than his legs. He holds his hand out to view it. He sees the sword, as before, but now it is held by a shiny metal clad gauntlet.

"Whoa!! This is awesome! It's beyond anything that I could ever imagine!"

He looks at his brother, who is armored from head to toe, as he too is examining the armor that covers him.

"It's light as a feather!!Just like the sword!!!"

Lucas poses with the sword in a defensive stance then thrust his sword out before him. He swings his sword in a wide arc and exclaims, "Take that you foul dragon!! Hey, Letete, I believe that we can do this! With the armor and the sword, I feel invincible!"

Letete looks at the sword in his hand, still growing and shrinking as before, he begins to feel the same feeling of strength waxing inside of him.

"Yes, Sojourners, indeed you will be just that." Neuma Ru chuckles at the boy's refrain.

"And the key Lucas is in what you said. You must always believe and never fear! Fear is the enemy and will strip you of this same armor! Be strong in this knowledge of me and the armor that I have endowed you! Now, turn and face each other. I will instruct you in the use of the weapons in your hands."

The boys spend what seems like countless hours under the instruction of Neuma Ru. The armor gives them the strength and ability to learn the ways of warfare against a dragon in combat.

"Now boys, it is time for your first test. Just south of this place, a few miles away. There is about to take place an attack on a small village of people, men, women, and children. You must go and stop this attack. Help those who have no hope! Be brave in the knowledge and power I have given to you! Honor me by defeating the enemy with my weapons of warfare! Use what I have shown you and you will be victorious!"

The two men of iron look up at the spiraling cloud. Letete motions to the cloud like that of a student in a classroom, raising his iron-clad hand to be noticed.

"A few miles you say, but how will we get there?"

Neuma Ru, the cloud bends just before the two warriors to be.

"I have a question to ask you both. Will you answer?"

The boys nod in agreement.

"Yes, we will."

The cloud swells and glows.

"Do you trust me? Will you move into action when I ask it of you?" The boys answer without hesitation.

"Yes, we trust you and will move when you instruct us!"

Lightning arcs cascade towards the two brothers and then instantly, laying just in front of them are two shields, seemingly made of the same metal as the armor.

"Pick up your shields young ones! These are the symbols of your trust in me! Use them, and they will protect you. Never lay them down. Keep them, and they will keep you! Now let's go on that quest, the hour is at hand to do battle! You shall move in that direction, due south. You will know when it is time to strike. Trust the armor; it will carry you!"

The boys look at the horizon towards the south.

"It seems so far away," they think to themselves.

They take one step, then two. Just like before when they drank the crystalline water, they begin to bound effortlessly across the plains. At that moment, the spiraling cloud seems to leap into the sky and land in between the two brothers who are now in full stride covering several feet at a time. At that moment, the cloud expands, and the boys begin to run in an ellipse, mirroring the spin of the cloud which now envelops them both. They appear as two objects in orbit of each other. The cloud accelerates, spinning across the landscape and disappears into the horizon with the two brothers inside.

This is indeed a day of adventure for them both. A day of adventure to trumpet. What more could two boys request?

SEVEN

Two Heroes, a Village and a Dragon

As Neuma Ru takes a moment in time to teach and instruct the boys in the use of their weapons, another event unfolds miles south of their location. Positioned atop a modestly constructed wooden high-hide placed at the edge of a dense forest, a young man sits and watches anxiously. The hide is covered in broken tree limbs and leaves to camouflage it from view. The apex is just above the tree line giving one standing inside a clear panorama in every direction. The young man has covered himself in trappings of the forest as well as a ruddy, oily looking clay paste. The paste is smeared over his face, arms and legs as well his clothing. Just to the west, about one hundred yards or so in the middle of clearing there is a small wooden platform. Affixed to the center of the platform is a broad, thick wooden beam with a series of metal rings at the top and what appears to be chains that hang toward the base. The wooden structure looks worn and has the appearance of being scorched all over. The young man sits staring at the structure. He fixes his gaze for moments on the structure, then another moment to the north, then the next towards the south. The young man, visibly nervous for some reason begins to speak aloud to himself.

"By the Kraken! What can be taking them so long? Why are they not here with the Gibbous Indulgence? It must be here before the appointed time arrives. And it is very near! Oh, woe, woe, woe to the people in the village if we do not have the Gibbous Indulgence here before the set time! If they are not here, the Ash Breather may decide to take his wrath out on me."

At that notion, the young man becomes even more shaken.

"I only pray that this Snarksen paste can mask my presence from the Ash Breather. Oh, where can they be? The time is almost at hand!"

Snarksen paste is a concoction derived from the sap of the Snarksen Tree in this unknown world. The fluid is viscous and sticky. It has a pungent smell which is a great base ingredient to mask the scent of a man. The young man brilliantly constructed the tower of Snarksen wood from the surrounding forest. The paste also has red clay, Browden's tree fungus and the blood of a particular potato beetle that smells similar to that of a rotten ripe onion. This stench of the paste is tolerable when you consider the alternative of being scented out by a dragon. Ranke looks wearily at a makeshift sundial that is attached to a wooden plank that protrudes just beyond the tower landing. The setting sun begins to cast a long shadow across the face of the solar dial.

"Ohh we are almost at the Gibbous Hour; the sun will set shortly. Where can they be?"

The young man reaches into a shoulder pouch and pulls out a rudimentary spyglass to search the path on the southern horizon to see if anyone is present. He sees something just over the hill in the south. It looks like someone riding a horse and riding it hard.

"What is this? Curious, I only see one rider on a horse. But where is the Gibbous Indulgence? Could the Gibbous be traveling alone? What a strange notion! They usually have to be dragged screaming in protest to the Gibbous Post. Wait, I see! It's Doldren! Doldren! What is he doing here without the Gibbous Indulgence?"

Doldren, the rider on the horse which is swift and quick, covers the distance rapidly. The passenger can now be heard screaming and shouting something as he gains ground on the high-hide.

"What is that dolt thinking? Coming here at this late hour without the Gibbous Indulgence! He will doom us both!"

The rider swiftly arrives at the base of the high-hide. His horse slides to a stop on the forest floor. He is still screaming and shouting to the young man in the top of the tower as he ascends towards the top landing.

"Ranke! Ranke! The Gibbous is not coming! The Gibbous is not coming! There has been a revolt among some of the families and the council. They refuse to participate in the Gibbous lottery."

Ranke, the young man in the high-hide, retorts back angrily, "Whhhaattt!!!Whhhhaaatt!! This decision cannot be! That is against the rulings of the council! Yes, all be it is harsh to one, that they would meet such a terrible end, but better for one to perish than the many! The Gibbous hour is almost upon us, and the Ash Breather will be here soon! We had better be careful here! I must think this through! The hour is almost upon us! And you, screaming like a wounded banshee, here with no Snarksen to cover your sent! What are you thinking? If the Ash Breather appears and scents you out, he may find me as well!"

Doldren, in sheer despair, places both hands on the side of his head and replies.

"Yes! Yes! I know that this is possibly the actions of a madman, but I wanted to inform you of what is going on in the village. There are some of the families who are questioning the old ways. They have some allies as well on the council who agree. The Old Man in the tree, the Seer, influences them, Ranke. Our Foster! I felt that you needed to know that the Gibbous was not coming! You needed to have at least fair warning! What are we going to do?"

Ranke, who was kneeling on one knee in the high hide, now stands up and says sternly, "We! What do you mean we? The Snarksen will cover my scent, and the Ash Breather will not scent me out!   But as for you, I cannot say that you may share the same good fortune if you do not leave here before it arrives! You must go now! The hour is almost here!"

Doldren, who is now in a full panic, grabs hold of Ranke's cloak that is coated thickly with the Snarksen paste. Doldren's face expresses fear at the demand of Ranke to leave so near to the Gibbous hour.

"I cannot and dare not leave! The Ash Breather may scent me out and devour me! Is this how you repay me Ranke for not wanting you to perish? You are supposed to be my friend, more than a friend even. We have known each other since we were children! Will you cast me aside to save your paste covered hide my childhood friend? Besides, I don't think that I would make it back in time! That beast will come and in all probability scent me out after he realizes that the Gibbous is not on the post!"

Ranke kneels again, to reply to Doldren's question.

"Yes, I would cast you aside as you say to save my hide! Someone will have to chronicle what happens here. I am the one who will do just that! Sometimes one must sacrifice the smaller things to accommodate the larger good! So, you had best get on your horse for your own sake while you still have time! Friendship aside, someone must keep track of the beast out of sight and out of harm. You being here, not covered in the Snarksen, will put me in peril and that all-important task of chronicling the Ash Breather! Leave now Doldren while you still have a chance, if you value your hide!"

"The larger good? The larger good! You dullish Brute! Throwing me in harm's way so that you can cower here is your idea of the larger good! The truth here is that you do not want to return with me to face the Ash Breather on the terms of battle! For surely as the Gibbous is not there on the post, that beast will in no doubt descend upon the village with his full strength and wrath! You would rather shrink here in the trees like some smelly Bog Ape! I hope that you accurately chronicle your cowardice! Good evening to you Sir, you dullish brute!"

Doldren, fully realizes that Ranke has no plans of helping him and will not consider returning to the village. He quickly descends the tower and calls for his horse. His horse appears, and Doldren in one motion ascends onto the saddle. He looks back up into the tower and gives a look of disdain to Ranke.

"I wish you good fortune Ranke, childhood friend! My brother!" He shouts.

At that moment, Doldren's horse is alarmed by something. He begins to try to regain control of the horse quickly.

"Somethings spooking you girl?"

He tries to calm her; his words do not comfort the horse who is now very visibly shaken.

"Oh no! The Ash Breather must be near. The Gibbous hour is almost here!" Doldren says in fear.

Doldren immediately calls his horse into action. He takes off like a dart, back towards the path for the village. He begins to talk aloud to himself.

"Ride Laurel swift and sure! I surely hope that the Ash Breather will not scent us out here in this wide-open terrain. Good fortune is with us as we are riding downwind with the breeze out of the north. A high drift during this season. Such an odd thing it is, the breeze is usually not this quick this time of the season. Usually, the air is still and dead during the Gibbous hour. But we will accept the gift of the elements won't we girl. Hah Laurel!"

Doldren, with the increasing gust of wind at his back pushing him southward, seemingly glides over the terrain back towards the village.

"Ranke is such a dolt! Dullish, dullish brute! I did not have to ride at such peril to give him a warning. I could have left him with no explanation out there to whatever fate he deserves. He is intolerable! It's amazing to me that I still refer to him as a friend. Friend indeed! If it was not for the promise, I made to his mother..."

Doldren instantly pulls back on the reins tightly causing Laurel to slide on the gravel path throwing grass and dirt into the air.

"The Promise! Oh, what a wretched person to attach a life promise. I cannot believe that I am doing this! Forgive me, Laurel."

Doldren steers Laurel back around towards the direction of the hide.

"Hah!" He commands his horse back into the direction of the tower as the Gibbous hour is at hand.

"I am genuinely a madman for hurtling myself directly into harm's way. All for Ranke, the dullish brute!

Ranke reaches into his shoulder pouch once again to view the south path on the horizon. This time he sees his friend Doldren on his horse clearing the horizon line and disappearing over the hill. He removes the spyglass from his face and looks a little puzzled.

"Amazing enough," Ranke says to himself.

"Doldren seemingly left in a swifter fashion than he arrived here. I'm sure the thought of being here in the open air without Snarksen to cover your sent from the Ash Breather as it nears would motivate any man to imitate the wind in retreat. As I ponder my predicament here in this precarious loft, I wonder if I should have moved upon Doldren's plea to leave this place before the Ash Breather arrived. Hhhmm yes, indeed! Maybe my actions are the actions of a madman. Crouched here in this tower of wood, alone with no ally but a smelly paste and no weapon but the covering of trees. But I can't have that now. It' too late to second guess myself. For it is near to the Gibbous hour. I notice that even now as the hour approaches, a strange wind blows from the north. What will the beast do in the absence of the Gibbous? Of course, I know what it will do. It will surely catapult itself into the clouds with the intent of showering its fiery wrath down upon the village. Doldren dared to suggest that a ragtag gathering of men at the village could sway the tide of battle against the beast. That would be a fool hearty endeavor. For this reason, the Gibbous was formed to protect the people of the village. The Gibbous gave us a respite from the terrible raids on the village from the Ash Breather. It was a truce of sorts, although tenuous at best. But what else could we do?''

At that moment, a large black malformed shadow cast itself across the tree line from the north. The shadow shapes and reshapes itself over the treeline of the Snarksen forest.

"The Ash Breather cometh! That must be the dark omen of the beast casting its shadow about the tree line."

Ranke says to himself shakenly. Just as quickly as the shadowy image appears, it disappears towards the south. It reappears towards the west and in like fashion fades. The shadowy specter fades into a more dimensional shape; It is significant, dark and ominous. It circles back around towards the north and makes a sharp turn towards the clearing near the place of the Gibbous post. It lights itself approximately fifty to seventy yards in front of the stake. It is even more imposing and lethal in appearance fixed on the ground than in the air. The beast from the top of its head to the base of its neck at its chest stands three or more stories tall. From the same chest area to its tails tip spans the length of two school buses. The body of the beast is encased in thick plated scales that resemble shields of armor. Each scale is a greenish-gray hue. It has piercing yellowish eyes with a mouth full of glass like teeth that curl to a point. The tongue of the beast hangs intermittently between the rows of glass like daggers in the beast's mouth.

"Behold the Ash Breather!" Ranke thinks an ominous thought.

At that moment, the beast turns in the direction of the high hide tower as if hearing the thoughts of Ranke. The young man takes in a large gulp of air in sheer terror.

"Impossible!!" Ranke thinks to himself daring not to speak or utter a single sound. The beast looks and scans the forest line. It pauses for what seems like an eternity then in an instant focuses on the Gibbous post. It covers the distance slowly towards the post. It arrives finally at the stake and inspects it, bending its massive head towards the pillar, sniffing it with flaring nostrils.

Suddenly the beast opens its mouth and lets out a shriek in response.

"Where is the Gibbous growwwwwwlllllummmmpf?"

The sound of the creature speaking sends a chill down the spine of Ranke. He is utterly still, frozen in horror as he looks on.

At the moment the beast shrieks out in anger, Doldren is arriving at the base of the hill just out of the sight of the creature. The sound startles Laurel. Doldren is just as shaken.

"By the Zule!! The Ash Breather is here! I cannot panic for it will certainly mean my demise. Think man, what should you do?"

At that moment, he realizes that he is still upwind of the beast. He notices the forest edge arcs around the ridge to the East.

"I'll flank the beast by riding towards the outer edge of the trees. I hope that will be enough to mask my scent until I reach the tower."

Doldren steers his horse towards the Eastern ridgeline. He disappears into the thick underbrush then turns due south towards Ranke in the high hide tower.

"I can't believe it! I am headed back to try to help that, nere do well! And the Ash Breather no doubt will explode into a beastly fit because of the absence of the Gibbous. Steady girl, steady."

Doldren carefully maneuvers Laurel between the trees, ducking low limbs as they both race back to the Hide.

"I am quite sure that Ranke is in a better position than I am now. Here are surely the actions of a madman, a madman indeed! Hah! Laurel."

The wind is starting to pick up from the north. It is brisk and cool, not at all the usual dead air that takes place at the Gibbous hour.

"This is a little harder girl, heading back into the wind as we dodge tree and limb."

Like a weaver's needle, the two, rider and horse, weave an intricate path towards the Hide. Then something strange happens in a quick instance. The wind dies abruptly and becomes still. Doldren, fully realizing what this could mean, pulls back on the reins and steers Laurel behind a large tree.

"Oh no! The wind! It has ceased! That beast can scent us out! Whoaa girl! Be still!"

He peeks around the tree to see if he can see the beast beyond the forest edge. He sees just parallel to his position about 200 yards or so the dark form of the beast, pacing about the post. Doldren thinks to himself that this is not a good predicament.

"I pray that the wind will pick up again to help hide our presence here. Whoa girl! I know that you agree but be still so not to give us away."

At that moment, Doldren steers Laurel away from the tree and begins to move towards the Hide Tower slowly. All the while keeping an eye on the dark, ghastly figure in the distance. After a few minutes, he thinks that he can see the Hide through the tree lines. Travelling through the brush and foliage, that Tower does appear as natural a fixture as a tree itself.

"Ranke did accomplish that feat, dullish brute that he is."

Doldren thinks to himself. As he inches closer towards the Hide with Laurel, suddenly, the wind picks up just as brisk as before. Doldren immediately realizes that something has just terribly gone wrong. The wind instead of blowing from the north has now changed directions. It is now blowing from the East. Doldren realizes his position is due east of the beast.

"Oh no! This turn of events is not good, not good at all! The wind will inevitably carry our scent over to the beast. He will surely scent us out!"

The Ash Breather with each passing minute is becoming more visibly agitated and animated. Its massive body being carried by sturdy, muscular and sinewy legs that end in claws with glass-like tipped points. It paces around the platform, growling and snarling.

"Grroowwllll sssssssss! Where is the Gibbous!! Why is it not heeerrrreeee!! Being late with the Gibbous, growwwwlllssssssss, is not acceptable. It is egregious to the construct of the Gibbous agreement! If it is not here, then the fleshies will feel fire and claw. Growwwlllll ssssss! How dare they defy me, an emissary of the one that I serve!"

The Ash Breather in that instance takes a massive claw and slams it on the base of the platform, breaking wood and beam, sending, dust, shards and splinters into the evening sky.

"How dare they!! How dare they!"

The Ash Breather examines the post again. He takes one finger-like claw and inspects the chains and rings, inspecting them closely.

"Curious? Maybe the Gibbous managed to free itself from the post? I like a little sport from time to time. I should be able to sniff them out easily, even though that cursed Snarksen weed covers this area of forest. Hmmm, aaaaahhh,yesssss! The wind has shifted for a moment. If they are here still, I will scent them out."

The beast lifts its head into the air as if to sniff it for all its content. He suddenly looks to the west forest clearing, parallel to where it is standing on the ground.

"I can smell some remnant of the nasty little fleshy. Yesss! Yesss! Let the sport begin!"

The beast says ominously. It sniffs the air again and around the base of the stand. It screams an ominous-sounding threat.

"Nasty little fleshy! I am coming for you. You cannot escape, and you cannot deny me the Gibbous."

At that moment, the beast releases a blood-curdling roar, raspy and bellowy.

"Growwllooorllooff!!!"

Ranke, who is looking at the beast in the high hide trembles at the sound of the roar as it echoes through the tree line. He hears what the beast is saying about scenting out the Gibbous.

"The beast must be scenting the remnant of Doldren's presence. Even with the Snarksen, is it possible that the beast could discover me here following Doldren's scent?" He thinks to himself.

At the moment, he inspects a connected taut line of rope that is high, fixed to a post on the top of the tower. Ranke, who is a tinkerer of sorts, when he constructed the tower with the help of some of the villagers, also had them to build another one hundred feet or so from the tower. The other tower is smaller in height but is still about the height of the tree line. He instructed them where to place tall, thick Snarksen posts on the same line from the taller tower to the smaller. Ranke constructed a wheel apparatus with a hand guard to provide a quick departure from the tower if necessary. He could easily slide over to the other tower in an instant if needed. He is beginning to wonder if that time has arrived.

Doldren pulls back sharply on the reins of his horse, Laurel.

"By the Kraken!!! I fear that the beast has scented us!"

He can hear the taunts of the beast in the distance, although the sounds of the beast don't seem to be getting closer. The wind has shifted and not in Doldren's favor.

"I don't think that the beast can fully scent us out as it appears. Probably because of the Snarksen forest. Coming back to save Ranke, this is a fool hearty endeavor. I should have never turned back to assist that, simple-minded Ranke. Should I turn back now? No! No! That would not be wise. The Snarksen forest gives us a little cover. Maybe I will continue towards the tower."

Doldren slowly moves his horse towards the tower. Continually keeping watch towards the west clearing where the Ash Breather is looming. He looks again towards the direction of the tower and back again towards the clearing. He can plainly see the dark silhouette of the beast, moving from side to side and around the stand.

"I can see the form of the tower. I can't make out Ranke from this distance." Doldren says to himself. He looks again to the west clearing, keeping check of the terrible form of the beast. He looks again towards the tower and returns his gaze to the clearing. This time, the figure is gone, to his horror.

"Wait a minute! Dear powers that be! The beast seems to have gone. Curious thing!"

He looks to the sky and scans the treeline but sees nothing of the beast. Then suddenly, he hears what sounds like leather sheets flapping in the wind. The sound echoes throughout the forest. At one point the sound dims then increases. Then suddenly, and horrifyingly, The Ash Breather lands just at the edge of the forest and the clearing.

"What have we here? Do I smell a fleshie?"

Doldren's body tenses in sheer terror. He is almost thrown from his saddle by his horse Laurel who is shaken by the sudden presence of the beast at the edge of the forest. Even though it seems apparent that the beast has picked up a scent, it appears that the beast does not know exactly the location of Doldren because of the dense Snarksen forest canopy.

"Just stand still human, and I will pick you out! If you don't run, I may be merciful... or should I say somewhat!"

The beast releases a fiendish, guttural, chuckle. At that moment, Ranke who has been a spectator the entire time to this beastly theatre reaches into his pouch again to pull out his spyglass.

"The Ash Breather has moved just due south of the where I am in the tower. Maybe he did not scent Doldren to this location after all. What could he be looking for there at the edge of the forest? I'm quite sure that the Snarksen Trees are agitating him a bit. Let's just take a look see here in my sight glass. Hmmm, need to adjust a little, Wait! It's Doldren! What is that simple buffoon during here? I thought that he retreated to the village."

Ranke looks towards the beast who is approximately 50 or 60 yards away from Doldren who is hiding behind a large Snarksen. Good fortune would have it that the tree's trunk is massive and almost completely hides Doldren and the horse. Even with the Snarksen fragrance in the air, it won't fully mask his presence from the Ash Breather.

"Foolish endeavor, foolish endeavor. Now I might have to intervene pursuing another foolish endeavor helping that dolt! Just what was he thinking of coming back?"

The Snarksen forest is very dense with a thick canopy that covers the forest floor. The foliage is dense and thick. Large trees provide an excellent cover and deterrent for such a massive beast to attempt to navigate. The creature is having a little difficulty navigating in between the gigantic tree landscaped forest. But eventually, that still won't be enough to protect Doldren if he does not move from his present location.

"This cursed Snarksen weed. The stench of these tree weeds is almost unbearable!" The Ash Breather belts out a complaint.

"Fleshie! I will find you! I can still smell you even in the midst of this weed-filled forest. The trees will not be enough to protect you."

At that moment, Doldren pulls hard on the reins of his horse and begins to race towards the High Hide. He sees another sizable tree and races toward it to hide himself and his horse from the ever-increasing threat of the Ash Breather. Laurel slides to a quick stop at the base of the trunk of another large tree. Doldren pulls hard on the reins to force Laurel to keep still and quiet as the Ash Breather tries to scent their location in the dense forest. He quickly jumps to the forest floor, while holding the reins in one hand, he gingerly peers around the large Snarksen. He is being extra careful not to slip and fall on the large root base of the tree that is providing temporary sanctuary for him and his horse. But unfortunately, that thought causes him to do just that. Doldren in an attempt to make sure that his footing was secure and steady, slips on a large root that is protruding like a loop from the base of the tree. He slips, hits the base of the trunk, and rolls into a line of sight of the Ash Breather. His blood runs cold; he instantly becomes drenched in sweat. Fear coils up his body like that of a constricting serpent. But the fear does not paralyze him; it fuels him. He immediately jumps up from the forest floor, flinging leaves and twigs in every direction. He scolds himself sternly.

"Stupid! Stupid! Idiot! I have surely given away my position to that behemoth! He will surely be upon me; I have given destruction a personal invitation!" He thinks to himself.

He knows that he cannot stay at this location for a second more.

The Ash Breather is looking and sniffing the air in every direction. Then it hears twigs breaking; possibly the sound of something or someone struggling after falling. It looks in the direction of the noise. It sees nothing. The wind picks up again briskly and has shifted anew but not in Doldren's favor. The wind is now blowing from the position of Doldren and his horse. The Ash Breather begins to stand up on its massive, sinewy hind legs. It lifts its long scaly neck into the air appearing like a green, scaly, castle rook. It sniffs the winds content and cascades back to all four legs. What he says next, sends shivers down the spine of Doldren.

"Ahh, yeeessss grooowwwllssss! I have scented you out Fleshie! I can smell you and your horse; I must say that the horse smells better." The beast in response releases a fiendish chuckle.

Immediately without hesitation, Doldren takes off like a rocket towards a massive Snarksen just in front of him about 50 yards. He thinks to himself.

"If we can just make it to that huge Snarksen, we will be o.k. Ride Laurel! Hah!" He says to his horse. He also knows that he can't ride in a straight line to that massive tree. The beast would surely overtake him.

Heavy, tremor filled footfalls that cascade throughout the forest can now be heard and felt. They are increasing in frequency with shorter intervals. The beast is evidently quickening its pursuit.

"I am coming for you fleshie! Even this Snarksen weed cannot protect you for long." The Ash Breather shouts as he is in pursuit.

He catches glimpses of Doldren and Laurel who are moving with surprising swiftness and agility. Doldren pulls hard on the left side of Laurel's reins. She turns on a dime. Then Doldren draws on the right side, and Laurel repeats the same. The two are zigzagging through the trees to through off the beast. The Ash Breather is having a terrible time maneuvering its massive body through the dense forest. It scrapes limb and trunk. The sound of breaking wood, snapping like toothpicks, can be heard just behind Doldren and his horse.

Doldren leans forward, standing up in the stirrups, and says to Laurel, "Good Girl! Now run!"

She takes off like a comet, clearing the remaining distance in minutes. Doldren pulls sharply on the reins of his horse and pulls around the opposite side of the massive tree. He instantly bounds from the back of Laurel and takes a tight hold of the reins. He motions to her to be quiet and still.

"Whoa, girl! Shhhhhhh!"

He rubs her on the head and begins to peer around the massive tree to get a fix on the location of the beast. He hears the breaking of limbs and the cracking of trees. The tremors from each step have increased. Then suddenly there is silence. The silence itself seemed deafening. Even the wind became still. Doldren feels that the pounding of his heart can be heard throughout the forest. He swallows hard, sweat beads on his head then gathers as a cascade down his brow. He knows that he must find the courage to peer around the tree to make sure that the Ash Breather has not attempted to flank him. He musters the courage and gingerly steps towards the base of the tree, edging its circumference to get a view of the beast's position. He tries to get his footing again, careful not to repeat the same mistake as before, but as fate would have it, he slips just enough to stumble into a root pocket on the other side of the tree. He thinks to himself.

"Again, a stupid mistake!"

As he is adjusting his footing again, he looks up for what only seemed like a millisecond to catch a glimpse of a horrifying sight. The Ash Breather is positioned just to the right of a line of trees that lead directly to Doldren's position. Fear, for only a moment, stiffens him in place as he and the Ash Breather make eye contact.

"Ohh dear powers that be!" He says to himself.

Doldren can see every single fine detail of the beast who is looking at him, glaring at him with yellowish eyes. He can see the green scales of the creature and his massive chest, heaving in and out with each intake of breath. He can even see the beast breath as it exits his flaring nostrils. Immediately, in sheer panic, Doldren snaps out of the deadly trance and races back to the other side of the massive tree where Laurel is visibly shaken, sensing the presence of the Ash Breather. He leaps on the back of the horse with an animal-like ability and snaps Laurel's reins firmly.

"Hah, Hah! Quick!"

Laurel again takes off like a bolt with the Ash Breather pursuing closely behind. Doldren, to his credit, is always thinking even under pressure. He sees another large Snarksen even closer.

"If we can make it there to that tree, I think that I might have an idea." He thinks to himself.

He pulls tightly again on the left side of the reins of Laurel who just as before turns on a dime. The Ash Breather for a time loses sight of his fleeing prey. Then he sees the two appear again from behind a large Snarksen in rapid retreat. The Ash Breather takes in a large gulp of air and roars at Doldren and his horse.

"Enough!!!Grrowwlsssshhhhrrrrrrroarhwhoooooosh!"

A thick, fiery flume erupts from the mouth of the beast overflowing its jaws. The great flume of fire shoots just in front of Doldren and Laurel who slides to a stop, just before the scorched forest floor and trees. Doldren pulls hard on the reins and Laurel swings around then is off again in the opposite direction. The Ash Breather breaths out another billowy flume of fire, repeating the same effect, pinning Doldren and his horse between two lengths of the scorched burning earth. Doldren spins around pulling on the reins of Laurel and shouts a command.

"Hah! Ride Girl! Ride!"

He races toward the large tree that is just before him. There are other smaller trees that Doldren manages to maneuver around. The Ash Breather is following closely behind in quick pursuit but is still having a bit of a time navigating the forest. It could easily catapult itself into the sky, but that would entail breaking through the thick canopy above. It would surely lose sight of Doldren and his horse, exactly the reason why Doldren retreated to the dense forest. The Ash Breather releases another blast of flames, this time directly towards Doldren. Doldren could hear the beast stop to a slide on the forest floor to inhale a large intake of breath. This motion was a sure giveaway that the beast was about to release his flame. Doldren in anticipation, dashes behind a large Snarksen, not as large as the one he is racing towards, but large enough to deflect the flame.

"Whhoooooo! That was closer than I would like! I could feel some of the heat from those fiery billows."

Doldren says as Laurel does not break her stride in retreat. Doldren's senses are compelling him to turn to see where the beast could be, but the fear of being swatted from the back of Laurel by a low-hanging limb overrides that impulse. He leans into Laurel, kicks into her upper thigh and snaps the reins.

"Run! Haaah!" He says as he can see a massive tree just a few feet ahead.

He knows that he will have only one shot at successively carrying out his crazed plan.

"What else can I do? I have no weapon to make use of and if I did what use would it be against such a behemoth as that Ash Breather? No! This action will work! It must work if only to gain just another bit of time before my demise. At least it can be said that Doldren used his wit until the end. I wonder if that dolt of a so-called friend is documenting this rabbit's hunt with me playing the role of the rabbit."

Doldren can hear the beast behind him.

"He seems close," Doldren thinks to himself.

What Doldren does not know is that the beast in a fit of rage, leaped half the distance between it and his present position. It has grown weary of the sport and desires to end this quickly.

"Stand still little Fleshie! Stinky fleshie! The end is almost near. Can you sense it?"

The beast says mockingly.

Doldren has reached his marker; he has but mere seconds to decide whether to retreat to the left or the right of the massive tree. He will have only one shot to pull this off. He pulls hard on the right side of Laurel's reins and leans hard to the left. The beast had managed to clear the last breadth of space between it and Doldren by springing from its hind legs. It opens its cavernous mouth to devour Doldren with one bite. It snaps its jaws shut! "Snaappp!"

The beast lunges, just missing Doldren by a hair as he and Laurel retreat around the massive tree. In that last lunge, the beast loses its footing and slams hard into the base of the trunk of the tree head first. In a flash, Laurel darts like a comet in the opposite direction back towards the area from where they retreated to the massive tree. Doldren is now low on the neck of Laurel as she opens to a full out gallop through the forest.

The Ash Breather now more furious than before is in a great deal of pain, dazed from the blunt blow of the tree trunk, rights itself releasing an angry roar. The sound of it makes the hair stand up on the neck of Doldren. The beast immediately begins its gruesome pursuit, even more, determined to capture its prey. Doldren is now in an all-out panic as he can hear the creature begin to flap its leathery wings. He can listen to the beat of the wings intermittently with heavy footfalls breaking limb and turf.

Ranke is watching the frantic spectacle below in the distance. He begins to pace back and forward in the high hide.

"Foolish, foolish, Dolt!! I can't believe what I am considering! Oh if it was not for the promise that I made to his mother. That foolish, foolish promise!"

He pulls out a makeshift telescope that he fashioned from items that he scavenged. He takes in a large gulp of air after viewing what was taking place in the forest below.

"By the Kraken!!! That buffoon of a man! He is bent on being a meal for the beast! Foolish promise!"

Ranke collapses the telescope and places it on the inside of his heavily coated cloak. He climbs a small ladder that is stationed in the center of the high tower. Once he reaches the top rung, he reaches up and pulls on a rope-like cord. The cord unravels and releases a thick tarp, coated in Snarksen paste. The removed tarp reveals a hidden contraption of an apparatus. It, as an apparatus, has a series of large pullies, springs, and coils. At the bottom of the apparatus, hanging at its base is a horizontal stick wrapped in leather with a brace and harness. Ranke quickly starts to attach himself to the harness. He tugs at the apparatus to check to see if it is secure. He kicks open a wooden box, laying just to the right. Ranke reaches into the box and pulls out several bladders containing Snarksen paste attached to a rope. He ties the rope around his waist, making sure that is tight. He reaches into the box a second time and pulls out another one of his tinkerings. It appears to be a medium-sized hand weapon. It is a crossbow, small and compact. Ranke reaches again into the box and pulls out several half-sized arrows of sorts. Instead of sharpened arrowheads on the tips, they seem to have bladders, like the ones tied to the rope around his waist, in the place of arrowheads.

"Never know when these may come in handy," Ranke says to himself.

He reaches under his cloak and tosses one side of it over his shoulder, exposing a small elongated leather cylinder strapped to his back. Ranke places all arrows into the barrel except for one. He inserts it into the bow carefully, not to break the bladder of Snarksen affixed to its tip. He pulls on a lever that is fixed to the base of the bow and extends toward the front. He pulls hard as the lever torques and snaps into place the cord of the bow. He catches a small latch into a position that secures the arrow with its contents in place. He reaches again into his cloak and hangs his tinkered weapon on a fastener affixed to his belt.

He takes the cloak that covered the apparatus and folds it secured by a cord, quickly attaching it as well to his belt. He looks up at the above system of coils and pulleys. He then turns his gaze to what appears to be a taut line that seems to be coated in a thick oily paste, even more, viscous than the Snarksen concoction. The taught line seems to go on through length of the forest of into the outer edges of the Snarksen Forest. What is hidden from view is a series of towers thinly hidden by leaves and vines, the trappings of the forest below. Ranke looks at the apparatus then at the tree line above followed by a gaze at the unfolding scene of the cat and mouse chase below. He pulls out again his telescope to get a view of where the pursuit must lead.

"Doldren, where are you? You stubborn Dolt!"

He adjusts his telescope a bit for a better view.

"There! There he is, and it's not looking well. He'll end up as Ash Breather kibble for sure. Stupid of me to make such a promise, such oath, a pall of an oath!" Ranke exclaims.

He again collapses his telescope and places it again inside of his cloak. Ranke reaches up and pulls down a lever affixed to both sides of the apparatus. He begins to crank the device frantically. Ranke places both hands on the horizontal stick and places one foot into the hanging placement on the pole affixed below the apparatus. He uses the other foot to push off the side of the high hide platform.

"I haven't had the chance to test this invention, I hope it works," Ranke says to himself.

"It has to work! All this peril for a promise kept."

At that moment, in a blur, Ranke disappears just below the tree-line in the distance.

Doldren is now in a state of extreme panic. He has tried everything that he can think of to out-maneuver the massive reptilian pursuant. He knows that Laurel is becoming weary and he is not sure how much longer she can keep up this exhausting pace.

"Hah! Keep moving girl! I know that this is trying, but we must not slow the pace now" Doldren says.

He can hear the Ash Breather behind him, leathery wings followed by hissing growls and snarls mixed in with roars and taunts. Doldren sees just to his left a clearing with a winding, worn path. It's the path that leads towards a road to the village.

"If I could make it to the clearing, I just might have a chance to reach the village where reinforcements could help me."

He is devising another plan to through off the Ash Breather following close behind him. The path is just to his left. He decides to have Laurel to stop and then turn swiftly toward her left in the hope of throwing off the pursuing beast. The place to turn is rapidly approaching. He counts to himself looking to make his move at the count of six.

"One, two, three!"

The beast is starting to close in again. He bellows a massive stream of fire. The fiery plumes strike a large Snarksen just as Doldren and Laurel dart around it.

"Whoooa! That was close! Four, five." Doldren exclaims.

He sees his mark, the tree, quickly approaching.

The Ash Breather is starting to close the gap again.

"Closer, closer, almost there." He states.

At that moment, the Ash Breather lunges forward and flaps his wings and immediately tucks them close to his body. He opens his mouth and turns his head sideways to devour Doldren and his horse with a snap of his jaws.

"Six!!!!" Doldren exclaims.

He pulls hard on the left side of Laurel's reigns and leans in the same direction. The Ash Breather misses again. The beast slides to a stop on the forest floor. He looks and sees Doldren heading at full gallop towards a small clearing. He thinks that this is his chance to end the cat and mouse chase finally. He lunges towards a massive tree and digs deep into the bark of the tree with his huge claws. His large talons dig deep into the wood releasing Snarksen sap onto the bark of the tree. The creature protest in anger as he begins to smell the irritating aroma of the substance.

"Cursed, repulsive fluid!" He shouts.

He peers to see exactly where Doldren is in the forest. He then leaps to another large tree and then another. He begins to move quicker, as he leaps from towering trunk to towering trunk, protesting each landing. Doldren is now just entering into the long clearing of the forest where the path leads to a road to the village. Doldren turns and looks behind him to see where the Ash Breather is at that moment. To his horror, he sees the Ash Breather leaping from one large tree another, covering large distances with each leap. As Doldren turns around to look forward, a medium sized limb is protruding just in front of him at about the height of his head. The limb catches and strikes him across the top portion of his crown, knocking him violently backward in a full torqued flip off of the back of Laurel.

"Owwumpff!!!" Doldren slams onto the forest floor.

Laurel continued towards the path without her rider. Doldren now full of paralyzing terror jumps up immediately to his feet.

"Stupid of me to take my eyes off the path before me. This lump on my head will be a reminder of this hard lesson. I pray that this will not be the final lesson."

He whistles loudly for Laurel. She slides to a stop and then turns and races back toward Doldren. Unfortunately, the loud whistle has also caught the attention of the Ash Breather. Doldren feels the blood in his body begin to run cold with fear. He cannot deny the impulse to turn around to see where his pursuant may be. Giving in to this impulse, he turns to see where the beast may be. Astonishingly enough, he does not see the beast. Now he realizes an aching dread. He turns in every direction looking all around but no Ash Breather. Then suddenly, the silence in the woods is broken by the horrid words of the Ash Breather.

"I have you now, Fleshie! This Ash Breather's sporting pursuit is finished as well as you. I will devour you!"

Doldren turns quickly to see where the beast is located. To his horror, the beast is located just a few feet from where he is standing, not on the ground but scaling the side of a large Snarksen tree. Doldren can see the beast's large yellowish eyes and can see his breath as it exhaled in and out. The beast releases a fiery billow, just missing Doldren as he ducks behind a large Snarksen. He looks and sees Laurel darting towards him. He instinctively runs towards her as the Ash Breather is in close pursuit behind him. Laurel slides to a stop just a few feet in front of Doldren, turns and kneels on her front legs. Doldren in running motion leaps onto the kneeled steed's back who also fluidly jumps to her feet and takes off like a rocket. The Ash Breather is right behind them. They are entering the clearing where there are only small Snarksen saplings. Not enough to deter a beast of this size and girth.

"Hah! Girl! Ride!"

The Ash Breather is rapidly closing the gap between it and the rider.

"Can you feel it Fleshie? Can you feel your imminent demise? I will pick your scorched carcass clean. You cannot escape me fleshie!"

The Ash Breather taunts! With each passing second, the beast closes in on the rider. The beast, now sensing the moment has come to end this drama, once more lunges forward to devour the rider and his horse. At that moment, a dark figure descends from behind the beast. It's moving at a speed that is faster than the beast and in mere seconds, is now in front of the creature. The figure reaches at its side and pulls out an item. He turns to look forward and then back again at the pursuing beast. He points the item at the creature and then pulls the trigger. The device releases a dart of sorts directly into the left nostril of the beast. The beast instantly recoils, stumbles and trips violently on the forest floor dislodging turf and saplings. The figure in the same motion lands onto the back of Laurel behind Doldren in one motion.

"Keep riding! The Figure shouts.
"Ranke? Ranke! But how and why?"
"Just keep ridding Dolt! And stop when I tell you!"
Ranke looks back to see what has become of the beast. It is on the forest floor, snarling, cursing, hissing and shooting burst of fire from its mouth and nostrils.
"What was that Snarksen paste?"
"Yes, but a more concentrated potion then the original. I added some other pungent secret ingredients."
"What other ingredients did you add?"
"Trust me you don't want to know. Stop here!" They slide to a stop.
"Quickly, take these bladders, break them and pour the contents out and spread it all over your body and clothes. Make sure to put some on your horse as well. Good!" Ranke exclaims!

"Take this tarp and cover your horse as well as yourself with it."
Doldren has Laurel to lie down on her side. He covers her with the tarp and lies down next to her. Ranke runs to a nearby tree to see if he can find the Ash Breather still in pursuit. He pulls out his telescope and looks to see if he can see the beast. He runs back to the where Doldren and Laurel are located. He gathers quickly leaves and handfuls of soil, tossing it hurriedly on the tarp. Ranke slides quickly under the tarp.
"Where is the Ash Breather? Did you see him?" Doldren ask.
"Shishhhh! He is still out there but he is dealing with a face full of my strongest Snarksen. If we are quiet, he will not be able to find us or scent us out."
A few minutes pass and there is still no sign of the Ash Breather. Then suddenly, there is a loud thrashing of leaves and limbs. The Ash Breather in a moment of rage has broken through the canopy of the forest above. He has a nostril full of Snarksen and is very angry to say the least.
"Fleshies, can you hear me? I am not done with you both. After I destroy the village for the insolence you have shown towards me and the Master, I will come back to finish what I started with the two of you. For the insult of soiling me with that accursed sap of the weeds in this forest, you shall pay and pay dearly."
The beast taunts as he circles above the canopy. Then in an instant, it can be heard with a flap of its leathery wings flying off towards the direction of the village.
"We must warn the villagers immediately!" Doldren exclaims.
"We have to do no such thing! If they had not violated the agreement of the Gibbous Indulgence, we would not find ourselves in this horrid predicament."
"Ranke, are you insane? We have loved ones there. We cannot be idle in this thing for it is a horrid thing. They must be warned, even if I have to leave you here in the forest."

"If we leave this forest, we are as good as dead!"

"You heard the beast! If we stay here, we are as good as dead! He is coming back for us! Better to be among many unified against a common enemy than to stand alone, weaker and separated."

"Dullish, dullish brute! Why do you care so much?"

"Why do you pretend not to care so much? Make note friend, if you refer to me again as a "dullish brute," I will not be responsible for my actions. I have had the most harrowing day of my entire life, so my frayed patience is to that to the core. And if you did not care for another soul, why did you come to my aid?"

"We shall not speak of it again. Maybe it was some sort moment of insanity, a not so lucid moment or something that I had eaten that soured on my stomach. In any case, if we are to head to the village to be harbingers of grim news we had best leave now!"

Both Doldren and Ranke climb atop Laurel and are off towards the path that leads towards the village. They ride towards the clearing that leads to a make-shift gravel road that leads to the village. Laurel instinctively accelerates as she enters the path towards the village. Ranke affixed behind Doldren on the back of the galloping Laurel notices the sky above.

"The weather seems to be taking a strange turn. Storm clouds seem to be gathering. Odd, it usually does not rain as much during the Gibbous. I think I heard thunder in the distance, strange indeed."

The three race as fast as possible to attempt to reach the village before the Ash Breather.

"This is futile! We will never make it to the village before the beast! It has a head start and can fly faster than we can ride!"

"Yes! I am aware of that, but we must try to get there to see if we can be of help. We managed to evade the beast using wit and a bit of luck. Maybe we can bring a little with us to the village." They race to the end of the path that leads to the road towards the village. Laurel swiftly covers the distance of the road that leads to the entrance of a small valley that leads to the village.

"Whooooa girl!" Doldren shouts bringing Laurel to sliding stop.

"What are you doing? Why are you stopping?"

"We need to run up to the top of the ridge to see where the Ash Breather may be. It could have been a trick to lure us out of the safety of the Snarksen Forest." Doldren responds.

"Aaaahh! Good thinking, good thinking. We cannot be discovered by the beast so far away from any covering."

They both dismount Laurel. Ranke tells Laurel to stay. The two young men quickly begin to hike to the top of the hill. At that moment, Ranke stops and begins to look around.

"Doldren, do you hear that sound? It sounds like thunder in the distance, but oddly enough, it seems to be coming closer."

"Yes, I can hear it as well. The sound seems like it is changing direction. Look at the clouds; they are churning something fierce!"

At that moment, a strange glow begins to appear in the northern sky. The full moon peeks from behind a swirling, shadowy cloud. Then in an instant, it vanishes behind the billowy cloaks. Just at that moment, appearing over a ridge in the distance, a thick, fiery maelstrom appears. It is moving at a purposeful pace. Fire and smoke congealed into a swirling mass that is moving towards the south, towards the village.

"By the Kraken and everything above! What manner of apparition is that?" Doldren shouts.

"A curious sight, a curious sight indeed!"

"Is it the Ash Breather? No, it could not be! I have observed the beast before, and it had never manifested any such ability, to cloak itself in fire and smoke" Ranke says. The fiery flume of smoke appears to pick up speed and disappears over a hilly ridge towards the south.   The fiery glow on the southern horizon begins to subside.

"Come on! Let's follow it! We can run over to the top of that ridge in the distance to get a better view at that, that thing. The ridge will give us a useful vantage point."

"Yes, yes indeed! This one thing I will agree. We must see what has manifested on this strange Gibbous evening."

The two wearied trekkers sprint to the ridge to get a better vantage point to view the fiery apparition that has appeared. As they arrive at the base of a hill on the ridge, they slide to stop and begin to crouch down and crawl towards the top of one of the tallest hills on the ridge. The eerie, fiery glow still can be seen in the distance.

"It appears to be headed in the direction of the village. We cannot wait here; we must try to make our way there to offer our hand in battle!"

"I don't know what we could expect to accomplish between the Ash Breather and the apparition."

Ranke ponders as he looks at the mysterious glow in the distance. He voices what he is thinking,

"A curious thing, a curious thing indeed."

The people of the village are gathered together at the center near an old snarksen tree. The tree is knarled, twisted and bent. It has a personality of its own and is the epicenter of the village where the people gather, discuss, trade goods as it is the pulse of the people. This eve is no different for the people have made a decision that has driven the following course of events.

"We have doomed ourselves to destruction at the claw, fang, and flame of the Ash Breather because we have chosen to ignore the Gibbous agreement!" A male villager states.

"We will surely feel the wrath of the beast once it discovers that the village did not provide the Gibbous for its sport." Another villager replies.

"People, people, calm yourselves. This moment is the very hour that we need show our resolve to stand together against the Ash Breather! We cannot and will not faint!" The Patriarch of the village speaks.

He is reverently referred to as "The Old Man." He has a given name but rarely is it used. He is not necessarily the oldest man compared to other patriarchs, but he is one of the wisest of men in the commune. He belongs to the village assembly and is the Chief Advisor. Irony would have it; He is the principal catalyst for the revolt. He has a hidden reason for igniting the rebellion against the Ash Breather and his master.

"Yes, Chief Advisor, we all know where you stand on the matter of the Ash Breather, but that will be of little protection from the wrath that is sure to come! I think that we should leave this domicile as soon as possible before the beast arrives which surely will take place! He has warned us repeatedly of what would happen if we failed to offer the Gibbous. We can leave under cover of night, start over again and rebuild." The young man states animatedly.

"That is not wisdom, but fear speaking and if you are correct as to the Ash Breathers imminent arrival, you will not have enough time to escape! And as for where I stand on the Ash Breather, I loathe that scaly blithe on this village! It is evil incarnate! Numbered are the creature's days!"

"What do you mean Old Man? How could that beast's days be numbered? Are you referring to that wretched prophecy that our parents use to tell us? Mere stories to keep us entertained as children? The creature, it is a prolific, ravenous, relentless being! No man or any number of men can defeat it! It is real and not fiction! And it is a fool's notion to think that we can withstand its wrath when it arrives! We should have presented the Gibbous when it was required. Maybe we could still yet offer up the Gibbous to assuage the beast's wrath just yet."

"Nooooo! That is not an option to consider! We cannot offer up kindred and friend to that disgusting beast, and its Master! We will choose to stand together and if need be, fall together!"

The Chief Counsel's thunderous response causes a raucous banter between two groups of people, those who agree with the young man and oppose the Chief Counsel.

"You cannot speak for all of us! We do not share the same sentiment Chief Counsel! I am not staying here one more moment! I am leaving with my family immediately and will leave those behind to their fate! If any of you are wise, you will join me and leave this doomed place!"

"That is not wisdom!" Says one other man standing in the crowd.

"No, it is not wise; the Ash Breather will certainly be here shortly! To leave this village without any cover or protection is folly!" The Chief Counsel expounds.

"We will take our chances! Tonight, we are leaving! And if any of you have any smarts about you, you will leave with us, but I and my family are leaving, now!"

"Trilleon, do not make this grievous mistake! I implore you!"

The young man ignores the pleas of the Chief Counsel. He and his family walk away from the gathered crowd at the center of the village. Trilleon along with his wife, Drayden Keywna and their little girl A'Sureth Keywna begin to head towards the gate. Trilleon motions to the Watcher in the tower to unlock the gate. The Watcher triggers the mechanism, fashioned by Ranke that sets in motion weights and pulleys that moves a large beam from latches mounted on the inner portion of the Snarksen wood gate. Trilleon pulls on the leash attached to reins on a dusty, spotted grey mule, tethered to a small cart. The cart is laden with all of their belongings. His begins to walk towards the opening. He stops for a moment and turns to look back at what was his home, his sanctuary. The Chief Counsel walks hurriedly towards him, holding his staff, and leans on the side of the cart near where Trilleon is standing.

"Trilleon, please rethink this decision! We can get through this together if we stand together against the terror of this night!"

As Trilleon begins to reply, the Watcher begins to stand up and peer through a make-shift looking tube towards the northern night time sky. He squints and adjusts the device then takes in a large gasp of air. He stumbles as he tries quickly to run to grab a large pole that has cloth wadding that is saturated with dried Snarksen sap and wax on one end. He rights himself and strikes repeatedly a large hollowed out Snarksen log with a large metal sheet that is tied suspended within the hollowed log. The resulting sound is guttural, tonal sound that reverberates throughout the entire village.

"Whuuummmlllmm!! Whuummllllmmmm!" He strikes the tonal log sharply. What he shouts next sends the entire village into a momentary shock.

"The Ash Breather comes! The Ash Breather comes! Ready yourselves!! "Whuuummmlllmm!! Whuummllllmmmm!" He strikes the tonal log twice again.

The Watcher drops a thick pole that is attached by a cord and it catapults him towards another pole that is vertical and adjacent to the tower he is standing in. He slides down the pole in quick fashion and joins the villagers who are now in full retreat to their various dwellings. Just in the distance, a shadowy figure appears for an instance then disappears behind a cloud bank. Its shadowy outline is made even more ominous by the backdrop of the waxing Gibbous moon in the night time sky.

"The Ash Breather is coming, run and take cover!" One man shouts.

Certain men in the village run frantically towards canopies that are rolled up like scrolls above many of the huts and enclosures. The Village is nestled alongside a small ridge. On the side of the ridge are a couple of smaller cave-like openings that were moreover hollowed out by the villagers for livestock and feed storage. Today it will also act as a makeshift bunker for some of the families.

"Women and children first, followed by the elders, gather into the alcoves now! Come along! The Ash Breather is upon us! We only have moments! Quickly! Quickly!" The Old Man says.

Now, on a small mount approximately 1000 yards or so, the Ash Breather lights upon it. It spreads its wings and releases a blood-curdling shriek of a roar.

"Rrooooaarsssshhhh!!! Destruction is upon you for your defiance! The Gibbous was not offered and all of you shall perish under fire, fang and claw! I will give your carcasses to the Master and he will have his fill! Fear and dread will be your companions this night! There is nowhere to hide, nowhere to flee! Roarsssshhhh!!!"

The beast roars his threats of harm. Instantly, after the creature releases his roaring intimidations, it extends its large, leathery wings into the night air and is instantly catapulted into the stratosphere.

"Brace yourselves!" The Old Man cries.

"Be steadfast men in your courage! The Ash Breather is upon us!"

In that instance, the shadowy form of the beast can be seen plummeting and arching itself in and out of amorphous clouds in the night time sky. At one arcane moment, the ominous form of the beast is accented by the backdrop of the Gibbous moon. Suddenly, the beast tucks its wings and nose dives with frightening speed towards the village. Preceding it in mid-air, spilling out of its mouth is a flume of fiery hot projectile and smoke. It levels itself and rakes the fiery flume through the center of the village.

"Break open the bladders!!" The Old Man shouts.

The bladders are tied throughout the village, large and swelling all filled with a mixture of sand, water and Snarksen sap. This was implemented at the suggestion of Ranke the tinkerer. Some of the villagers were reluctant to place the bladders on their homes and around the village but now they are not regretting the decision. The Snarksen concoction is working well. The flames are extinguished but not before damaging some of the modest structures made of wood and earthen clay.

"The beast is not done with us, it is returning again from the north!" One man shouts who scurried atop a smaller tower within the village. The beast in like fashion swoops down through the skies and rakes fire through the village. The fire deluge on the second assault causes more damage than the first. Some of the modest, earthen structures seem to almost combust into mushroom clouds of smoke and flame. The people scatter to avoid the flame deluge. Some drop and roll on the ground in agony enveloped in flames while others try to douse the tongues of fire that attach to them like a ravenous animal. The spotted grey mule being spooked by the mayhem of the winged creature manages to break free of its tether that is weakened by flames. The beast runs in a panic to and fro throughout the village.

"Get those flames extinguished, douse them with the Snarksen water and do the same for those aflame. Careful now, be ready for the beast will surely make another pass!" The Old Man exclaims.

And sure enough, the beast does just that. Its shadowy form arcs and dives through the night time sky. As the night advances on, the Gibbous moon's illumination casts an eerie glow on the form of the beast.

"The Ash Breather is making another pass!" The young man in the tower exclaims.

"Take cover!!" The Old Man shouts, as he himself ducks into a shallow alcove in the side of the hill where the village resides.

He pulls down a Snarksen laden tarp and quickly ties the sides to poles affixed inside of the alcove. The flames of the beast pour out like water through the center of the village. The sheer force of the blast feels as if a fiery vortex has lit in the center of the hamlet. The Old Man turns his face towards the back of the small space towards the rocky back of the alcove to avoid the flames that flow around the sides of the Snarksen covering. Once they subside, he immediately leaves the makeshift keep to extinguish a small residual of flames that has affixed to his right shoulder.

"Counsel, you are injured by the flame!" One man shouts. The Old Man grabs a small bladder of Ranke's Snarksen water and breaks it open onto his right arm immediately extinguishing the flames.

"Awww, its nothing, nothing at all. The Snarksen water has provided a quick remedy!"

Suddenly the young man in the tower exclaims loudly, catching the attention of the men who are working feverishly to extinguish the flames.

"The gate is breached! The gate is breached!" He exclaims excitedly.

The gates of the village where fashioned by the villagers of Snarksen wood. With several of the beams weighing enough to take ten men to carry and set into place. While the Snarksen provides an excellent barrier to resist flame, they are not indestructible. The Ash Breather during its last assault swooped low and gouged a breach with its massive tail through the center of the gate, raking it as well with flame. The breach is massive and leaves the village in a dire predicament. Trilleon, who managed to cover his wagon with a Snarksen tarp and hide his family in one of the adjacent alcoves, sees this as a chance to flee the fate of the village. He calls to his wife and daughter after quickly attaching a horse to the wagon.

"Come, Come now! We have a small window of opportunity to leave this place while the beast is setting itself for another assault!" He says to the wife.

He places his wife into the wagon, then carefully his small daughter setting her alongside her mother. He quickly runs to the horse and grabs the reins.

"Come on girl, come!" Trilleon commands and coaxes the nervous animal.

"Nooo, Trilleon, what are doing? Have you taken leave of your senses? Would you take your family directly into the path of destruction?" The Old Man exclaims, grabbing the arm of Trilleon.

"Leave me, Old Man, to stay here would put my family in harm's way!" Trilleon rants as he snatches his arm from the grasp of the Chief Counsel.

"Now leave me be! Hah, horse!"

Trilleon hurriedly runs through the gaping breach at the gate. His wife looks back with trepidation into the eyes of the Old Man holding her daughter close to her.

"Trilleon, I beseech you, stay with the gathered here! You will not be able to survive alone an encounter with the Ash Breather. You are placing all of your lives in peril!"

Trilleon ignores the pleas of the Old Man and continues to pull the horse-drawn wagon through the gate into the clearing in front of the village. He hurries along tugging at the reins of the horse. Suddenly, the horse stops in its tracks and begins to rear up on its hind legs, snatching the reins out of the hands of Trilleon.

"Whooa girl! Calm down! Calm down! Whooa girl!"

Trilleon is not successful in calming the horse because it senses an approaching danger. The horse in an instance of panic breaks loose of the harness and runs away into the forest. The husband in sheer fear grabs the little girl and helps his wife down from the wagon.

"Go now, take A'Sureth and run back to the gate! I will push the wagon back to the village!" He motions to his wife.

"Nooo, I will not leave you! Leave the lot of it here! Flee with us!" The wife responds to her husband.

"It is everything that we own! I will not leave it!"

"No, it is not! We are everything that you have!"

"Go now! I will follow!"

She begins to head in the direction of the gate where a crowd of the villagers has gathered, beckoning them both to run for the gate. At that moment, the young man who was in the gate tower scurries again to the top of the tower. He screams words that send cold fear through the bones of Trilleon. Words he did not want to hear while standing in the clearing in front of the village.

"ASH BREATHER! It's coming again! Take cover!"

The people scatter again, all except two, the Old Man and a young man by the name of Drash'Ur. They are beckoning the trio forward.

"Run! Run! Run with all your might! The Ash Breather is coming!"

The wife manages to make it to the gate first. She hands the little girl to the Old Man and turns immediately to run back towards her husband. She screams at Trilleon to leave the wagon where it stands and run. Stubbornly he tries to push the wagon towards the gate.

The young man in the tower shouts aloud, "Take cover, take cover! The Ash Breather comes!"

In that instance, a fiery flume rakes the ground first behind the wagon then snakes a scorched path around to the front of the cart between Trilleon's wife and himself. Trilleon falls to his hands and knees and covers his face from the flying, fiery turf. His wife does the same, screaming his name in horror.

"Trilleon!!!!"

She screams his name repeatedly as she cannot see him over the wall of flames. He also cannot see her but can hear her screams as he is looking down towards the ground, shielding his face from the heat, a heat that is surprisingly intense. He notices a shadow on the ground, being cast by the Gibbous moons light. The shadow moves, darts, pauses, then begins to grow larger, then more substantial and then finally expands to meet the thing that is the source of the shadow. The beast lights onto the clearing floor in a surprisingly gentle fashion likened to that of beastly moth, affixing itself to a branch without fanfare. But as the beast begins to move, Trilleon could sense and feel each step as a micro-quake. With each movement taken by the creature, a hint to the massive size and proportions of the dangerous beast is revealed. The Ash Breather arrogantly struts over to where Trilleon crouches low to the ground. In sheer terror, mustering the courage to move his fear stiffened body, he retreats under the wagon. He motions to his wife, who he can now see him as the fire has begun to subside, to go to the gate of the village. She is fixed and motionless, frozen in fear. She manages to shake her head in a motion to say no to his request. At that moment, the Ash Breather approaches the wooden refuge of his prey. Trilleon is frozen in place and gripped with fear; his heart is racing faster and faster. He can see the beast's massive body stop at the front of the wagon. What happens next almost causes his heart to stop functioning in cardiac distress. The creature lowers its head below the frame of the carriage and peers under it to find itself eye level with Trilleon. It makes eye contact with the now whimpering man. Trilleon looks into the piercing yellowish green eyes of the animal. He is so close to the creature that he can even see the pupils dilate as they fix a gaze directly on him.

"What have we here? Do we have the Gibbous offering ready to be retrieved? Are you offering yourself as an oblation aye fleshie?" The beast mockingly taunts the terrified man.

The creature places one scale clad claw under the carriage of the wagon and in a quick torque of its arm, flings the cart several feet away sending it crashing and sliding on the open clearing floor. His wife, just a few feet away, screams in horror. Trilleon without the covering of the wagon is now facing the mocking, scaly figure. His increasing adrenalin causes him to attempt an escape albeit feeble in its execution. He stumbles and repeatedly falls as the beast mocks him in his attempt. The Ash Breather does not pursue him initially but merely insults his effort.

"Amusing, the sport of the chase. I have had enough sport for this night and have worked up an appetite." The taunting beast exclaims.

In an instance, it is airborne and hovers over the stumbling Trilleon. The Ash Breather descends with a thud, pinning the stumbling man to the ground underneath one of its massive claws. His wife shrieks in horror.

"Going, somewhere are we? Come now fleshie, we can't have that!"

The beast says mockingly and arrogantly.

At the same instance, the Gibbous Moon becomes obscured by gathering clouds; And the wind begins to arise.

"Odd, there are usually no storms during the Gibbous season." The beast says, looking around into the night time sky.

"But never the less, it is an omen of your doom and to this village of vermin."

The beast bends its scale clad neck bringing his massive head close to the face of Trilleon pinned below his claw.

"I am going to toy with you Gibbous."

The beast looks up to where Trilleon's wife is crouched low to the ground, tears streaming down her face. She is pleading for the life of her husband. The beast laughs mockingly.

"Fleshie, is that your mate that pleads on your behalf? Mercy she says? A cry for mercy? I don't have a desire to give you mercy or her. But I do have a desire to taunt you beyond strain; I will make you watch as I release a fury of fire and smoke upon her fragile frame!"

Trilleon screams and hurls insults at the beast. The Ash Breather laughs mockingly at his response.

Ranke and Doldren finally make it to the top of the high ridge mount overlooking the valley clearing leading to the village. They crawl the remaining distance to the top with their mouths agape viewing the spectacle of the burning storm that is cutting its way through the forest and eventually towards the edge of the valley.

"What could it be? The trees do not burn at the storms touch!" Doldren exclaims.

"I have no earthly explanation!" Ranke replies.

"My first thought went to another apparition of the Ash Breather, but that does not seem to fit an explanation."

"Look! There in the distance at the crown of the valley near the place of the gate or what's left of it. It's the Ash Breather!"

"It looks like he has someone under one of his claws and another just before him in his sights!"

At that moment, the fiery maelstrom seems to change direction sharply and begins to arc fiercely in the course of the Ash Breather.

"Look, the whirlwind is changing direction and heading towards the beast. Wait, I see something else. It looks like shiny, fiery projectiles encircling the vortex." Doldren says.

"Yes, I see them; it looks like two of them. Look the whirlwind has suddenly subsided hurling the two projectiles in the direction of the monster. They are changing direction! Do my eyes deceive me?" Ranke says.

He pulls out his looking glass to get a closer look.

"They are men or metal men of some sorts, flaming and running swifter than any terra gazelle I have ever seen!"

"Give me that glass!" Doldren replies.

He plainly can see the outlined image of the two speeding objects.

"What manner of apparition are they? The earth even burns under their feet." Doldren says to himself as he and Ranke look on at the unfolding theatre below.

The Ash Breather hurls insults at Trilleon and taunts his wife. The beast strafes the valley floor with his tail, back and forward. He breathes foul, ash-laden puffs of smoke through his nostrils almost suffocating Trilleon from the stench.

"Do you hear your mate's sorrowful cries fleshie? Ohh please, oh please, spare my husband!" The beast says in a tone mocking Trilleon's wife's plea.

"But who will plead for her life?" The Ash Breather says.

He presses down ever so lightly with his claw on the chest of Trilleon preventing him from speaking. Such a mockingly evil gesture by the loathsome beast.

"Can you hear her voice, aye fleshie? Now you will hear her screams as I bathe her in a deluge of flame and smoke."

Trilleon manages to muster a scream at the beast as it begins to inhale deeply preparing to exhale its pungent, fiery maelstrom of destruction upon the frail form of Trilleon's wife. The Ash Breather emits a flood of flame in the direction of Trilleon's mate. He screams aloud her name.

"Elsabeth, Elsaaaaaaabeeetthhh!"

Trilleon screams until he feels almost as to faint and lose consciousness. He looks up into the face of the beast. Its eyes, glowing a yellowish illumination, look void of compassion and are filled with anger and hate. The beast, drunk with mayhem, releases a fiendish chuckle rearing its scaly head back while still spewing fire and smoke into the night-time sky. A flaming column lights the entire valley floor.

"Look fleshie; she is no more. Fire and smoke consume her. I am Ash Breather!!"

The arrogant oaf of a lizard exclaims.

The beast looks down toward the grief-stricken Trilleon and taunts him further.

"Aye fleshie, no words? Is your heart torn and ripped with despair? Do not fear, I will end your suffering shortly but first look at the remains of your beloved mate. The fire still has her, but soon it will subside and reveal the destruction."

The beast lifts its claw releasing the trapped Trilleon from under its foot. Trilleon manages to stand briefly to his feet then falls to his knees sobbing uncontrollably. Repeatedly he cries his wife's name,

"Elsabeth, Elsabeth, Elsabeth!"

He musters the strength, the courage to lift his head to see the grim specter of the tragedy of his beloved's demise. He looks into the flames as he hears the mocking laughter of the Ash Breather. He squints to adjust his eyes for only a moment because he sees something odd and even peculiar in the midst of the subsiding fiery torrent. It appears metallic, but he can't be sure. The Ash Breather obviously can see the strange object as well because its mocking laughter has ceased. As the fire begins to subside, Trilleon notices that the wind has increased significantly. Then suddenly he hears Elsabeth scream and what appears to be another voice speaking beyond the subsiding flames. Intuitively, Trilleon screams her name, "Elsabeth!"

The Ash Breather is confused and again pins Trilleon to the ground under its claw.

"Silence Gibbous!" The beast shrieks.

The beast looks at the object in complete confusion then suddenly the object shrinks in size to reveal what appears to the beast as a metallic creature, shiny, and positioned with the metal object attached to its arm. The metallic interloper is standing between the beast and the woman.

"What manner of creature are you metal one? And do you dare defy me my mayhem? Speak and give me an explanation, the Ash Breather demands it!" The beast exclaims.

The metallic creature does not respond to the brute but kneels down to lift the woman to her feet. He seems to say something to her, and she initially shakes her head in disagreement but the metallic creature points toward the gate of the village, and eventually, the woman flees towards the entrance. She takes a brief glance back at her husband who is still pinned by the beast.

"What? Do you dare? Woman stand your ground, or I will devour you and your mate!"

At that moment, the metallic creature speaks in reply.

"You will do no such thing dragon! We will not allow it!"

It is Letete who is speaking to the dragon and who saved the woman, Elsabeth from destruction. He stands in a defensive pose and reaches behind his head to reveal the sword of Neuma Ru, bright, shining and covered in a bluish green flame.

"Tiny thing, you dare defy me!"

The Ash Breather in a fantastic quick motion inhales a massive gulp of air with the intention of blasting the defiant metallic creature. But more amazingly, dashing even faster than what the beast can respond to, Letete covers the distance between it and the monster and strikes it with the middle portion of his shield directly in its snarling agape mouth. It gasps, expelling muffled puffs of fire and smoke as a result of the blow. Letete's motion precedes scorched flamed markings on the grassy turf. He, after striking the beast squarely, torques and flips backward near the place where he stood. The delivered blow catches the creature off guard, snapping its head back violently and causing it to be lifted off the ground and falling backward with its feet sprawling awkwardly into the air. This strike instantly frees Trilleon who was pinned face down by the beast with one of its claws. Trilleon manages to rise to one knee and look back at the sprawling monster. He then turns to face the metallic, man-like creature. Letete quickly makes his way to the injured Trilleon.

"Are you okay?" Can you walk?"

Startled and confused by his small-sized savior Trilleon nods an affirmative. Trilleon turns again to see that the beast has just righted itself and is visibly angry. It is screaming and puffing while all at the same time hurling insults in a language that is not understood at all by either Trilleon or Letete.

"The audacity to strike me! Strike me! The Ash Breather! I will crush you both and level that fleshie infested village! My fire will reduce it to ash and cinder!"

Letete takes hold of Trilleon's arm and shouts to him, "Run!"

Trilleon runs as fast as he can towards the village. He stumbles and limps his way in that direction. His wife is just outside of the village gate with others beckoning him on. Letete turns to brace himself as he hears the heavy footfalls of the beast behind him. The monster is running at full gape with its wings tucked tight behind him. Letete plants his left foot first then instantly the ground below him ignites in a greenish blue flame. He is running directly towards the beast. Letete is staring directly into the eyes of the Ash Breather who has now tucked his head low running with every intention of destroying his metallic assailant. Time seems to slow almost to a stop then suddenly Letete notices a glow that is increasing just to the left of the best. The object is moving at an incredible speed. It arcs alongside the beast then like a bolt of lightning flanks toward the head of the creature striking it cleanly across its face slicing it over its left yellowish eye. The blow, hard and concussive, torques the beast in the opposite direction causing it to slide uncontrollably on the clearing turf.

"Arrrrgghhhhssssssssgrooowwwlllsssss!"

The beast exclaims as it rolls on the grassy clearing floor. Letete slides to a fiery stop as he sees his little brother Lucas slide in the same fiery fashion almost twenty feet with his sword poised in a position as one who had completed a sword-stroke. He stands motionless for a moment as if posing for a camera snapshot to be taken.

"Show off!" Letete responds.

"You haven't seen anything yet!" Lucas replies.

The Ash Breather finds itself in a predicament it has never experienced before, bested, injured and confused by an enemy that he has never seen. It rights itself again and in a berserk rage charges Lucas, leaping into the air, it wants to reach and rend this metallic assailant into pieces.

"Circle him!"

Letete thinks to himself knowing that his brother can hear his thought, another unique ability given to them by the wearing of the armor. They find themselves in complete unity. The two brothers begin to run fiery circles around the charging beast that is confused and does not know which assailant to attack first. The creature slides to a stop as a bluish-green blaze encircles him. Then suddenly, Lucas breaks the circling arc and bullets again towards the beast, clipping it on the lateral of its massive scaly head. Lucas spins and torques like a gymnast and sticks a landing on the opposite side of the beast. Letete follows suit. The creature, in a state of exasperation swings at the metallic blur missing it with the scaly swipe of its claw. Letete slides effortlessly alongside his brother.

"Arrogance and sacrilege!! You dare strike me!!! Who are you? Are you minions of the Master sent to test me? To test my loyalty?" The Ash Breather says uncharacteristically.

"Serve a scaly frrreeeak like you or anything that looks like you, not a chance Barney!" Lucas says mockingly.

Letete chuckles uncontrollably at his brother's insult of the beast.

"Then what are you? What manner of beast are you?"

"We are more than mere beast dragon! The true ruler of this world has sent us, Neuma Ru and has empowered!"

Letete responds audibly to the query of the beast and speaks a thought to his brother, "Remove your helmet for just a minute."

Letete and Lucas simultaneously remove their helmets to reveal who they are to the beast. The Ash Breather is in shock at the revelation of the children under the metal facades. It screams in response to the unveiling of its otherworldly foes.

"What? This apparition cannot be! How can this be? Fleshies? You are mere vermin of the same type in this village. Vermin pestilence! You shall die this night!"

The Ash Breather shouts. Lucas looks to his brother and asks him a simple question.

"Letete, what is a vermin? It doesn't sound too good."

Letete responds keeping an eye on the Breather as it begins to strafe the ground with its tail and snort puffs of smoke and ash out of its nostrils.

"Vermin is another name for a rat or something like that."

Lucas' eyes stretch large at the explanation, and he releases a response the only way that Lucas could.

"Heeeey! Who you callin' a rat? Barney! You know I don't like being called a rat!"

The Ash Breather hurls another threat in response.

"I will call you scorched and destroyed soon you vermin simpleton."

The Beast begins to inhale a large gulp of air. Its chest expands rapidly seeming as if it would even burst through its scaly confines.

"Whooooaaa! Put your helmet on now!" Letete shouts.

Almost a second later, the two metal clad liberators of the village are completely bathed in a blanket of fire and scorching heat. The villagers gasp and recoil as they see the two warriors disappear in the deluge of fire and smoke. The Ash Breather releases a fiendish laugh that echoes throughout the night-time sky. He turns to taunt the villagers gathered at the gate.

"See, your would-be saviors, my fiery breath devours them!" he scoffs.

The flames of the Ash Breather illuminate the entire valley clearing. What remains is a bonfire of smoke, cinders, and ash. The villagers begin to despair as the Ash Breather continues to taunt them and mock their would-be protectors. Moments later as the blaze starts to subside, the young man in the gate tower strikes the tonal log and shouts excitedly.

"Look, in the midst of the fire! The two are still standing! The two are still standing!"

The Ash Breather turns to see the two brothers standing with their shields extended. The shields appear larger than before and shrink back to their original state before the fiery deluge. Their armor is glowing red hot from the fiery deluge of the beast, but they are unharmed.

"Impossible!" The Ash Breather shouts.

"My fire is unrelenting, unforgiving! How can this be?"

The two brothers each pull their swords from their sheaths. The swords instantly grow in size, a size that is so unnatural in appearance that the two boys should not be able to weld them. But weld them they do. Letete responds first.

"You want fire?"

Then Lucas follows finishing Letete's sentence.

"We will give you FIRE, DRAGON!!"

The two brothers leap as if propelled into the night-time sky and in unison swing their massive, fiery swords overhead and they both strike the very ground in front of them. The ground shakes and ignites, ripped by a massive arc of fire and lightning. It zigzags its way towards the Ash Breather, striking it before it can respond to avoid the immense energy discharge. The fiery release races its way towards the beast and dislodges it from its stance, knocking it several feet from its position in the clearing. The fire scorches the creature directly across its massive chest. It screams in agony because of the searing pain. The intense heat energy discharge stings the beast violently. It is a pain like no other pain the Ash Breather has ever experienced. It rights itself, still enveloped in the searing fiery discharge, and in a berserk move charges the two brothers standing in the clearing. It clears the distance between it and the two brothers in a surprising fashion. It lunges with its mouth wide and agape seeking to devour one of the two brothers. The assailed brother takes a giant leap backward while the other lunges forward with his sword and strikes at one of the beast massive scaled legs. The beast roars in pain and swings its enormous tail like a whip to attempt to swipe the older of the two brothers, Letete. Letete ducks and flips over the Ash Breathers tail while his little brother attacks the flank of the beast. The Ash Breather in a full panic attack lunges, swipes and claws at his bee-like assailants missing them at every turn. One swipe comes too close to Letete for his comfort. This near miss enrages his brother Lucas who screams, "This ends NOOOOWW!"

Lucas manages to side-step one of the beasts deadly attempts to claw him and draws his sword and strikes with deadly accuracy hitting the right claw of the animal severing two of its long glass like claws from the joint. The beast screams in agony and recoils. It grabs its wounded claw and accesses the damage. The creature, in a quick, instinctive motion, exhales a burst of flames on the wounds to cauterize them. The pain causes the beast to tremble then strike its wounded claw on the grassy turf.

"No! No! No! Vile, vile vermin! My claw, you have maimed me. For that, you have gained an enemy for as long as you live!"

"What makes you think that you will live to see the light of day, dragon?"

Lucas threatens as he draws his sword and it grows to a massive size. In that instance the beast bellows fire and smoke in every direction. Instinctively, the two brothers raise their shields to protect themselves from the fiery burst. When they lower their shields, the Ash Breather is gone. They look up to see the shadowy form of the beast flying towards the south. It shouts a threat as it lifts away in retreat.

"This is not the last time we shall see one another, Fleshies! I will return with others of my kind! And I have a score to settle with the little one!"

Lucas lifts up the visor on his helmet and replies to the fleeing beast's threats.

"Oh yeah, Barney?" He shouts.

Lucas holds up one hand with his fingers in the shape of the letter "L."

"Loser, loser! Who's the vermin now?" Lucas shouts as the two warriors stand in the clearing with their fiery swords drawn as they watch the wounded beast fly off into the moonlit sky. Letete lifts his visor and begins to laugh uncontrollably.

"Well, I guess that's that!" Lucas states. Letete responds to his little brother's edict.

"Unfortunately, Lucas, I don't think that is it. I feel that we will see that beast again and others like it. I'm a little concerned about this Master the dragon kept referring to."

"I'm not worried about nothin'! Did you see how we fought? We were awesome!" At that moment, a voice responds to Lucas' declaration and speaks to both of the two young warriors via their thoughts.

"Remember humility young warriors. Remember to be humble." The two were startled for a moment but instantly knew that the voice they were hearing was that of Neuma Ru.

"Yes, we understand." The two brothers answer in unity.

"Lucas, we must always be careful here in this strange world. Remember, we are not from this place, and there is still so much that we do not know about this world."

At that moment, the villagers begin to file out through the broken gate and gather in the clearing just before the entrance. They are a little cautious in their approach.

"Lucas, sheath your sword, we do not want to frighten the people."

The two metal-clad boys place their swords into their sheaths. The swords instantly shrink to size to fit perfectly snug into place. The two stand and face the growing crowd of villagers who are gathering to see what manner of beings have rescued them today. All are astonished and surprised by their visit except one, the Old Man.

"My eyes feed my heart with this joyous spectacle of the Ash Breather defeated and sent fleeing. My mind tells and reminds both my heart and eyes of the foretelling of their coming in the prophecy written so long ago in the tree. What a glorious day, a glorious day indeed!" He says to himself.

The Old Man begins to shout a chant in honor of the two. The villagers immediately follow suit, remembering the stories of the prophecies and the 'Hero's Song' known and taught to all children.

"Trumpet the heroes that come, trumpet the heroes that come, trumpet the heroes that come and put the Ash Breather on the run!!!"

Letete thinks a thought to himself knowing that his brother can hear it.

"This is a true adventure. The adventure of helping others just like Dad taught us. Trumpet the adventure!

"Trumpet the Adventure indeed, big brother. Trumpet the adventure indeed!"

EIGHT

The Old Man and the Prophecy

The villagers flow out into the clearing, some carrying torches and oil lamps though hardly needed. The Two warrior's armor emits a bright, warm glow. A fiery flame encircles the heart-shaped insignia on their chest plate. In like fashion, their swords and helmets are aflame and cast dancing shadows on the ground. The villagers still chanting the new song of victory are now gathered into a circle around the two. Some of the men have right-sided the overturned cart, tossed aside by the Ash Breather. Surprising enough, it is still in working condition. They push it slightly and then join in the festivities of the jubilant crowd of villagers singing the new song of victory. Letete motions to his brother to remove their helmets. Once removed, the sight of men in this strange armor, albeit little men, ignites the gathered villagers into a raucous cheer.

"Look, they are people like us, even children. Amazing it is, absolutely amazing!" One of the jubilant villagers shouts.

The two warriors sheath their fiery weapons, and instantly the chanting and singing crowd fall upon them. They are lifted up on the shoulders of men and carried in a victor's trek around the wagon cart nearby. The throng hoists the boys onto the bed of the cart. At that moment, A'Sureth presses through the crowd and reaches up towards the two. Instinctively, the two reach down and take one hand each and lift the little girl effortlessly as a feather into the cart. She grabs Letete and motions for him to lean forward.

She says to him, "Thank you both for saving my Mama and Peh-Paah!"

Both Letete and Lucas reply to the little girl's show of gratitude.

"You are welcome!"

At that moment a horse carrying two riders can be seen coming from the south bearing down rapidly on the gathered crowd.

"By the Kraken! We have beheld a great spectacle, none of which has ever been seen by man nor beast before in this place!"

It's Ranke and Doldren. They both dismount Laurel while continuing their tale.

"A glorious thing, an astounding thing to say the least! Metallic beings have come to our aid to defeat the Ash Breather! Where do you hale from metallic beings? Are you beast or other?" Ranke asks.

"We are definitely not beasts!" Letete retorts.

"We are people just like you, boys to be exact!" Lucas responds.

"Boooys? Boooys!! How is this possible? How can mere boys perform such mighty and wondrous acts of heroism?"

"It's not because of us; it's because of the one who sent us!" Letete responds.

"Mighty are his weapons in battle!" Lucas shouts as he stands on his feet unsheathing his fiery sword thrusting it high into the Gibbous night sky. This action garners a resounding response from the gathered crowd. They shout with jubilance and begin to chant again. Letete leans over to his little brother and whispers something in his ear.

"You are such a show-off!"

"I'm not showing off Big Bro', I'm excited beyond anything! We wanted adventure, and we found more than that. We found a purpose!"

The gathered crowd of villagers escort the iron-clad champions through the damaged gate. They gather around the two as they stand and view the damage left by the marauding beast.

"We should have gotten here earlier." Letete thinks to himself. A voice whispers to him in response.

"It was in my timing that I sent you. Do not fret."

The Old Man begins to instruct some of the gathered men both young and old to start making repairs to the gate and some of the damaged buildings. Letete and Lucas volunteer to help. They lower little A'Sureth down carefully into the arms of her mother. They leap from the cart in an instance and join a small caravan of men who venture towards the Snarksen Forest.

"We will run on ahead of you and cut down a few of the trees to make them easy to transport back to the village," Letete says.

Lucas and Letete run ahead of the group. Quickly, in a flash, they are at the edge of the Snarksen Forest. They draw their swords and effortlessly cut down some of the large Snarksen and trim the limbs. They cut the trees into timber for easy travel and construction.

"Hey, Lucas, cut the trees like the Lincoln logs back home. I'm quite sure that the men should be able to build some great structures with these life-sized Lincoln Logs."

"Good idea!"

The amazing blades with surprisingly little effort slice through the Snarksen. The fragrance of the trees fills the air. When the men arrive, they marvel at just how many massive trees were cut down. They begin to load some of the cut beams onto the wagons. When they arrive at the village, they make quick work of the repairs and even enhance the gate with the help of the two brothers. Hours pass quickly. The men, except for the gate, almost complete most of the repairs.

"We will finish the repairs to the gate on the morrow. Let us stop and celebrate with an impromptu feast in honor of our guest." The Old Man Thaddeus states.

"Come here young warriors!"

He looks first to Letete and asks him his name.

"Young man, what is your name?"

"I am Letete, and this is my little brother Lucas."

Thaddeus smiles in response.

"Hmm! Unique names Letete the Elder and Lucas the Younger. Welcome to our humble village. We celebrate you by inviting you to a banquet in your honor. It is a meager harvest, but we gladly offer it to you as our honored guest. Doldren! Ranke! Set the places for our honored guest."

The two warriors are astounded by the appearance of the structures that were not damaged by the Ash Breather. The structures have different designs; some built of wood and what appears as thatching and stubble while others are constructed of earthen material. There are oil lamps placed throughout the village that add warmth to the simple domiciles. Shadows flicker and dance throughout cascading off the walls and nook places within sight. The two are being led to the banquet by Thaddeus who begins to talk to them about their experiences since coming to this strange land. Thaddeus motions to the two brothers for them to wait by the entrance to the place where the banquet will take place.

"Wait here for the moment young warriors. I want to make sure that all is prepared and proper."

Letete looks at his brother who in turn looks at him.

"Are you thinking what I am thinking?" Lucas asks his older brother.

"I heard your thoughts. Remember, the armor allows us to hear each other's thoughts. You want to take off the armor right?"

"Well, it's not that I don't like it. It is very comfortable and lightweight. It's very lightweight. I just wish that I had something else to wear."

At that moment the armor, starting with the helmet then the breastplate and down to his iron-clad footings begin to fold into itself like the reverse shuffling of a deck of cards. The armor all but disappears except for the heart-shaped portion of the breastplate that remains in place suspended by a cord around his neck, hanging like a fiery pendant. The shield follows suit and transforms into a shiny metallic bracelet. Lucas and Letete simultaneously respond to the metallic spectacle.

"That was awesome!"

"How did you do that?"

"I don't know; the sword is still kinda floating behind me. I just said that I wish I had... Hey! That's it! Just speak to your armor."

Letete does just that, and in like manner, his armor folds into itself exactly as his younger brother's armor had done a minute before. Letete reaches behind him to grab his sword. He pulls it from its invisible sheath, and it instantly shrinks to a size smaller than the fiery heart pendant handing his neck. Letete raises the shrunken sword to get a better look at the strange spectacle. At that moment the sword, like a magnet is stripped from his hand and attaches itself to his heart pendant.

"Whoa! That was awesome too! Let me try that." Lucas shouts.

And just as before, the sword finds its way to Lucas' pendant. Both boys are amazed as they stare at their clothing which is similar to the clothing of villagers.

"Is this cool or what?" Lucas shouts to his brother who is just as amazed at what the armor can do.

"Cool it is, Lucas. Cool, it is!"

At that moment the Old Man returns and looks at the boys in amazement and confusion.

"You managed to change out of your armor. Excellent! Your clothing is much richer in quality than our meager attire. But none the less, we are willing to serve and welcome you tonight. Come now, enter in, enter this place of rejoicing."

The three file into the place where the gathered villagers are, young and old alike. They are all singing the song from before and chanting the victory over the Ash Breather. They all stop and look at the two warriors, clothed in similar but not so regular clothing. The people look on in amazement as the two look, even more, know like mere children, boys even who are travelers from some distant land.

"Come now, sit here in this place of honor next to me. I want to hear everything about how you came to us from your world."

The boys both excitedly tell of their journey to this strange place. They tell of the wishing well and the shiny placard with the inscription they dare not say at this point. They also tell of the fragrant forest that smelled of chocolate and the river of strange, gem-like water that ran uphill against all laws of nature. They also, of course, told everyone about Neuma Ru, the one who sent them to deliver them from the claw and fang of the Ash Breather. Doldren and Ranke stand up and shout at that point of the story in an awkward show of enthusiasm that makes the gathered crowd laugh.

"Aye, that's the spirit lads!"

"This is truly a night to remember, a night to rejoice in. The night we were delivered from the clutches of the Ash Breather!"

The villagers all begin to cheer at the Old Man's declaration. There are so many wondrous things about the two hero's story, one's mind cannot comprehend them all. The villagers are amazed at what they have heard. Ranke the Tinkerer musters the courage to ask the boys a question.

"If you would pardon me kind gentlemen, you mentioned that you fell upon a visit to a place of wonder, blue colored grasses, and trees that smelled of what did you say? Ah yes, choc-u-let. Pray tell, what is this choc-u-let you spoke of?"

Lucas replies to Ranke's question and tells him of chocolate and his favorite candies and cakes back home.

"Of course, my mom always has to slow me down from eating too much but I really like it. Maybe someday Ranke you will get a chance to taste some choc-o-late!" Lucas laughs as he replies to a wide-eyed Ranke.

"It sounds like an interesting treat, this choc-o-late!"

As the festivities begin to wane, Thaddeus motions to Ranke and Doldren to come to him. He whispers something to them, they nod in agreement and leave hurriedly to carry out their assigned task. Thaddeus then turns to the Letete and Lucas and addresses them.

"Letete the Elder and Lucas the Younger, come with me, I want to speak to you about a matter."

The boys arise and follow Thaddeus out into the night time in front of the eating place.

"Gentle warriors, I want to share something with you concerning what happened tonight. I always knew that you would come."

"You knew we were coming? Does this have anything to do with this prophecy that spoke of earlier?" Letete asks.

"Yes, Letete the Elder. You are correct. The prophecy spoke of two young deliverers that would defeat our oppressors. I have heard the stories since I was a lad."

"Just how long have you had to deal with the Ash Breather?" Lucas asks.

"For many generations. I don't know if the beast you defeated this even is the same beast from our past, but they all seem like the same to me from tales and sketchings. Until recently, no one ever really looked upon an Ash Breather and lived to tell about it. We have Ranke to thank for that, building his high hiding places in the Snarksen forest to learn more about the beast. He used his discoveries to create the bladders of paste, Snarksen sap and water that were used this eve to quell the fires of the beast. I am thankful for the creation of the concoction."

"Thaddeus, tell us more about the prophecy." Letete asks.

Thaddeus continues speaking of the prophecy and how that boy's appearance exceeded his expectations. He escorts the two brothers through the village. Emblazoned oil lamps and torches dot doorways and posts throughout, but there is another concealed source of light, a bluish green light that is beginning to adorn the trees and the adjacent rock face of the valley where the village sits. The lights seem to be moving. Letete looks around and sees the strange apparitions. Lucas, in the usual form, asks Thaddeus a question.

"What are those weird lights and why are they moving?"

Thaddeus chuckles and replies.

"Ahh yes, yes! That is a good sign. The Scaly Gems are returning. We have not seen them in many generations of Gibbous seasons."

"Scaly what?" Letete replies.

"Not Scaly what, but Scaly Gems. Come, come, let's get a closer look at our well-adorned friends. They are proof of the prophecy that I will share with you."

The Old Man walks over to an adjacent rock face and motions to the boys to come over. Letete and Lucas stare in amazement at the small luminescent creatures.

"Again, to ask if you pardon me, what are they, Sir?" Letete asks with curiosity.

"No pardon needed. I take it that these creatures are alien to you both. They, my friend are called "Scaly Gems." They are a tiny welcomed guest to our humble village. They lived in the forest ages ago. They would come out at night to feed on the Snarksen flies that are in abundance in this region."

"Snarksen Flies? They are like what we call in our world, "Fire Flies or Lightning Bugs except your Snarksen Flies are twice the size!" Lucas retorts.

"You have such interesting names for creatures in your world. I like the name Fire Flies!"

"Continue telling us about the Snarksen Flies and the Scaly..."

"Scaly Gems, my curious young heroes. Here, come see."

Thaddeus looks around and notices a small swarm of Snarksen flies that have a faint glow themselves gathered around an oil lamp.

"Ahh, yes. Got you!"

He manages to grab a few of the bluish bugs in his hand. He hands one each to the boys and then takes the remaining Snarksen flies and offers it to the gathered Scaly Gems. One of the larger creatures sniffs the air and scurries over to the outstretched hand of Thaddeus. He approaches rapidly then slows to a cautious crawl. Thaddeus reassures the tiny creature with verbal queues. It is a beautiful creature. It is lizard-like in appearance. Each scale seems to luminesce individually. Surprising as well, the lizard has wings that appear to have tiny, little points of light all over them. The small creature in startling quickness devours the offering from Thaddeus.

"Whoa! He sure is quick, quick as lightning!"

Letete responds.

"Can we try?" Lucas asks excitedly.

"Yes, you can, just simply reach out your hand and they will come to you. See, like this."

Another Scaly Gem crawls out towards the outstretched hand of Lucas. Because of Lucas' short stature, the Scaly Gem compensates by climbing out on the end of a dead branch that protrudes outward near the boy's extended hand. It sniffs the offering of Lucas, but instead of snatching and running away with the gift, it devours the Snarksen fly on the spot.

"Whoa, this is cool!" Lucas whispers not wanting to startle his little guest. Letete follows suit and the two boys instantly are entertaining several of the luminous amphibians. Children throughout the village can be heard laughing and playing with the luminesce creatures, both Snarksen Fly and Scaly Gem alike.

"Come now boys; I want to share words with you from the prophecy."

As the three walk towards the center of the village towards Thaddeus' place, one of the Scaly Gems separate from the bright reptilian lounge. It runs and then leaps, using its modest wing-like appendages to glide from tree to limb following close behind the three. It stops for a moment and releases a loud shrill followed by a series clicks. It is surprisingly loud for such a small creature.

"Whoa, what was that?" Letete responds.

"It looks like you have made a friend." Thaddeus replies.

The creature continues to make the cacophony of sounds, becoming even more animated as it notices it has an audience. Letete notices another swarm of Snarksen flies hovering around an oil lamp. He reaches out quickly to grab a handful of the darting insects. He manipulates a few of them between his fingertips and offers them again to the clicking creature.

"Here you go little guy, I won't hurt.... hey!!"

The creature in quick fashion devours the offering from Letete even before he can finish his sentence. In the process, he nips him on his finger.

"Watch it, buddy, that's a finger you know!"

Letete and Lucas chuckle at the tiny creature's tenacity. It clicks and shrills and in a surprisingly swift move, climbs up the back of Letete, circles his abdomen, and lights upon his right shoulder. It releases another series of clicks as if showing its approval.

"Whoa!! What are you doing?"

"Be still; it will not hurt you. it seems to have taken a shine to you, if you pardon the pun." Thaddeus smirks.

The three, now four continue towards the center of the village. They arrive at the large Snarksen that stands as a sentry in the middle of the multitude of people. It is knarled and twisted at its base and springs upward into the night time sky. It has the appearance of a large hand with twisted fingers reaching towards the heavens. There are Snarksen lamps hung about the lower branches. Thaddeus beckons the two brothers to follow him to the backside of the large tree. Thaddeus walks up to the base of the tree and steps in between two large roots that are about knee high. He takes a piece of kindling and lights it from the flame of a lamp on the other side. He uses the kindling to light a larger lamp that is hanging just above eye level on the tree. The resulting light reveals a small door that has a strange symbol on its face. Thaddeus unlatches the brass hook on the door, removes the lamp and enters the dark nook of the Snarksen. The boys and their new friend stand looking at each other.

"Come in boys, watch your step, and follow me. I have something to show you."

The boys and their scaly companion enter the tree. Once inside, they look around in amazement at the interior. It is larger in appearance than one might expect. It has a fragrance that reminds the boys of a fresh cut Christmas tree. Their Dad would take them to choose one to bring home for the holidays.

"The tree has a different smell than the other Snarksen in the forest," Lucas says.

"It has a sweeter smell because of its age. It is an ancient tree, almost completely impervious to fire. Legend has it that it is the first Snarksen tree and that all Snarksen comes from its fruit. But that is not why I called you here. I wanted to show you something. Something that speaks of your purpose here and the one who sent you." At that moment, there is a knock at the door. Thaddeus walks to the door and opens it. Two figures are standing in silhouette. Thaddeus lifts his lamp to reveal who they are. It's Doldren and Ranke.

"Father, I see that we have guests. I would like to speak with them. I have many questions I would like to ask them." Ranke exclaims.

"I am sure you do Ranke. Come, come inside, the both of you."

"You have sons?" Letete ask.

"Yes, they are my sons, victims of circumstance and adopted by a motion of the heart. But I will share that story in a moment. Now, where were we before the interruption? Ahh, yes, I have something to show you. Ranke pass me that shade on the mantle behind you. Thank you, kind Sir."

Thaddeus places the shade over the lamp and the interior of the tree-dwelling fades to black in an instance. It takes a moment to focus as the darkness becomes as black as ink. Then in a moment, images begin to trickle into place, then brighter and brighter the images become. The images fix, and glow then reveal what appears to be some strange writing that spans upward toward to the top of the interior. Symbols also are seen; one large symbol matches the one on the door of the dwelling.

"Wow!" The two brothers exclaim, looking on in amazement.

"What is it?" Letete asks as his scaly companion clicks and shrills in response.

"It is a prophecy, a prophecy about two gleaming heroes that defeat the Ash Breather. "Trumpet the heroes that come and put the one that breathes ash on the run!" It reads."

"Hey, that's the song the people were singing!" Lucas exclaims.

"Yes indeed. I have told of that song to man and child alike. No one believed the prophecies to be true until this Gibbous night. This night that the Ash Breather was defeated, and prophecy made true."

"There seems to be a lot of strange words and symbols here on the wall of the tree. It has to tell more than just that small line of a song." Letete retorts.

"Yes hero, it does speak of more. You both will have to go on a quest, a quest that will place you both in harm's way. But it will not be for naught. You will do this for the sake of others, to deliver them from the clutches of the enemy. You will deliver us. But you will not be alone. It will be a trying journey for you both. The journey will be necessary to break the stronghold of the dark threat that wants to destroy my people." Thaddeus states, pointing to the writings and symbols on the wall of the tree.

"Is it the Ash Breather? I thought that we defeated the beast once and for all?" Lucas responds.

"No, this is a threat that is far more ominous than the return of that beast. He is only an emissary for some greater threat. The Ash Breather has a master."

Thaddeus squints and motions towards the two young men. He points towards the glowing pendants hanging around their necks. That symbol around your neck, it is very similar to the symbol on the door of this room and the walls. This conjunction is further confirmation of the prophecies scripted on the walls of this place."

"This is true. Your words are very similar to the ones spoken by the one who sent us. He gave us the power to defeat the Ash Breather." Letete responds.

"And we will defeat the dark threat to your people with his help as well," Lucas says confidently. Thaddeus nods his head in agreement and motions to Ranke to remove the shade from the oil lamp. He motions to the young men, and they follow him out into the open night time air.

"Come with me gentlemen, and I will show you to your quarters for the night."

NINE

A Story of Adoption

Thaddeus motions to the young men to follow him around the sizeable Snarksen dwelling to a small landing that reveals a series of steps that lead to a platform that encircles the Old Man's lodging. Thaddeus walks around the platform to another door on the side of the tree. He opens the door to a home that is more inviting and warmer than the previous. There is a hearth located in rear and small alcoves filled with make-shift bedding. There are nooks and shelving filled with scrolls and oddities. Oil lamps that are burning fragrant variances of Snarksen and other viscous blends.

"It smells like Christmas and cakes!" Lucas says with a chuckle. Letete nods his head in agreement.

"Christmas? What is this cake you mention of?" Thaddeus responds. Letete and Lucas wax on about the holiday in their world and the great experiences they have enjoyed on that special day.

"That sounds like a joyous holiday! Maybe we can remember this day in the very same way!" Ranke and Doldren nod in agreement with Thaddeus.

"That would be a glorious celebration indeed!" Thaddeus motions to his adopted sons to bring blankets for their two quests.

"Young Heroes, you can sleep here for the night."

Once settled, Doldren and Ranke begin telling of their ordeal. They tell of how they had seen the Ash Breather descend on the Gibbous offering platen and how it sniffed out Doldren and Laurel. They wax eloquent about the terrifically horrible chase sequence as they ran for their lives from the creature. They tell of the amazing image of the fiery maelstrom that moved with great speed towards the village and awesome spectacle of the defeat of the Ash Breather.

"It was a thing to behold! I could never have imagined mere mortal men defeating the beast!" Doldren exclaims.

"No! It was not by our strength but by the one who sent us!" Letete responds.

"Mighty are his weapons in battle!" Lucas retorts.

"It would also appear Doldren and Ranke that our two guests weren't the only mere mortals to have victory this night over the Ash Breather."

Ranke and Doldren smile widely at their Guardians statement.

Letete and Lucas begin to tell everyone about how they entered this world by way of the wishing well. They tell about the peculiar blue grass and the trees that smelled like chocolate with orange colored leaves. They tell of the crystal-like water that ran uphill to a point where they found the floating, spinning sword. And of course, their first encounter with Neuma Ru.

"What a glorious tale of adventure!" Doldren shouts excitedly.

"You tell of things that we could never imagine. How is it that you have seen such things here in this land that we have never seen?" Ranke asked.

"What do you mean never seen? The grass, the trees, these things do not exist here? But we saw them!" Letete responds.

"Ahh yes, things that you both could have only seen. You both experienced "the quickening!" The prophecies spoke of this. I don't fully understand all their meaning, but I am thankful to be alive to witness such a great day."

"You have never seen Neuma Ru?" Lucas asks.

"No, I have not had the privilege, but I still believe in him though I have never seen him. But you have seen him and received his gifts and counsel. What a glorious honor that Neuma Ru has bestowed upon you both. I would cherish the opportunity to see him myself."

Letete and Lucas turn to look in the direction of Doldren and Ranke.

"How did you become his children, his adopted?" Letete asks.

"Well it's a long story, Thaddeus, Father, would you like to begin the story?" Ranke replies.

"Ahh yes, a story of adoption. I will gladly tell the story to our two young heroes. It is the crux of the reason or should I say purpose to their being here. It began almost 12 years ago; I was a part of the council but not the head. Two well-respected families were members of the council. There were a mother and father, Syanthea and

Criswele, a most lovely couple. Also, a young man by the name of Demstel. Both families had one son each, these two gentlemen you see before you. It was a time before the Gibbous Indulgence accord had been struck with the Ash Beast. I was always against the accord along with several others on the council, but we were not the majority. One fateful event lead to the Gibbous accord, an event that set the village on a dark course. In the still of one dark evening, the beasts descended upon our village like a flood. There were winged breathers and some groundlings that walked upright like a man bearing weapons as such. We took heavy losses and damages. A few of us banded together to take a stand; we even managed to take out a few of the marauders. Criswele, Syanthea, and Demstel were among the resistance. Criswele protested his beloved Syanthea desire to fight with him, but she believed that she had the heart to fight for everything dear to her just as he. She obviously was right because the two of them mustered the reserve to take out several of the groundlings during the mayhem. Then suddenly, out of nowhere, it appeared! The Ash Breather in full devastating wrath. Its flames ravished our humble dwellings like kindling. We had to fall back. We looked at the damages and our dead. Criswele, Syanthea, and Demstel were among the other souls who had given their lives to protect us. That is when the villagers struck that heinous accord with the Ash Breather. He and his marauding band could have easily destroyed the rest of us, but because of the creature's macabre desire to hunt us for sport or more so it's Master is the reason the accord was struck. That was also the night that I became a father to these two."

There was a silent pause that seemed to last hours but in truth last only seconds. Then Letete broke the silence with a question.

"You mentioned the family connection between their parents, but you did not mention the family connection of Demstel. He was your son wasn't he?"

Thaddeus held his head down for instance and quietly replied.

"Yes, yes he was. You are wise beyond your years Letete, the Elder. I recall that fateful day constantly in my mind. I am thankful that my wife did not see such tragedy even though she left me tragically just years prior. But even in that loss, I did find gain. These two are young marvels. Full of knowledge and courage."

The two young men nod and reply.

"Father, we are honored as well as thankful for your generous heart. We are thankful for your name as well."

Letete and Lucas stand silently looking at their hospitable host. Their hearts are heavy as they begin to think of their own family back in their world. Letete breaks the silence again with a question.

"You mentioned Thaddeus that we are to go on a quest, a quest against the breather and the dark threat."

Lucas places his hand over his pendant, and instantly a sword appears, fiery and luminous. He shouts a cry of affirmation in response.

"To war against the Ash Breather! Defeat the Beast!" The gathered group shout in reply.

"My father in my world tells us that the one we serve gives us deliverance over dragons. The only good dragon is a dead dragon!" Thaddeus nods in agreement.

"Yes, yes indeed."

TEN

Armor All!

The following day, the two brothers, Ranke and Doldren arise from a nights rest. They stir about being awakened by the aroma of simmering food and baked bread in a hearth. Thaddeus had awakened first to prepare an early morning meal.

"Did you rest well young heroes?"

"Yes, yes we did sir. The bed was very comfortable." Letete responds. Lucas still a little groggy, answered as well.

"Yawn! Yes, I slept well also."

Thaddeus motions to his two sons to set places at the table.

"Good morning young warriors. Arise! Let us eat to build up our strength. We must prepare for a long journey. A quest as such."

Ranke and Doldren look at each other with a question on their face. Then they reply in unison, "Us? What do you mean us? We are not heroes made of invincible metal; we are only mere men, boys even. How can we go on a quest, a war campaign against the Ash Breather?" Lucas and Letete are equally confused as well.

"Thaddeus, I thought that you said that the prophesy stated that we were to go on a quest. Does that include others as well?" Letete asks.

"Yes, or I am led to believe so. There is a portion of the prophecy that is not fully clear, but it would seem that you are to have friends to accompany you on this quest."

"An Army? We could be generals!" Lucas replies.

Letete touches his brother's shoulder and motions for him to be quiet.

"No, that is not a good idea, I am confident in our ability in our armor and the power of Neuma Ru, but to put others at risk, I am not too sure about that!"

At that moment, the fiery pendants around the boy's neck begin to glow even brighter like an ignited flame. Then suddenly the unmistakable voice of Neuma Ru is heard to the boys.

"Be encouraged young warrior; I am with you. Call a council with the villagers at the meeting place and wait for my instruction. I will tell you and your brother what to say when you are there."

Letete and Lucas asked Thaddeus to call a meeting with the villagers. He nods and smiles widely.

"You have heard from him, haven't you? He instructs you even now?" Thaddeus responds.

"I will move with great haste to make this so."

Thaddeus excitedly and hurried moves to the entrance of his dwelling and walks with great haste to the center of the village on the opposite side of the great Snarksen tree. He takes a wooden mallet and uses it to strike a large tonal log affixed to a wooden frame. The people come quickly and gather at the meeting place. There are murmurings and whispers among the crowd. Thaddeus waves to the gathered crowd and begins to speak.

"Gather everyone quickly, yes, yes indeed. Ahh, yes that is in good measure. I am pleased to inform everyone that our heroes have something to say. They have a message of hope from the one who sent them. I have spoken to you often about the one who sent them for many years. Even now, the excitement that I have can scarcely be contained! But none the less, I will show constraint. Letete the Elder and Lucas the Younger, gentlemen you have our ears."

Letete and Lucas walk to the center of the gathered villagers. They are a little reluctant at first, but a calming voice in their mind gives them comfort.

"Remember, I am always with you." The voice says.

Letete motions to the crowd to get their attention. Silence falls across the gathering. Letete says a simple prayer to himself, just like his father told him he does before he speaks.

"Hello, people of...what do you call yourselves?" He asks Thaddeus.

"We have no name for our village. It is one of the treatises of the accord with the Ash Breather. It is forbidden!"

Letete and Lucas look puzzled.

"Great people of this place. The place of victory. The place where you witnessed a great and mighty act! Not acts carried out by us, but acts carried out by the power and might of the one who sent us. He is to receive the glory for this triumph, and he is the one that will empower us all!"

Letete pauses his speaking at the response of the cheering crowd.

Letete hears the still, small voice of Neuma Ru who tells him "Well done young warrior."

At that moment one of the older men in the gathered crowd shouts a question to Letete from the rear of the gathering.

"You say that this Neuma Ru will empower us all. How can he do this? It's one thing that you two special aliens to our land have these special abilities, but we are mere farmers, tillers of the ground, how can we have such power?"

At that moment, Lucas steps forward at the urging of the voice that he hears.

"Those that hear our words, his words through us shall have power as well. He promises this, and it is his desire. Your time of deliverance has come!"

Now, there is murmuring and chatter among the crowd. Letete and Lucas look towards Thaddeus with concern and bewilderment. He steps forward to address the crowd again.

"My brethren, why do you doubt what you have heard! You saw with your own eyes what has happened just this latter eve!"

At that moment, both Letete and Lucas receive an instruction from Neuma Ru. The boy's motion to Thaddeus to stand back.

They place their right hands over the glowing fiery pendants hanging about their necks and in unison say these words, "By his power and might!"

Instantly their pendants expand, chest plates, chin coverings, gauntlets and helmets all fold into place. Lastly and amazingly the sword of Neuma Ru appears in a white flash of light that temporarily blinds the eyes of those that are gathered. They all look on in great wonder. The sword floats in mid-air, growing and shrinking just as before. The gathered crowd falls back, startled at the sudden transformation of the two young warriors. Letete steps forward towards the spinning sword and reaches in and pulls out his weapon leaving a spinning identical sword in place. Lucas follows suit. In amazement, the two brothers each have their own weapons but there still hovers before them a glowing, fiery blade.

The man who doubted previously says in response, "How can this be? Amazing!"

Letete lifts the visor on his helmet and responds.

"It is possible because of him. He will make his weapons available to anyone here that will believe in him and trust him."

Lucas follows suit, taking his sword and thrusting it into the air saying, "Mighty are his weapons in battle!"

The air crackles around the blade and a static charge can be felt by all surrounding the two brothers. Everyone's hair is standing up on their arms and head. Letete walks throughout the crowd, talking and pleading with the people to believe and trust.

"If anyone here will dare trust him, step forward and take your sword."

People can be heard murmuring, but no one moves in the direction of the fiery spinning sword.

"We are not warriors, we are mere farmers and gleaners. How can we stand against the Beast?"

One villager cries out the same mantra as the previous. Lucas steps forward holding up his sword again like a torch ablaze.

"How can two small kids like us have accomplished such a great thing as defeating the Ash Breather? It's because we trust the one who sent us. Look, we were frightened as well, actually terrified beyond belief."

Letete chimes in chuckling, "Yes, yes we were frightened but he has shown us that we have nothing to fear. You are more than farmers, more than gleaners, you are conquerors through him. If you are tired of the Gibbous Accord, tired of sending out your loved ones to this beast only to never see them again, step forward and take the first step towards a new day! A day free of fear, a day full of hope!"

At that moment, Doldren and Ranke step forward along with Thaddeus. "Ahh, yes, good measure lads!" Thaddeus exclaims.

"We will be your first recruits in this Army. No matter the number, large or small, our hearts will compensate for any lacking!" Thaddeus thunders!

"Well said, Father, we will stand with the heroes! Trumpet the heroes!"

At that moment, Ranke extends his hand then instantly recoils. The spectacle of the spinning sword slows his advance.

"Well, this is something, but a lot less frightful than dodging the fangs of the Ash Breather!" He exclaims!

He advances again and reaches out towards the spinning sword pulling back instantly his own which blazes with the strange bluish green flame. Ranke is in absolute awe of the strange blade. It is glowing and flaming. As he begins to examine the strange metal, something even more amazing happens. His right hand that is holding the blade is enveloped in a shiny metal. The metal spreads in a blink of an eye then just as quickly he is covered from head to toe.

"Outstanding!" He exclaims!

Doldren and Thaddeus follow suit and the metal reacts in like manner. Now there are five shinning warriors standing before the crowd. The gathered villagers step back a bit in complete awe of the transformations.

"The armor, it's light as a feather, even the sword seems lighter than air!" Doldren replies.

One of the villagers who doubted previously pushes his way to the front of the crowd.

"Let me through, let me through! I am no coward! I want to have a go at that armor as well!" He exclaims.

He stretches forth his hand and the same happens to him as the previous.

"Ooh my! How excellent an experience! A mere farmer, now a warrior! I want to take back what the enemy has taken! I will do so with the Armor's help!" He exalts.

"No good warrior, with the help of Neuma Ru, he will help us win this battle." Letete responds.

"Good young warrior!" Letete hears in his mind.

"Will there be another? We will leave two days from today at the break of dawn! When that moment arrives, we will not wait another day! We will train those who are willing. This time the fight will come to the Dragons!"

Many more follow the actions of the previous. At the words of Neuma Ru, Letete and Lucas begin to teach the small band the ways of the armor and the sword. Letete motions to get the attention of the men to address them.

"Remember what we have taught you this day and remember you must never doubt or lose faith. That would affect your use of the armor."

Joining his brother, Lucas shouts a closing refrain.

"Never lose faith! Never lose faith! Never lose faith!"

ELEVEN

Horses of a Feather

The gathered crowd begins to segregate miraculously; people stepped forward transforming from a farmer, son, and some daughters to a warrior. Shiny, excited and exuberant. Not all stepped forward. Some even a little resentful of the others that did. But all were in awe of the spectacle that was taking place before them. The two brothers stood before the crowd, a remnant now clad in armor. Thaddeus, Doldren, and Ranke moved through the crowd hugging and cheering on those who stepped forward. Thaddeus moves toward the two boys, now Generals of a small and unique fighting clan.

"Letete the Elder and Lucas the Younger, this day will be recounted of for generations! Sonnets shall be written and sung about the faithful few that moved forward to take the sword of Neuma Ru into battle. Freedom and liberation have begun this day! We are small in number but not small in faith! Amazingly, not all moved forward, but it will still be well with us because of who we serve!"

Letete motions to Thaddeus and his sons to come closer towards him and his brother. They form a small circle just a little distance from the remnant warriors.

"Thaddeus, Sir, we are being instructed to make you one of our Generals and your sons both to be made Captains. We do not have long, but we will train you in the same fashion as Neuma Ru trained us. As he speaks, we will tell you. As he teaches, we will teach you. As he instructs, we will instruct you. You will be a remnant, but a mighty army!"

Thaddeus bows his head and nods.

"As you speak it Letete the Elder, we follow as required Sir."

Doldren and Ranke acknowledge and agree with the words Thaddeus has spoken. They both respond in kind.

"Alright then, line up and follow me! We have some fighting to do and little time to prepare!" Lucas shouts.

"I'm going to enjoy this!" Lucas tells his older brother.

"I hope that he doesn't enjoy this too much. He really likes to fight!"

Letete and Lucas along with his chosen General and Captains lead the remnant through the gate into the open clearing where the Ash Breather was defeated. What irony to train an army of free men on the same ground where their oppressor was defeated. The group first mills about walking awkwardly in their new armor. All and everyone glisten in the morning light, living diamonds and gems in the rough. The boy's motion for everyone to take one knee. They remind the group of the purpose of their quest. A quest for liberation and justice. Justice against the Ash Breather and the unseen darkness that is behind the Breather's deeds. They instruct the remnant as Neuma Ru instructs them. The warriors are amazed at the wisdom and the power behind the words of the young men. Their speech is years beyond their ages. They each speak in turn and sometimes in unison. Letete tells the kneeling crowd to focus on him and his brother.

"Now we will show you some basic swordplay. But before we instruct in that area, first everyone stand. Good, now draw your swords!"

The sound of the drawn swords turns the meadow clearing into a symphony of metal, each sword reverberating each its own tone. Even the remnant warriors are amazed. In the distance at the gate, the villagers stand to gaze in awe at the spectacle. Letete and Lucas notice something different about the swords of the remnant warriors. Their swords do not have the same glow. They are glowing alright, but not the fiery presence of the two brothers. Neuma Ru speaks to the mind of the two warriors.

"Yes, you see correctly young ones, their swords are different and yet the same. Your swords are different because you are set aside for a different purpose than that of those who follow. Whom I call, I equip for my purpose and non-other."

Letete instructs the standing warriors with their metal torchieres to listen to his brother as he instructs them in knowing their weapon. "Listen, remnant, your weapon, and your sword will be your offense. It cuts one way and then another. Even its design and feel you must know. Get familiar with its construct and function down to the smallest facet. Now take your sword in your right hand. Good! Now place the blade flat and square into your left hand gently. Look at the blade, examine it. Feel how feather light the blade is. Now take your left hand and with your fingers and run them across the flat of the blade. Feel its vibration and coolness to the touch. Run your fingers into the grove of the fuller at the center base of the blade. This increases the strength of the blade. Neuma Ru placed this stripe on the blade to give it strength in battle. It also adds to the feather-light feel of the blade. Now run your hand down the groove of the fuller to the grip of the blade. Squeeze the grip with the right hand and look at the guard of the sword. Review every piece, every image, and filigree and commit it to your memory. This sword will be your offensive in the heat of battle. Trust it and never lose faith in it and it will be true to you."

The warriors all follow the instruction of the small warrior general. All nodding in as they examine their weapon of offense. Letete motions for the remnant again to focus on him.

"Good! Now my brother and I will show you some that swordplay that I mentioned. Lucas, stand in front of me. Let's show them what Neuma Ru has taught us."

The two warriors, Letete the Elder and Lucas the younger, draw their swords and give an exhibition in use of the mighty weapons of war. They also remember some of the moves that their father had taught them as well. Letete's mind drifts back to just a few days ago when he and his brother were wishing, hoping to find adventure in their new home and city. He remembers the moment around the well when he and his brother handled mere plastic and rubber swords, fighting imaginary enemies, leading imaginary armies against dragons. He smiles and begins to laugh to himself as imagination has given way to reality.

"You're thinking about the well, aren't you?" Lucas asks his brother.

"Yes, you read my mind, didn't you? This is awesome, isn't it brother! We wanted adventure, and we got just that!"

The two warrior generals parry, dodge, and block. Their swords clang and spark, casting arcs into the air. Letete raises a hand to his brother motioning to him to stop.

"Now, your turn!" He says to the remnant.

"Pair off into groups of two! Good, if any are not a part of a group, come towards the front and we will accommodate you."

One young man comes forth; He is the only one that is not able to pair off.

"You do not have a partner?" Letete asks.

"No sir, uh General, I do not."

"What is your name?"

The young man cups one hand over his brow to block the noonday sun.

"My name is Drash'Ur the Watcher."

Letete motions to Thaddeus to come to him.

"Thaddeus, would you mind pairing off with this young man?"

"No, indeed it will be an honor. He is the young man that stood in the tower to warn us of the coming of the Ash Breather the very night of your arrival."

The group, now paired off, practice the moves given to them. The sound of clanging metal echoes through the valley. Trilleon who did not move forward when the call was given stands at the gate and looks on.

"Look at them. They think that they are warriors. They are mere farmers, gleaners of the land. How do they think that they will be able to defeat the Ash Breather?" He exclaims. Another standing nearby hears his rebuke and replies.

"Aye, I think they will be able to do just that. Two young boys were able to defeat that beast and send it flailing into the nighttime sky wounded and bested. How could the beast hope to stand against several cut from the same metal? Oh, how I wish that I could stand with them in battle. But alas, I have the excuse of many years and old ailments that keep me from joining the fight. But you Sir, are without excuse! You were even saved, your family the like, by the two warriors and still you have a complaint and show apathy. Shame on you Sir and the example you show to other able-bodied men!" Trilleon looks on at the group without reply.

Letete and Lucas motion to Thaddeus and his two sons.

"We are being instructed to separate the warriors into three groups with each of you leading and instructing them. Kneel where you stand." Letete tells them.

Lucas draws his sword and lightly touches each shoulder and the crown of the three gentlemen's head with its broadside. Letete begins to speak the words that he hears from Neuma Ru.

"You are now set aside as General Thaddeus, stand and be ready. You Doldren are now set aside to be Captain under General Thaddeus. Stand and be ready. Ranke, you are now set aside to be Captain under General Thaddeus, stand and be ready. Good, separate the warriors into three groups and follow the instructions as given. May you be protected by the armor you wear, and may your faith grow with each passing day." Letete tells the three members of their newly formed military council. On into the early evening, the warriors train for the coming battle. They look more like seasoned warriors towards the latter part of the day than they did at its beginning. They wield their swords like men with years of battlefield experience. This is only accomplished with the presence that is with all of them. Letete and Lucas stand a stone's throw distance away from the group. He motions to Drash'Ur to come to him at the instruction of Neuma Ru.

"Drash'Ur, as the Watcher of the village, do you own a horn that you may have used in the tower?" Drash'Ur nods an accommodating motion with his head.

"Why yes, Sir I do. It is still in the tower at the gate. I keep it there alongside the tonal in the tower."

"Good, please go and get it. You shall always keep it at your side during this journey. Your skills of watching will be one of the tools used to defeat the beast that we will face."

"Yes, Sir! I have the eyes of a young Falcon, my father says. I can see farther and clearer than any man in the village!"

"Is your father among the fighters?"

"No, he's the older man there by the gate." Drash'Ur says proudly.

"He has been standing there this entire day, watching and wishing for younger years so that he could fight with us."

Letete and Lucas look to the gate and just as Drash'Ur had stated, they could see a wiry old man standing by the gate with a walking stick in one hand and waving with the other. Letete motions to the young man to retrieve his horn. Once he returns, Letete instructs him to blow into it to get the attention of the sparring warriors. "Warriors of the village, we shall stop for the day and start again at sunrise. Tomorrow, we shall leave this place and journey on our quest for liberation!"

At this statement, the gathered warriors cheer loudly along with others at the gate of the village. At that moment, clouds begin to appear out of nowhere. The cloud appears as combined with fire and smoke.

There are thunderings and arcings all around. Lucas looks to Letete and says, "We've seen this before haven't we big brother!"

"We sure have! But not exactly like this. It's a cloud but not a whirlwind. Is it Neuma Ru?"

"Who else could it be except Him?"

At that moment, the cloud pours itself, literally onto the ground and disperses in a concentric burst in every direction. The concussion pushes the warriors standing there back a few steps, even knocking some of the warriors to the ground. At the end of the burst, there is a bright blinding flash of light. What follows is a loud sound as of thunder. After the flash of light and the deafening sounds, the warriors begin to collect themselves. Drash'Ur, true to his vocation, squints and begins to reply to what he sees in the midst of the dispersing haze.

"I see three, no four creatures in the midst. Looks like horses of some kind but not like any horse that I have ever seen!" He exclaims.

True enough, these creatures were magnificent in their appearance. One horse appeared as being made up of fire. His long flowing mane appeared as burning flames, flickering and dotting in the wind. Smoke emanates from its fiery nostrils and lingers, bellowing wispy rings. The second seemed to have lighting draped across its form, its mane as the first is made of the energy that seems to drive it. The long hair of its main seeming almost alive is made up completely of lighting arcs. The third beast was as awesome to lay sight on as the first. It is a darkish, grey hue. Its mane appears as dancing, rolling billows of clouds. Small thunderings could be heard clearly by the assembled troop with each roll of its mane. And the final horse, no less awesome and majestic in its appearance, appeared to have a form completely made of water. It appears as crystal clear water that moves and ebbs like ripples in a pond. Its mane appears as crashing waves on the shore of a beach. Letete and Lucas not sure of what they are seeing, reach instinctively for their swords.

"Stay your weapons young warriors! We mean you no harm! We are sent by the mighty one who gave you use of His power! The horses all speak in unison, startling the boys and the gathered warriors even the ones at the gate. Their unified voice was loud and ominous shaking the very ground where they stand.

"You were sent by Neuma Ru?" Letete asks.

"Yes, young one, he has sent his wings to cover you!"

And at that moment, each creature rears itself and stands on its hind legs releasing loud whinnies and thunderings. Instantly, each horse sprouts massive wings from the center of their muscular backs. The boys and the band of warriors stand gazing in amazement. At that moment, Thaddeus begins to quote a line from one of the prophecies.

"To begin the quest, the quest the heroes did seek, the mighty one who desires to liberate will give them wings to cover them."

Thaddeus looks on in complete awe and stands as the others with his mouth agape. He stares and is humbled by the strange and awesome theater that is set before him. One horse, the one of fire, prances forward and comes to a stop. It begins to speak, not in unison as before, but alone.

"I call on the one known as Letete the Elder, come forth!"

Letete looks a little trepidatious in his stance. He does not move forward immediately.

He hears a small voice in his mind, "No need to fear, remember I am with you. I sent my wings to cover and keep you. You only have to trust me. Move and you will receive."

He moves forward and the beast nods in agreement.

"Good, Good, young warrior. You are the general of this band, the elder leader. For this cause I am pledged to your service. Take my bridle, stand in my stirrup and light upon my back."

Letete looks at the bright almost fiery brazen cord. It has an appearance of being almost molten. He is hesitant to touch it.

"Do not be afraid of my fire, my fire will not harm you young one, it will strengthen you! Only enemies need fear my flames. For I am forged of the power of the one who sent me!"

Letete looks and decides to do as the creature has instructed. He grabs the molten cord, expecting to feel some tinge of heat. To his amazement he feels nothing or better to say what he feels is not heat like fire that consumes but a warmth and tingle at the same time. He laughs aloud a child's laughter. He places one foot into the stirrup and bounds onto the back of the fiery beast. The fiery mane dances and flickers all about Letete's arms and his torso. The fiery steed rears itself and releases a flume of flame from its mouth. It startles the warriors and the people gathered at the gate.

Lucas begins to shout out loud, "That was sooooo cooool!!! Hey, do I have a horse?" He asks with anticipation. At that moment, the creature appearing to be made of lightning moves forward. He begins to say the same greeting as the first horse.

"I call to the one known as Lucas the younger, come forth! Good, Good, young warrior. You are a general of this band, second only to Letete the elder leader. For this cause I am pledged to your service. Take my bri..." and before the beast could finish his discourse, Lucas the younger was already in full stride towards the side of the beast.

He runs and bounds onto the back of the arcing creature. The move was so quick that even the otherworldly creature was caught off guard, but amazingly the creature releases a surprising sound. It could be heard laughing, even as a child would laugh.

"Veery Good, very good young warrior. I like this one, he has spirit and eneergy. A perfect match for me. We are kindred and I am pledged to your service!"

And just as the previous beast, the mane of Lucas' steed made of lightning arcs dances across the arms of the boy general and the ground. The beast rears itself releasing a massive arcing bolt of lightning from its mouth. After the creature rights itself, Lucas releases another shout, "That was soooo awesome!"

Lucas and the creature share a moment of laughter while the creature prances and leaps into the air. Letete makes a comment to himself that his horse also hears.

"Wow, he found someone just as crazy as he is, that can't be good." Letete's horse chuckles aloud at his comment. And replies, "You don't know the half of it. The remaining two horses follow suit just as the first and the second. Thaddeus is called out by the one creature whose appearance was that of rolling storm clouds. That creature is followed by the one who appeared as crystalline water. He calls out Ranke. All of the captains and generals have a creature to aid them except one, Doldren. The fiery creature with Letete atop, calls to Doldren to step forward. Doldren looks a little bewildered and asks a question when he is called.

"You have your assignment to the Head General of our army. Why do you call me out?" He asks.

"I am instructed by the one who sent me to have you bring forth your horse." Doldren nods in agreement and motions to a young man at the gate. In moments

Doldren's horse, Laurel is standing at the gate. Doldren whistles for her and in swift fashion she is standing at his side.

"Good, very good." The fiery beast responds. Laurel walks almost seeming to be drawn to the fiery steed standing majestically in front of it. It touches it's forehead to that of the flaming horse. "Greetings my sister of creation." The fiery beast exclaims. "Doldren, because of your valor in times of peril, we have been instructed to endow your steed, our sister of creation with power as well. Stand by her warrior!"

Doldren follows the instruct of the beast. Each creature stands at different points with Doldren and Laurel standing in the center.

"Now Doldren, stand clear! The creatures open their mouths and breathe the element of their creation upon their terrestrial kin, Laurel. She is bathed in fire, water, cloud and lightning. In an instance, she disappears in the deluge. The creatures cease the baptism of their kin. Once the deluge of elements dissipates and settles, a form appears, magnificent in stature. Laurel is covered from nose to hoof in metal, armor as it were. But there is an added form; she has a flaming horn protruding from the head of her armor. She rears herself, swinging her head from left to right with flames draping her newly acquired horn like a tattered banner.

"Whooooaaaa!" The two brothers say in unison.

"They made her into a Unicorn! How awesome is that?" Letete exclaims. Doldren walks up to his horse and places a hand on the side of her armored head.

"Astonishing girl! You have never looked better!" He says softly to her as she nods in agreement, bobbing her newly acquired horn.

Doldren places a foot into the stirrup of the saddle of his trusted steed and mounts the back of Laurel. She prances and whinny's in an excited fashion.

"Yes Laurel, I'm excited as well, my trusted friend."

"We get another crack at the Ash Breather! But this time on our terms!"

TWELVE

Sojourn

The gathered menagerie of creatures and warriors all standing in an awesome spectacle, encircle the two boy generals who are standing in the midst. The gathered group transforms the valley clearing into a facet holding in its setting glimmering gems of all colors and sizes. Each standing warrior has flames dancing about them. Their swords are draped about with the bluish-green effect. Their appearance is so striking in the setting as evening advances. The darkness approaches. It threatens to overtake them where they stand, like a shadowy stalking creature only to retreat from the ebbing glow that begins to illuminate the darkening clearing. Letete motions to the crowd. Some of the warriors still test each other's mettle with a trying of their newly acquired skills. Their swords clang and resonate into the evening sky. Letete motions to Drash'Ur to use his horn.

"Whuuu urrrrrrrrrrh!" The horn displaces the cacophony of sounds with its sharp clarion shrill.

"Warriors of this place… this place…" He pauses for a moment to think.

"Why should this place not have a name?" He thinks. Lucas hears his thoughts.

"It should have a name. Every place has a name. Even the park where we used to play in our old town had a name. Even a puppy is given a name by its owners. I agree with you big brother, this place should have a name." Lucas replies in thought to his brother.

"Neuma Ru, what do you say? Should this place have a name?" Letete says softly speaking to his benefactor.

"Why yes, it should have a name and I will for you both to name this place. What name you give it, I will sanction." Neuma Ru says into the mind of the two.

"Lucas are you thinking what I am thinking?"

"Already with you, go for it!"

The group stands looking at the two in a bewildered fashion, wondering what they are saying and why the long pregnant pauses in their discourse. Letete begins again.

"Warriors of this place... this place... this place where you have given up your security in times past to a scaly threat. In this place where fathers have lost sons and mothers have lost daughters. In this place where a horrible agreement was entered into, carried out by the one called the Ash Breather."

At the mention of the beast, the warriors and the gathered villagers at the gate began to murmur and speak insults toward the beast. Letete motions to them again and nods in agreement.

"Yes, yes! I agree with your thoughts. In this place that creature caused you to have sleepless nights. But also, in this place, even this very spot. Two strangers came to your aid by the command of one who wishes to see you liberated from fear, liberated from sleepless nights, liberated from the threats of dragons!"

The crowd begins to cheer loudly. Lucas now begins to speak where his brother stopped.

"It is at this same place a gathering of heroes will leave on a quest to rid themselves of the scaly threat of the Ash Breather and its Master!"

Letete picks up from where his brother ends.

"We together will leave this place, many put together as one! But we will not leave this place without a name and we will return to this place with the victory! We will return to this place which will be known as Rose Sharon[1]!

THIRTEEN

A Dragon Masters Plan

Two days ago, late into the Gibbous evening...

An ominous shadow moves over a clearing in the southern portion of the strange land. The Gibbous moon shines brightly in the night time sky. The source of the umbra lands in a clearing, flapping its leathery torn wings. It stumbles a bit as it lights upon the ground hurling curses and insults at the ones who were responsible. The beast clutches one of its left claws to its chest. The nail is scarred and knarled with three remaining claws curled inward.

"Cursed vermin! Cursed, cursed vermin! I will have my revenge! I will seek them out and destroy them! But I have a much larger concern. I am returning to the master without the Gibbous indulgence. He will not be pleased! Not pleased, not pleased at all. Not pleased to hear of how the villagers defied me, defying even him.

And to show my shame, I bear a scar, wounds even at the hands of, of those fleshies!!"

At that point, the Ash Breather releases a blood-curdling roar followed by a massive deluge of fire that pours like a running river from his gaping jaws. The clearing is scorched and aflame. The Ash Breather extends its wings and flaps in one motion becoming airborne again flying southward.

The Beast rolls and swoops in and out of darkened cloud banks drifting in the moonlit sky. The dark clouds outlines are silvery and yellowish, each appearing as animal-shaped balloons set afloat in the night time sky. Below the landscape is in constant flux, changing from clearing to a clearing. The scape below is flat and expansive occasionally giving way to rolling hills with darkened valleys. The landscape provides a macabre panorama; at its base, it appears to be a bog that ends in a strange, eerie vista. It seems to be a waterfall, but not like any waterfall seen in the world that is home to the boys. This waterfalls source comes from a small spring at the southern end of the marsh. The water cascades as it should over the sides ending or should it be said disappearing into a fine cloudy mist. No river or lake is a recipient of the watery cascade. It is an odd sight indeed. Only a cloud of vapor that gathers and floats several feet above the base of the falls bears witness to the cascade above it. The strange earthbound cloud cast an eerie shadow on the jagged, rocky floor below.

The Ash Breather swoops low then catapults itself like a rocket vertically into the night time sky. It reaches an apex then comes to a full stop for only a mere moment. It torques its body, bows its massive head and nose dives towards the edge of the falls. The Breather has done this on many an occasion to test his airborne skill. But tonight, it is hoping not to give away its arrival to the Dragon master's domain. It tucks its massive wings, accelerating at a breakneck speed. At the last moment a few feet above the surface of the marsh, the beast levels itself above the surface of the water. It clears the waterfall's edge and tucks its wings again torquing the creature over the side of the fall, parallel with the cascading water. In seconds the beast's scaly form pierces the mist cloud and levels itself just above the jagged, rocky floor of the valley below. The speed at which the beast propels itself is astounding. It zig-zags in and around what appears to be stalagmites protruding from the floor of the rocky domain. It is hot and reeks of sulfur and smoke. Magma pools dot the landscape of the other worldly terrain. No vegetation is seen anywhere in the region. Flumes of smoke and ash burst forth from fissures in the floor of the jagged canyon. The Breather takes one flap of its wings and accelerates upward into a high arch just at the base of a precipitous cliff. It opens its wings and holds that position as it gingerly lights upon the cliff face. The face leads to a vast open chasm in the side of the mountain. A smoky haze can be seen floating around its opening. Two lizard-like creatures can be seen standing at the entrance of the cave. The beings are tall and scaly. Their approximate height would be about seven feet. They stand upright like that of a man, but they have massive muscular arms and necks. They have mouths that are long with large yellowish eyes sitting on top. Inside of their mouths, rows of sharp teeth, crooked and facing different directions.

The Ash Breather folds its wings into place draping its back like a leathery cloak. It begins to walk, taking the first step gingerly. The beast grimaces and spews curses and insults again at the source of his injury.

"Cursed vermin!"

He limps toward the open chasm which is the entrance to the lair of his master.

"No gibbous, maimed, injured and bearing shame. The master will not be pleased, not pleased he will not be."

The two creatures are standing at the entrance staring at the Breather with curiosity. They notice that the Ash Breather is limping and appears wounded.

"Halt! Who goessssss there!"

One the beast shouts. Both beasts lock two long crooked spears into place as if to block the passage of the massive Ash Breather.

"Do you chance to mock me, servant! You must know with surety who I am!"

The Breather snorts a ring of smoke from its nostrils to punctuate its statement.

"The Ash Breather? You limp as a wounded thing, a prey that has been preyed upon. Like weak cattle to devour. Surely you cannot be the mighty Breather."

The two scaly creatures laugh mockingly at the beast.

"Aye, the Ash Breather would truly bear the Gibbous Indulgence on the night of the Gibbous."

The other creature retorts with sarcasm.

"Maybe the Gibbous turned on him." The other says as they both snicker in response.

At the statement, the two beasts begin to chuckle to themselves even louder. The Ash Breather lifts its massive head and begins to tremble violently.

"You dare mock the Ash Breather?"

In a swift motion, the beast descends upon the two creatures snapping them both with its jaw in quick fashion. The two monsters lay motionless on the ground as the Breather's form slowly disappears into the gaping mouth of the cavern.

The Ash Breather limps its way deeper and deeper into the cavernous abode of his master. The creature moves past what seems to be holding cells of a sort. It passes more of the lizard-like creatures that give it the right-of-way as he passes. It looks at the animals with a glaring stare as if waiting, almost daring them to make a sound. They scurry to avoid any contact with the massive beast. The Ash Breather pauses for a moment as it approaches a broadened portion of the castle-like cavern. On each side of a corridor, there are massive torches, bonfires of a sort that leads to an even more significant cavern. Smoke and haze fill the room. This opening is the entrance to the abode of his master.

"Cursed vermin! The worms have placed me in this dire predicament with my master. I will have my revenge!"

At that moment, there can be seen movement at the far end of the dark-void abode. The smoke which hovers all about like mishappened ribbons is displaced by the movement of the large creature positioned inside of the dark void.

"Ash Breaaatheer! Come closer to my abode." An ominous guttural voice speaks from the void.

The sound shakes and rumbles off the cavern walls. The voice visibly shakes the Ash Breather.

"Yes, ah yes my lord!"

He limps slowly and carefully towards the void in an attempt to not show his injuries at the hands of the two human kinsmen. He makes his way to the edge of the dark void with his head in a bowed position.

"Present the Gibbous to me for my indulgence." The creature bellows.

The Ash Breather, like a timid puppy, turns his head sideways to look into the void then quickly looks at the floor of the cave.

"Master, master. I have come before you without the Gibbous this eve. The fleshies have defied me, even us." The Breather retorts.

"Impudence!!!"

The creature in the void hearing this, roars angrily. The Ash Breather tucks its head under one of its wings in terror and trembles.

"You dare appear without the indulgence? And what is this about the fleshies defying you, even me? You are the Ash Breather! My emissary! You are a fearsome beast of power! How is it that the weak sacks of bones could defy scale and fang!" The void creature resounds.

"They had assistance, visitors even aliens from another realm. They outnumbered me!"

At that moment, a flume of unimaginable force and magnitude cascades from the smoky void, illuminating in outline the head and other portions of the void creature. Even in its void apparition, it is clear that the beast is almost three times the size of the Breather. The column of flame jets just over the head of the cowering Breather curled on the floor of the cave.

"Just how many of these aliens dared attack you on behalf of the fleshies? Twenty, fifteen, even ten?"

At that moment the void creature takes the first step from the dark. The motion reveals a claw of such massive size and density that the step even shakes the floor of the cave. The claw is scaly and large. Even on two or more of its talons, large golden rings can be seen glimmering from the light of the bonfire torches.

"Stand and come closer to me Breather. You did not answer me. Was it even ten, eight or even five aliens to our world that came to the aid of the fleshies that dared disrupt my Gibbous? Answer me know if you value your head!" The master retorts.

"Sire, it...it was but two."

The void creature takes a step backward into the smokey dark void.

"Two you say? Were they great in size as you or greater? Were they breathers of fire and ash? Answer with a sober reply!" The master shouts.

The Ash Breather pauses for a moment, but the fear of the threat of injury moves it to respond.

"They were of metal and of fire, fire like I have never seen."

"Fire! Fire? Ash Breather, you offer riddles to me? Did or did you not say that the beasts were not breathers like you? But how do you account for the fire?"

The Ash Breather begins to unfold his wings nervously and refold them likened to a nervous twitch. He stumbles over his words seeking the courage to answer his master.

"Well? Speak creature!"

The Breather is startled by the screaming retort of its master.

"Come closer to me beast! Now answer me as if you last breath depended on it! What manner of beast did these things to you, robbing me of my Gibbous!" The void creature screams again.

The Ash Breather pauses for a moment then out of fear answers with the words that it struggles to utter.

"They were not beasts my, my, master. They were fleshies!!"

The void creature snorts several concentric rings of smoke and ash in the direction of the Breather and releases a horrific roar.

A flume of fire escapes again from the dark cloudy void, but unlike the previous flume, it strikes the cowering Breather where he stands. The outline of the void creature still is illuminated. The beast begins to stand upright, displacing the ribbons of smoke that floated above and around its form. Before the Breather can right itself from the fiery concussion, a massive scaly horned tail unfolds and descends on the Breather like a giant serpent coiling around the Breather's torso. The enormous tail pulls the beast towards the void creature's position lifting it effortlessly into the air. As if that horror was not enough, a massive claw reaches out and grabs the Breather around the throat. It struggles to breathe contorting and gasping for air. The Void Creature leans forward exposing an enormous head with two large horns and scales that look like small shields. It pulls the Ash Breather even closer to its face and speaks again.

"Did you say fleshies? Fleshies! Those weak little beings did this to you? And it was only two?"

The Ash Breather struggles and points towards its throat with one of its claws as if signaling its difficulty in breathing. The Void Creature loosens its grip only so slightly.

"Yeees, mmmy master, two metallic like creatures with the face of fleshies." The Ash Breather struggles to reply.

"What manner of men could have done this thing?"

The Ash Breather clears its throat and utters the following words.

"They were not men; they were children master."

The Void Creature turns its gaze again upon the Ash Breather. The creature's eyes stretch full, and it releases a roar louder than the first if that could be possible. It flings the Ash Breather to the cave floor below. The Ash Breather slides a few feet and rolls once or twice from the force of the throw.

"Children!!! Children? How is it that two children could best the Ash Breather? Do you mock me?"

The Void Creature steps partially from the dark smokey mist. It pounds the floor and the walls of the cavern causing tremors and concussions to reverberate throughout. It swings its massive tail at the Breather who manages barely to duck its torque. The brush shatters and splinters a few of the torchieres nearby.

The Ash Breather, visibly shaken, rights itself from the assault of its master. It looks on as the void creature expresses rage at the news of the two new visitors to his realm.

The Void creature steps back into the cloudy mist. It again tells the Ash Breather to step forward. The Ash Breather reluctantly steps gingerly toward the direction of the void.

"Where are they now Ash Breather? Where are the children that bested you?" The void creature asks mockingly of the shaken beast.

The Ash Breather with its head bowed close to the cavern floor answers sheepishly.

"I, aah, I do not know Sire! I fled the village clearing before the aliens could visit more harm upon me."

"Yes, of course, you would not know because you fled like a wounded hen! Did you speak to these child aliens beast? Did they say anything to you?"

"Yes, I did my master. They spoke a thing of a word of which I am not familiar. They called me by a name that I have never heard. They referred to me as draa-guun. I thought it to be some form of insult or tirade."

The Void Creature places one claw on his chin and rubs the underside with one of its claws in a thoughtful manner as if it were pondering what the Ash Breather had stated.

"Hmm, yes! That name is foreign to this land but not foreign to me. I have heard that name before."

"What else did these beings say to you?"

"Nothing, nothing. As I stated previously, I..."

"Yes! I Know, you fled like a wounded fowl! I am very much aware of your failure."

The Ash Breather, still visibly shaken, musters a question, an utterance positioned to its master.

"Sire. Sire? I know that I have failed you! I have not brought to you the Gibbous Indulgence this Gibbous night! I ask and await my fate! What would require of me this night?" The Ash Breather sheepishly asks the ominous question.

"I should strip you to the bone and throw your carcass to the Ophidian clan! But I have a better scheme, a plan as it were. You will be spared at least for another day!"

The Ash Breather bows its head repeatedly and thanks his master for sparing him.

"Ohh thank you, master, thank you, master! I will have my revenge this eve on those vile vermin fleshies that maimed me and brought me to shame! I will take a chosen number of the Ophidian clan and will take unto us a Gibbous like none other ever seen by our kind!"

"No Breather, I have a different plan. If but two of these alien sojourners did this to my emissary, what should we do if there be more of their kind? No, I have a different plan. My minions come forth! Make yourself visible!" The Void Creature beckons.

Appearing from the shadows, materializing out of thin air as it would appear, three creatures, two are slightly smaller than the Ash Breather appear at opposite sides of the creature. The third creature's appearance causes the Ash Breather to step back as if startled by what it sees. It is another Ash Breather, identical to him except it has no injuries. The Ash Breather bristles and bears its fangs and snorts concentric rings of smoke from its nostrils.

"What is this, what are you? Who are you? There is only one! There is only one Ash Breather!" The Breather screams its threat.

It puffs itself up, pounding the ground and strafing the floor of the cavern with its tail. It begins to charge its doppelganger when at that moment, "Stop! Stay your ground Breather!" The Void Creature speaks.

He then calls the strange creature by its given dragon name in its dragon tongue.

"She is Spakov Darstis! She is kindred! Watch and learn Breather!"

The twin beast trembles and shakes its massive head and begins to change its composition instantly. In mere seconds it now looks identical to one of the other standing beasts that stood near the Ash Breather. It again shakes and trembles and turns into a small Scaly Gem.

"By the Gibbous! You are a changeling! I always thought changelings where a thing of fable and myth, but yet you stand there! And why do you appear as this frail lizard kind?"

"Ah, haa,haaa. That is part of my plan! This kindred has been a spy in the enemy's camp. This kindred will infiltrate the fleshies and find their weaknesses, and I will have my revenge, I will have my Gibbous! But first, I will send these two ahead to execute my plan; these two kindred, twins joined by a purpose of mayhem and destruction. One cannot exist without the other."

The Void Creature calls the two beasts by a strange sounding tone. It is a language that is difficult to alliterate in a human tongue. The translation of the name of the paled colored lizard would translate into a human tongue as "doubt" and the other blotchy skinned creature as "confusion." They are twin brothers who work their spells and conjurings together. Where one conjures, the other is near working in unison. The Void Creature motions with one of its massive forelimbs for the twin creatures to move closer to his misty sphere. He leans again out of the void exposing its large scaly head. He whispers something to both of the creatures and instantly they vanish.

He looks towards the Ash Breather and chuckles fiendishly. He motions towards the remaining creature who still bears the form of small Scaly Gem. He then motions to the Ash Breather to move forward. The Ash Breather looks somewhat puzzled but moves forward none the less. He stares at the shape-shifter who turns and stares at the Breather as well. The shifter in its present form looks like in every fashion as that of a small Scaly Gem. It looks identical to the numerous Scaly Gems at the village. The Breather looks and stares into the eyes of the shifter. It notices an interesting detail. The Ash Breather notices this flaw as it were and speaks of it to the Void Creature.

"Master, the creature is incomplete in its rouse. It is flawed and a pale vision of the original. The fleshies will surely see this error!"

After the Ash Breather speaks of this flaw, the shape-shifter begins to fly, hovering around the Breather like a bluish-green bee. It begins to shake violently and in mere seconds reveals its true form. It is a long serpent-like creature with four muscular legs, not as massive as the Breather but ominous none the less. Sprouting from the four legs are long sharp talons that appear as metal daggers. It has an iridescence to its scales. It coils instantly around the torso of the Ash Breather and places its face directly to the face of the Breather.

"Do you dare mock me beassst? I sssshould rend you where you sssstand!"

The Ash Breather instinctively takes his muscular claw and wraps it around the throat of the serpentine beast. The shifter reacts in kind slashing the Ash Breather across the left side of its head. The two are entwined in the clutches of each other. The Ash Breather who has not had the best of days reacts swiftly and violently. It swipes the snout of the serpentine-like beast with the back of one of its large claws followed by a concussive direct blow to the same spot where it struck with the other. This enrages the serpent-like beast and it begins to constrict its captive prey. The Ash Breather screams in pain, then reaches towards its torso and claws the serpentine beast with both of its bared talons. The serpentine beast roars in agony. The Ash Breather clasps the beast in its mouth under the soft-side of its neck near the head. It grips the beast by the neck with one claw while it still has it in his jaws. It torques and pulls the beast unravelling from its torso like that of a leather belt. It flings the beast toward a side wall of the cavern. The serpentine creature manages to right itself like a feline tossed in the air and slides on the stony cavern floor igniting sparks from its long sharp talons. Enraged, the Ash Breather begins to inflate its chest in a motion to incinerate its assailant.

"Be still!"

The Void Creature demands and strikes the Breather where it stands.

"Do not harm her Breather! I have need of her!"

The shape-shifting creature shifts again back to the form of the Ash Breather and bristles at the remark made by the Void Creature.

"Harm me? I don't think that loathsome, crippled creature would be up to that challenge!"

"Again, stand and be silent!" The Void Creature reprimands the shape-shifter.

"I see that you still have a killing spirit within you Breather. I hope that you can use that against the appropriate foe and not against kindred!"

The Ash Breather grimaces and growls at the other Ash Breather or better the shifter.

The Shifter responds by puffing a large ball of fire in a mocking fashion.

"We will work together for I have a plan even beyond that of the work that the twin beasts will carry out. Come closer both of you and bury your differences deep."

The Void creature speaks to each of the creatures standing before it, giving them specific instructions to be carried out.

"Now then, the plan must be and will be executed without a flaw! I know much about the heart of a fleshie! I have observed their kind for many a Gibbous season. It only needs to take an affliction here and a deception there to dissuade it! We will rob their hearts of hope! Once that hope is removed everything else will follow. Then we shall have our Gibbous again!"

It chuckles to itself and expounds again.

"There was one thing that was spoken of by the aliens to this land that caught my ear. I liked what they called our kind and kindred. It is a name among many names that I have heard spoken before in time past even in other dimensions. I, Tannin, the Master of this land and realm make this decree that from henceforth that all kindred of scale, talon and fang will be called dragon!!!"

FOURTEEN

An Enemy in the Camp

The gathered newly trained, newly empowered warriors begin to gather their belongings and supplies. A few more horses are chosen to pull wagons of supplies for the multitude of heroes preparing for a quest for liberation. A few of the elder villagers and some of the others who are not the fighting sort volunteer to serve and assist the band of warriors by commanding the supply wagons. Drash'Ur's father of advanced years still stands at the gate, cheering the men on with child-like vigor.

"Trumpet the Heroes of Rose Shar'On!"

His son, Drash'Ur, runs swiftly to greet his adoring father.

"Father, look at me! I am a warrior, just like the heroes who came to help us! I have a purpose now!"

Drash'Ur's father places a hand on the iron shoulder of his son's armor and looks with empathy into his eyes and states...

"No, my son, you do not have a purpose now, you always had a purpose even before you were born! I know my purpose as well. I only wish that I could go with you and your band of heroes but alas my advanced years prevent this from being so!"

At that moment, Drash'Ur unsheathes his sword and extends it hilt first to his father.

"Here Father, take my sword if even for a moment."

His father motions to his son shaking his head in disagreement. Drash'Ur insists. His father gives in to his insistence. He reaches for the sword and takes hold. It is surprisingly light. It begins to tingle in his hands, and the energy from the sword cascades up his arm through his entire body. Then suddenly, instantly, Drash'Ur's father is enveloped in armor. He drops his crutch and looks at his feet and legs. He is standing upright like a man of much younger years.

"By the blade of Neuma Ru! I am whole again!"

Drash'Ur embraces his father and squeezes him tightly. He whispers these words in his ear.

"Father, you have always been a hero to me, and forever you will be in my heart!"

Drash'Ur releases his father and they stare at each other and share a moment of laughter. Drash'Ur's father returns his sword to him, and instantly his armor disappears from his body. But surprisingly enough, a small, fiery heart is left hanging about his neck. They look at each other and laugh aloud again. The father looks at the crutch that lies on the ground before him. He glances at his now strong legs that are straight and renewed. He reaches down and grabs his crutch and in one swift motion breaks it across an uplifted thigh.

"I have no more need of this device!"

He begins to dance a jubilant silly dance to the triumphant tune that he had been singing all the day.

"Trumpet the heroes that come in the name of the one brings joy and dance to these old pants!"

Drash'Ur laughs and weeps at the same moment. He is most certainly joyous as his father's song exclaims. Trilleon who stood nearby witnessing the entire miraculous event is still as unsavory as before.

"This is some act of sorcery!" He exclaims.

"Sorcery? How can you say such evil? Is your heart so rock-like that common sense cannot seep within? Are there any cracks or fissures that will allow the radiance of hope or joy to shine inside? Oh foolish, foolish Trilleon! Instead of casting stones at the events that have taken place, you should be a part of it. Benefit from it. You should join the fray! I in my miracle will do just that. I may not fight, but I will stand with them and not against them!"

Drash'Ur's father agrees to assist with the command of the supply wagons. The gathered villagers and the heroes alike all rejoice at the good news of Drash'Ur's father. The two siblings both welcome him to the band. Trilleon considers the words spoken to him and decides to err on the side of betrayal.

"Maybe you are right, old man. Maybe I will join the fray. But not in the way that any of you will expect."

Trilleon at that point decides to go along with the band of warriors to assist or so it would appear.

"I will indeed go along with this merry troop. I will see to it to expose those two strange aliens for the rouse that they are playing on us all. I will wait for the proper moment to make my move. Then everyone will see them for what they truly are."

At that moment, Trilleon places a strained faux smile on his face. He walks over to the gathered thronged in the clearing and offers to join the band of warriors. Little do they know that there may be an enemy in their camp.

The gathered warrior band, some in shining armor, some atop otherworldly steeds and others in modest attire are almost finished with securing their needed supplies and belongings for a long quest. Some of the warriors as well as the villagers are becoming a little concerned about the arduous task in which they are about to embark. It is becoming more real as they are about to depart for the Dragon Master's lair. Letete is prompted by Neuma Ru to gather his Generals and Captains with their steeds to receive instructions. Letete motions to Lucas who is already atop of his horse celestial, Lightning Sky. Letete gives his brother instructions to deliver to the others. They all receive and accept their assignments without any complaint. Just the opposite, they are jubilant in their position and rank. Ranke, the Tinkerer, suggests the use of time devices made of glass and sand to carry out the patrol of the band. He gives a timing device to first the Generals followed by each Captain.

"Good! We can use these to rotate a patrol at each checkpoint as instructed."

"Lucas, see that they understand with the instruction of Ranke how to use the devices. I will take a moment to address the people to ease their fears. I will be a part of the first southern watch. You have your instructions."

Letete turns aside to address the gathered warriors.

"Warriors of Rose Sharon!"

When Letete makes this statement, the gathered troops erupt into a loud and enthusiastic cheer. Letete motions to the group to be silent for a moment.

"Warriors of Rose Sharon! I want to commend those of you who volunteered to join us on this quest for liberation! The journey will be difficult. It will have dangers!"

Some of the crowd begins to murmur in response to that statement.

"But you have nothing to fear! Neuma Ru is with us and shall give us the victory over the Ash Breather and his Master!"

The group erupts again even louder than the first time. Letete quickly motions to the crowd again.

"But I must warn you. You must never lose faith, you must never fear because this will weaken you and the armor will not remain with you. You were not given fear as a gift, but you were given the armor of Neuma Ru to keep you if you believed and you did! Never lose that faith!"

The crowd cheers and applauds the statements made by Letete. He hears the voice of Neuma Ru again and nods in agreement.

"I have a request of you. I need ten warriors to volunteer to stay behind and protect the village while we journey on to face the Ash Breather and his master."

The group begins to murmur among themselves.

"Yes, I know that this may be disappointing but for those who remain behind, your task and calling will be no less important. The ten that stay will be commissioned to watch over all that you hold dear. The homes and more importantly the families that you all are fighting for."

At that moment, one of the younger men steps forward and exclaims, "I will stay and protect Rose Sharon' for the warrior, family, and friend!"

Letete gestures to the young man, who appears to be an older teenager, tall and stately.

"Because you have stepped forward first without complaint, I will name you the captain of the ten."

Letete unsheathes his sword which ignites. The young man immediately drops to one knee in response. Letete touches first the young man's left shoulder then his right. He gestures for the warrior to stand.

"What is your name Captain?"

"My name General is Katsin Sar! I am in your service!"

"Captain Sar, you are to lead the nine that follow. You have been chosen and charged! Lead well!"

Katsin nods in agreement and moves a few steps backward.

Others step forward, offers a nod to the General and follow suit, lining up behind Katsin. Soon the remnant of ten is chosen. Letete gestures sternly towards Ranke.

"Good! Ranke will quickly tell you the locations of the different devices that can be used to help protect the village in case the enemy attempts to flank our army. Rose Sharon' shall never fall!"

At that declaration, the villagers and the gathered warriors all cheer loudly. The remnant of ten line up and head towards the village gate with Katsin leading the way.

"Now, for this group of warriors, liberation awaits! On towards the dragon's lair and on towards victory!"

The cheering band of warriors, beasts, and villagers begin the journey towards the lair of the Dragon's. All faces are bright and vibrant. On every face, joy and anticipation can be seen, except for one. Trilleon scowls as he stares at the pair leading the way. "Imposters, Aliens! It should be me that the village adores and not mere children. I will have my day!" He says to himself quietly.

"I will have my day!"

Letete and Thaddeus have the first watch together in the southern portion of the group. Lucas along with Drash'Ur is located in the north at the rear of the band while Ranke has an eastern point and Doldren the western point. Both Doldren and Ranke also have a designated warrior to assist. Each assisting warrior is assigned to rotate clockwise to the next checkpoint to alternate with the previous. Letete takes to the sky with Fire Sky while Thaddeus is atop Thunder Sky below. Letete's fiery steed, Fire Sky, is a sight to behold. It appears like a tattered banner of flames in the noonday sky. Even in the brightness of day, it appears as bright as a comet in the sky with a tale of flames and smoke behind it. Lucas's horse in the rear of the band is no less spectacular in appearance as well as the ominous billows of the horse Thunder Sky below with its rider Thaddeus. Those images combined with the shimmer of mirror-like armor gives the gathered group the appearance of a glistening gem in the clearing below. The spectacle of the milestone event is not lost on the gathered band. They all look in awe at the wonders all around them. Fear is not observed present in the hearts of any one of the warriors or villagers. But betrayal lurks in the heart of one. The group begins to chant the victory song that has become their mantra.

"Trumpet the heroes that come!"

The miles seem to pass by unnoticed. The rotation by the Generals has been completed at least seven times fluidly. They have traveled far in what seems like mere moments. Thaddeus, now back to his original point in the rotation, looks strangely at his surroundings. Letete lands his horse for a moment to speak to his Captain.

"Thaddeus sir, you look concerned, is everything ok?"

"Everything is fine young General. It is only my fascination and awe at what is transpiring. In all my years, I never dreamed that I would ever see beyond the edge of the Snarksen Forest. I have always wondered how the land would appear. No man woman or child has ever ventured this far from the village. The Ash Breather expressly forbids it by word of his master. I never thought in my wildest imagination that I would be able to venture freely through these plains. We are truly set free!"

"Yes, you are free Thaddeus. That freedom with the completion of this quest will be permanent. We will defeat the beasts. We will tear down their strongholds and take back what they have stolen!" Letete retorts thinking back to one of his father's sermons.

"Speaking of that Thaddeus, I remember when we were in your home back at the tree, you spoke of villagers that were taken or either missing even after the Gibbous accord was agreed upon and set into place. Do you have any idea what happened to those people?"

"It is a mystery; a horrible affliction carried out by those sympathetic to the Ash Breather and his master."

"Those sympathetic to the Ash Breather? What do you mean?"

"The Ash Breather has enlisted the aid of some of the other creatures in this realm or so we believe. They always seem to strike at night under cover of darkness. We have lost so many of our loved ones to this blight. It is a burden on our spirits to have the threat of the Breather coupled with the threat of these other seemingly almost invisible creatures."

"Invisible? You can't see them?"

"We say invisible because no one has ever been able to say what they look like. If you see one, you are not left to tell about it."

"We will continue to post the rotating guard after nightfall. We will also enlist others to be a part of the rotating watch. We will lose no one on this quest if I can help it!"

"This is a good spot Letete the Elder to make camp for the evening you would agree?"

"Yes, I agree."

Letete motions with a raised hand for the glimmering multitude of warriors and beasts to stop for the evening in a clearing that has a small lake.

"We will make camp here for the night!"

Letete motions to the others on point watch to meet him at the front of the gathered band.

"We will continue to rotate the guard, but we will rotate every three hours instead of one. We will also replace the guard of two men with two more rested men in their place. We will need twenty-four men to create the rotation."

Quickly, Letete and Lucas choose twenty-four men, and the rotation begins immediately. The original guard of eight does not take the first watch. They rest their horses, although the mysterious beasts don't seem to need the rest, and then begin to settle in. Some of the men on the wagon start a large bonfire in the center of the camp. Other smaller fires are lit as well in front of smaller sub-groups of people. Before long, the wagoneers prepare a tasty but humble meal of lentil-like beans for the evening. These lentil-like beans are not exactly like the beans from the world of the two young generals. They are bright orange but have a distinctive taste. A modest bread is prepared to accompany the strange orange colored pourage.

"This is pretty good stuff!" Letete says.

Lucas nods his head as well in agreement.

"It's not so bad, but I would rather have a cheeseburger." Lucas responds.

Both brothers share a moment of laughter. The gathered warriors, generals, and captains ponder what is said and ask questions of Lucas about the strange sounding food that he begins to describe. Everyone gathered is amazed at the description of the culinary delight. Letete motions again to the crowd. He gets the attention of Lucas and tells him about the accounts of the "invisible" threat that has taken villagers by cover of night.

"Yeah, Big Bro, I do remember Thaddeus telling us about that at the tree. Do you think that we need to be concerned?" Lucas asks his brother.

"Just to be safe, Neuma Ru has instructed me to step up a rotating guard."

"I agree! Nothing can happen to this group and nothing will under our watch!"

"Young warriors, I suggest that you both rest for the evening, we have enough guards on post to take care of that task. Plus, your presence in the camp will help sooth any fearful concerns."

"Then it's settled! We will sit around the fire and tell stories. I can tell stories from our world, stories that our Dad has told us!"

"I want to hear more about your world's "Han-bear-gers!" Doldren responds.

"Always thinking about your stomach as usual Doldren." Ranke says as the group laughs in response.

The gathered settle in for the evening and the first watch rotates without any difficulty. Letete, Lucas, Thaddeus and the others are positioned around the bonfire. The horses are positioned not too far off, closer towards the lake. The night time is a perfect backdrop for the glowing stable of the otherworldly beast. By the end of the second watch Letete, Lucas and Thaddeus are the only ones who are not yet asleep.

"Young warriors, I know that you are concerned and want to oversee the men, but you should get your rest. We still have a very long journey ahead of us." Thaddeus says with a fatherly tone.

"Yes, I agree. I just have this strange feeling. I can't shake it." Letete responds.

"You too Big Brother? It's like someone or something is watching us."

Thaddeus looks out into the darkness just beyond the camp.

"Letete the Elder and Lucas the Younger you do not need to be overly concerned. You have posted a rotating guard around the camp. All is well. Get some rest. I will continue to be vigilant until the end of the third watch."

The boys agree and nestle themselves in for the evening. Before falling off, they both recite a prayer that their parents had taught them, taken from Psalm 91.

"We shall not be afraid of the terror of the night or things that stalk during the day. No evil shall befall us; it shall not come near our dwelling, protect us in His Name, Amen."

A few moments later, both young men fall soundly asleep. Thaddeus is attentive and ponders what the elder of the two boys had stated. He feels a slight unease within the darkness. At that moment, farther in the camp, someone rustles about and stands to their feet. They are careful not to awake the others around them who are sleeping. They begin strolling towards the supply wagon. It's Trilleon. He walks slowly and purposely.

"Now is my chance. I will cause a commotion in the camp. I will expose those alien children for who they are."

Off in the distance, beyond the outer edge of the camp, there appear three shadowy figures just outside of the glow of the campfire shrouded in the darkness. Trilleon is unaware of the maleficent presence of the shadowy figures. At that moment the rotating guard changes point, and the replaced guards are heading near to where he is standing. In a panic, He runs toward a small bush, just on the outside of the camp. He slides to a stop and rolls just behind the bush, out of the sight of the patrolling guard. The bush is just the right covering for Trilleon. It is dark, and it is a good staging area for what he desires in his envious heart. He seeks to bring shame to the two young generals. Just in the distance about 30 yards behind Trilleon, he is unaware of the three shadowy forms that appear in the cloak of night.

"A fleshie! And like the others who were our prey, he is alone and separated. We should take him!" One of the darkened forms states ominously.

"Nooo! You sssssimpleton! Remember the wordsss of our massster. We musssst ssstay on tassssk! That fleshie will be our puppet! Can you smell the stench of deceit and envy in his heart? He is ripe for manipulation!" The serpentine Slither says.

Slither motions to one of the dark, shadowy figures and calls him by his dragon name in their dragon tongue. To the human ear, the translation is not understandable or pronounceable. The translation of this reptilian apparition is simply "Doubt," and the other larger blotchy scaled beast is "Confusion."

"Doubt, move silently and in your shadow form next to the flesshie and tell him exactly what I tell you word for word."

"I do not take orders from you shape-shifter! I only listen to the master and his emissary The Ash Breather! You dare..."

At that moment interrupting the objection of the beast called Doubt, the serpentine beast holds up one of its claws exposing on one of its fingers a golden ring with a strange moniker embossed into the band. Doubt immediately responds and removes a threatening scowl from his face.

"The signet of the master! How can this be?" The dragon called doubt retorts.

"He hass put me in charge of thiss campaign! And if you dare defy me again beasst, I will rend you into piecess and sscatter your remainss to the wind! Now move with hasste and sstealth, Our masster commandss you!"

The beast called Doubt bows and complies as ordered. It teleports from its standing position instantly appearing next to Trilleon undetected. It bends its massive scaled head towards the right ear of Trilleon and whispers small wisps of smoke with words peppered throughout that enter the ear and mind of the unsuspecting Trilleon. Trilleon repeats aloud the words spoken to him by the shadowy form. Doubt teleports again and appears before Slither.

"It is done as you have commanded!"

"Confusion sssss, wait for my command, I will tell you when to sssstrike!"

The shadowy trio watch Trilleon stand and quietly begin to maneuver his way towards one of the supply wagons. He pauses for a moment to reach down and pick up a small dried branch that is lying on the ground. He begins his trek again towards the wagon.

"Sssee, the flesshie iss predictable. Fleshies can be eassily manipulated if they are not pure of heart!" Slither says ominously.

They watch as Trilleon takes the dried wooden branch and places one end into the flames of a nearby fire pit. He quickly places the burning ember into the wagon near the rear where dried spices and kindling is stored, hoping to find the best resting to start a fire. He lifts up a loose tarping and pushes the ember deep within and moves quickly back to his bedding. Moments later, as Trilleon has made his way back to his pallet, he feigns a slumber with one eye open and focused on the wagon which is beginning to smolder. Someone nearby the wagon which was asleep begins to stir. They sit up and begin to stretch and yawn. Trilleon begins to see the smoke accumulate and then small tongues of fire at the rear of the wagon. The person who was stirring nearby stands to his feet immediately after smelling smoke and seeing the source begins to yell the expected phrase.

"Fire! Fire! The wagon is on fire!"

Trilleon, who really was not sleeping, took the opportunity to scream a dire warning to exacerbate the situation even further.

"The Ash Breather has returned! The Breather is here!"

Slither motions to the beast called Confusion to move at the shouts of Trilleon and the other man.

"Now beast of Confusssion, move in sssssshadowy form throughout the camp and ssssspread your ssseedsss of fear throughout the mindsss and heartss of the flesshiess!"

Confusion moves swiftly, cloaked, and invisible to the startled village warriors. Unrest starts to move and spread. The burning ember of doubt begins to ignite and spread throughout the camp. The Two Brothers along with Thaddeus and the others move in quickly to assess the calamity and noise coming from the center of the camp. Thaddeus is the first to speak upon arriving at the scene.

"People, warriors stay your panic! What is the matter to this unrest? Quickly form a fire line of men and buckets from the lake nearby."

The men gather quickly with buckets to form a line to the nearby lake. The fire just as quickly as it was started is now extinguished. Thaddeus motions to the crowd to hear and look towards the two brothers who are now in full armor, there chest plates set ablaze in a blue-greenish blaze.

"People, warriors do not fear! The fire has been put out. Does anyone here know how this could have happened? I don't believe that it was the Ash Breather as was said because the fire and its damage was too small compared to what the Breather could have done with its flames." Letete says.

"Does anyone have any answers as to who or what could have done this?"

At that question, Slither motions to the Beast called Doubt and again to Confusion.

"Go now with stealth, cloak your form and cast your shadows through the crowd."

The two ethereal beasts swiftly carry out the orders of the dragon called Slither. As the forms of Doubt and Confusion fade and disappear into vapor and mist, the shapeshifter, retreats slowly backward into the dark of the forest out of the light of the fire of the camp. Amidst of fog begins to form and gather as wisplike specters throughout the camp. The beasts make their way first to Trilleon because treachery is great in his heart and gives off a scent and stench as it were to the beasts that attract them. They begin to whisper words of doubt, confusion, and discord into the mind of Trilleon.

"How can you be sure it is not the work of the Ash Breather?" Doubt whispers into the ear of Trilleon.

Trilleon is instantly entranced by the words of Doubt and repeats them all.

"How can you be sure it is not the work of the Ash Breather? We can't be sure, now can we?"

At that moment the two unseen phantoms run through the camp spreading their poison to the unsuspected gathered. Murmurings and talk begin to increase. The crowd begins to become uneasy.

"How can we be sure that this is not the work of that beast, returning to have his revenge on us because of those strangers to our land? They are not one of us, but yet you trust them blindly!" Trilleon continues.

Some of the villagers nod in agreement while others are not convinced.

"How can you say these things? You of all people should be grateful that these young warriors arrived to help us when they did? Did not these two save your wife, even you?" One of the warriors asked.

"Enough!" Thaddeus retorts.

"We are not this group, this mob! We are not under the attack of the Breather! We all remember what that type of attack looks like, it is fresh in all of our minds!"

At that moment, Letete and Lucas draw their swords, each extended and flaming.

"There is something not right here! There is something here, and it is not the Ash Breather!" Letete says.

"Yes, big brother, I can feel it two."

Thaddeus looks at the heart-shaped insignia on the chest plates of the warrior's armor. The flame is brilliant and begins to increase in intensity to a white-hot glow. He also draws his sword sending the entire camp into a state of readiness as the entire warrior clan draws their swords in response.

"Men, warriors, I sense that we have an enemy in the camp!" Thaddeus exclaims. At that moment Trilleon responds to the proclamation. Letete motions to his captains and Lucas his general to man their posts and patrol the perimeter. He motions to the crowd to get their attention.

"No, we are not under the attack of the Breather, but I sense something, and I am not too sure what it may be. But we will patrol the perimeter to ensure the safety of the camp."

Letete motions to his horse, Fire Sky, and fiery steed appears instantly, lighting upon the grassy area near him. He quickly mounts the beast. He motions to Thaddeus who joins him as well on his thunderous steed. Lucas patrols with Drash'Ur who climbs on the back of lightning sky with him.

"I am going to need your eyes Drash'Ur, are you up for a quick patrol?" Lucas asks.

"Yes, indeed General!"

He quickly bounds onto the back of the beast with Lucas riding in front.

"Ride Lightning!"

The horse whinnies and then instantly catapults itself into the air. Letete and Thaddeus fly the perimeter in the opposite direction. They quickly pass the other warriors who are riding the perimeter by air or by land. After three trips around the perimeter, he motions to Thaddeus and lands his fiery steed on the clearing floor below. Thaddeus follows in kind.

"Thaddeus, Sir, what do you make of what happened here? I could sense something, but we did not find anything. Isn't that odd?" Letete asks.

"Yes, yes indeed. I felt a strange presence as well."

"I feel that there is still something amiss here."

At that moment, just outside of the camp's fire glow about twenty feet into the darkness of the forest, there is what appears to be an explosion. A small mushroom-shaped ball fire cascades upward through the forest line into the darkened sky.

"By the Snarksen!" Thaddeus exclaims.

Letete instantly and with speed atop Fire Sky dashes towards the flume of fire. His brother also atop Lightning Sky is also is headed in the same direction.

"Drash'Ur, use that vision of yours to see what could have caused that ball of fire in the forest!" Lucas exclaims.

"I started gazing into the forest the very moment the fire erupted from the forest floor. I do not see anything that could have... wait; I see something in a clearing on the ground! Head in that direction!" Drash'Ur instructs the small-sized general.

Letete is already at the spot of the flaming ball, but he does not see a possible source. Thaddeus is just behind Letete and has dismounted to investigate the matter.

"This is strange indeed; nothing is here to show what could have caused this strange event."

Letete, still atop Fire Sky and in full armor looks around and peers into the darkness. He sees something that seems to be stirring in the distance about ten or more feet from the spot of the fire flume.

"Wait! I see something moving in the forest over there in that clearing!"

Letete dismounts his horse and swiftly like a gazelle bound towards the direction of the moment.

"Wait, young general; we don't know what we are dealing with!" Thaddeus exclaims.

But it is to no avail. Letete and his bright vesture is already the clearing area. He draws his sword instinctively. He slides to a stop in the clearing area. What was there before is not there at the moment he arrives. He can sense something is watching him. He hears something break a twig nearby.

"Gotcha!" He says to himself.

He leaps covering the distance in one bound. He swings his sword at the middle trunk of a small sapling that had grown up through a large bush. The sword slices through the sapling like butter with no resistance. It is displaced without effort along with the top portion of the bush. Leaves and bark are shattered in every direction. "Awwwweeeeerrrrrrrrr!" A scream emanates from the remnant of the bush.

Letete freezes motionless in place holding his flaming sword still. It is not the scream of a beast or animal. He recognizes that sound because he has heard it so many times before either in his old town or at church picnics.

"Is anyone there? Who are you?"

Thaddeus rushes to the side of Letete and moves forward to inspect the remnants of the charred tree. He pushes aside the branches and peers behind the bush.

"Careful Thaddeus!" Letete exclaims with his sword still drawn for the worse. Thaddeus nods in agreement. He draws his sword, using its glow to illuminate the surrounding area.

"Young General, I think you need to come and see what we have here!"

Letete walks quickly to his side and peaks through the bush. What he sees astonishes him. His eyes are stretched far because of what he sees.

"Whoa! I can't believe it! It's, it's a girl!"

FIFTEEN

A Girl Named Qrueinen

Thaddeus and Letete look on in amazement at the visage of a scared young girl. She appears to be approximately about twelve years old. She is curled on the forest floor, scared and trembling.

"Don't hurt meee! Please don't hurt me!" She screams in a terrified voice.

Letete sheaths his sword as well as Thaddeus. Thaddeus motions to the young girl to show that he means her no harm.

"Young one, we mean you no harm. We will not hurt you." Thaddeus says in a trusting voice.

"Come, reach for my hand. Letete, the Elder, come to her side and assist her to her feet."

Letete quickly moves to her side to assist her to her feet. He feels guilty about almost striking the young girl with his sword. Thaddeus and Letete assist to her feet.

"Owww!" She exclaims, and she falls to the forest floor.

"My ankle, it hurts me stand on it!"

Thaddeus bends to a knee to get a look at her ankle.

"It looks like a sprain. I don't think that it is too bad."

Letete notices a red stain on his armored right arm. It appears to be blood. He knows that he was not injured so he looks to see if it could be from the girl.

"You have a cut on your arm; it's bleeding!"

Thaddeus looks at it quickly. He reaches into a small pouch that is hanging around his neck to pull out a piece of cloth. He tears a strip of the cloth and ties it securely around the wound. The young girl grimaces as Thaddeus ties the makeshift bandage.

"There now, you will be good as new shortly."

Letete looks at the young girl with sympathy.

"I am very sorry for injuring you. I would never hurt anyone on purpose! I am so, so sorry!" Letete says.

"It's not your fault, but I would like to leave this forest as soon as possible before they come back!"

"They!" Lucas chimes in on that note.

"It's a girl! What is she doing here?" He shouts.

Thaddeus responds quickly.

"Letete the Elder, Lucas the Younger, I recommend that we take this discussion back to the camp and leave this area as soon as possible taking the advice of our young maiden friend. We can get more answers to questions in the morning which is not too long from now!"

"Agreed!" Thaddeus motions to Letete.

"General, can you carry this young maiden back to the camp? Lucas, General, we can cover the rear as we leave this forest."

Lucas nods in agreement. Thaddeus and Lucas draw their swords as Letete effortlessly lifts the young girl into the air. She clutches one arm around his waist, and the other is placed palm down onto his armor chest plate. He easily lifts the slender young lady. Letete is unusually tall for someone as young as he is. He has the appearance of being older than he is.

"You are soo warm!" The young girl exclaims.

"I am extremely sorry!" Letete says sympathetically to the young girl. Letete, Lucas, and Thaddeus all start walking towards the camp edge. Their horses are gathered there along with Drash'Ur who stands in their midst.

"It is a young damsel!" Drash'Ur exclaims.

"Yes Drash'Ur, your keen sight has not failed you again." Thaddeus exclaims. Letete with a wave of his hand motions to his horse. Fire Sky immediately lights next to where Letete is standing holding the young girl in his arms. As the horse approaches, the girl appears startled at the sight of the mysterious beast. She turns her face inward into the shoulder of Letete's armor.

"He won't hurt you. He is my friend. Fire Sky fly the perimeter along with the other horses and keep watch!"

The fiery beast nods in agreement and takes to the air in one beat of its powerful fiery wings. The others follow in like fashion.

"Come, let's take her to the camp to tend to her wounds. You must be hungry young damsel!" Thaddeus exclaims.

The young girl nods and again covers her face. Letete says softly to the young girl,

"Hold on!"

He motions to Thaddeus, Lucas, and Drash'Ur. In an instant, he lunges forward and leaps covering several feet at a time being careful not to shake the young girl. Lucas and Thaddeus follow close behind. In moments they are all at the central part of the camp near the main campfire. Letete places the young girl gently down on a pallet on the ground.

"Here, lay here for a while."

Thaddeus moves in quickly, pulling out a pouch filled with different medicinal items, salves, ointments and oils along with stripping of clothes used for bandages.

"Let me take a look at your ankle." He says to the young girl.

She timidly extends her injured leg for Thaddeus to inspect. He motions to a young man standing nearby to bring him a bucket of water quickly. He dips a small cloth into the water. He carefully rings the excess water from the cloth. He begins cleaning the ankle of the new guest.

"Now there, that is done. All better?" He asks.

The young girl nods in approval.

"Now, let's take a look at your arm."

The young maiden reluctantly extends a small, frail arm. Thaddeus examines the wound closely. The wound is a little more significant than the other wound. He takes a small cup and adds a powder to it, stirring it briskly.

"This may sting a little, but it will clean out the wound and make it heal quicker." He says to the young guest. She grimaces as he pours the contents over the wound. He cleans it and bandages the wound securely. A small group has now gathered to peer at the camps new visitor. Letete the Elder and his brother Lucas, Drash'Ur, Ranke and Doldren are gathered as well starring at their new quest with great intensity. She is visibly uncomfortable with the attention. Thaddeus can sense her level of discomfort.

"Ranke, Doldren and Drash'Ur, why don't you join the others on the patrol of the perimeter. We can attend to our quest."

"Why Father, we would not dare leave you with such a pretty...uhh hmmm... I mean a cumbersome task alone." Doldren states.

"Yes, I am sure of your valor and willingness to help. It is for that very reason I command you to go and carry out the task that is before you. Go, take leave, I will hear no more."

The young men leave the place of the newly arrived guess with reluctance. The three remaining generals now turn their gaze upon the petit guest.

"Now there young maiden, how did you arrive in such a precarious condition and position? You can begin by telling us your name. Do you have a name?" Thaddeus asks with a carefully positioned tone.

"Yes, yess, yes. My name is Qrueinen."

"What an unusual name you have. I have never seen you before. You are not from our village. Where are you from?"

"I think that it is a pretty name!" Letete responds.

The young girl looks at Letete with a small grin on her face and then turns to Thaddeus to respond. She pulls back the cloak from her face. Lucas is the first to respond.

"Look at her eyes! They are two different colors! That is strange!" Lucas retorts. The young girl looks a little embarrassed and uncomfortable but replies first to the statement of Lucas.

"Yes, yes they are. It is a birthmark. My parents thought it to be a good omen or sign of a special purpose. To answer your question sir, I am from a nearby village towards the west. I am not altogether sure about how I arrived here in this area. I was walking in the forest gathering Tijera berries and other fruits for a special meal later that evening. I went a little too far into the forest. It is there that I encountered an invisible creature of serpent-like proportions. It appeared out of thin air or it would seem. It grabbed me and subdued me. I was like that of simple rag doll in the clutches of the beast. As I lay pinned to the forest floor. I saw it... I saw a beast of such massive size and power fly above and past me towards my village. I could see a flume of fire bellow up through its mouth. It flew over as that of a shadow." Lucas responds to her description.

"The Ash Breather! Scaly freak!"

Qrueinen continues.

"I could hear the cries of my people. The beast that held me absconded with me in its clutches. I was helpless to do anything. I was so afraid. I was taken to the lair of their master. He called himself "Tannim", their master and king. I was given to their master as his captive. He threatened to harm me if I did not cooperate with his wishes. I managed to escape or at least it seemed as if I had at first. I was unable to navigate the harsh terrain of their domain. I was soon discovered. But strange enough, I was not taken back to their master's lair but to this forest area. It is only now that I have realized that the beast that found me only wanted to have some sport, to hunt me down before...before..."

At that point, Qrueinen begins to sob uncontrollably.

Letete moves to her side to comfort her as she places her face into the fold of his shoulder.

"You don't have to worry, you are safe now. Nothing can hurt you here."

At that point, Thaddeus moves towards the young girl and places his hand on her shoulder.

"Come now, Qrueinen, get some rest. I will stay here with you until the morn, which is not long from now. You can rest in one of the wagons as we journey on."

She looks up into the face of Thaddeus and nods. She utters a simple question to the older general.

"Yes, that would be fine. As a query Sir, where pray tell are you going?"

The gathered group looks at each other and in-kind look to the frail young maiden.

"We are going on a quest of liberation...to the Ash Breather's Lair."

Qrueinen recoils into a fetal position and shrieks in response.

"No, no we cannot go there! I cannot return that place! Tannim will destroy us all!"

Qrueinen sobs and cries herself to sleep as Letete kneels next to her holding her hand.

"Thaddeus, Lucas, what do you think about what she said? We now have a name to attach to this Dragon Master. Thaddeus have you heard of this Tannim before." Letete asks.

"Well you General that is a name that I am not familiar with. It was never shared with us. The Ash Breather was the only beast that we dealt with directly. We of course were tormented by those invisible creatures she talked about. Lucas the Younger, what do you think of our guest?" Thaddeus asks.

Lucas places an armored hand on his chin. He stares down at the sleeping girl. There is a long pregnant pause. Then he says what he is pondering only in the way Lucas can, succinctly.

"I don't trust her. There is something not right with her story. Thaddeus, you said that no one ever came back to tell of attacks by these night creatures. How did she escape? What is special about her?"

"Lucas, I think that you are paranoid! She is a victim and you are treating her like an enemy! That's not fair at all!" Letete fires back.

"Hey, don't get mad at me! You asked me what I thought, and I told you! There is something not right about her story! Not right at all!" Lucas storms off towards the south of the camp.

He calls for his horse Lightning Sky who appears instantly. They both take flight into the early dawn sky. The young guest stirs and rolls onto her side. With her face turned away from the warriors, she opens her bi-colored eyes which reflect the flickering flames of a nearby campfire and smiles a crooked grin.

SIXTEEN

Divide the Conquerors

As the sun begins to rise over the horizon, it cast long shadows through the forest in the distance. The sun's rays create bright orange and yellow ribbons on the face of the lake nearby. Songbirds begin to sing their morning songs at the sun's arrival. Small forest creatures can be seen scurrying in the distance. A soft breeze picks up, kissing the faces of the slumbering band. But not all sleep within this gathering of warriors. Thaddeus looks on over the gathered band. His mind is racing because of what had transpired just hours before. He is pondering the statements of Qrueinen and Lucas. He wants to believe the girl but also has the same trepidations as Lucas. Letete begins to stir nearby. He made a place to sleep, not too far from the young maiden who was still fast asleep. Thaddeus motions to Letete to come to him.

"Letete the Elder, General, pardon my forwardness by beaconing you to come to me. I am concerned, and I wanted to speak with you regarding this matter. I wanted to talk to you away from our slumbering guest."

"It is not a problem Thaddeus, but I wanted to ask you first, have you seen Lucas? He left our conversation pretty upset with me. I thought about it, and I wanted to apologize to him."

Now, a familiar voice chimes in from above.

"Did I hear that someone wants to apologize?" It is Lucas who drops from the sky on the back of his horse and with Drash'Ur with him.

"Shhh! don't wake her!" Letete exclaims.

"Oh, here we go again. I think that we should wake her and ask her about her story and why there are holes in it!"

Letete looks at Lucas with disdain while Thaddeus motions to the two young generals.

"Generals, you must show a unified front. You do not want to give the warriors any reason to doubt or lose faith. You stated so yourself that would not yield positive consequences."

"I just want some answers, that's all. I don't know why my big brother is being so defensive of someone he doesn't even know!"

"I'm not defensive! I just feel sorry for her because of what she has gone through. And to top that off, I cut her, accidentally of course, but I still hurt her."

"Look Big Brother; you shouldn't be so hard on yourself. I care about the people here, and I care about you too. I just want to be careful and make sure that we are extra careful."

"Letete the Elder, General, I too have some questions about our young guest's story. I think that we should be watchful of her just to be cautious. These are strange times, and we have experienced so much." Thaddeus states.

"Yes, I agree. I don't mean to be defensive. Lucas, I apologize for getting angry."

At that moment, Qrueinen awakens abruptly screaming in terror. Her screams awaken and startle those sleeping nearby. The trio quickly runs to her side with Letete leading the way.

"Qrueinen, Qrueinen, are you okay?" Letete asks as he kneels near the shrieking young girl.

Thaddeus responds as well and calls to the young girl, placing a reassuring hand on the girl's shoulder.

"Nooo, don't hurt me! Don't hurt me!" She yelps.

She finally becomes more coherent and clear-headed. She clutches Letete's thigh as he kneels near her side.

"What's wrong?" Letete asks.

"I, I had a horrible dream! I dreamed that I was being chased through the forest by... a shiny creature of sorts."

"A shiny creature?" Letete retorts.

"Yes, a shiny metal like being. When it apprehended me, it threw me to the ground and struck me. After the creature struck me, it revealed itself to me. It was him!" Qrueinen points a petit, trembling finger at Lucas standing before her.

"Me!! What do you mean me?" He shouts.

She recoils at Lucas' response and clings even closer to Letete kneeling next to her.

"That's crazy; I would never hurt anyone...anyone except a dragon! Are you a dragon?" Lucas says sarcastically.

"That's not funny; can't you see that she is scared?"

Thaddeus pulls the young girl from the side of Letete and stands her to her feet. He motions to Letete and Lucas to get the camp ready to move as the day begins to break and others begin to stir.

"Young Generals, the day has begun, and the sun is beginning to rise above the tree line. We should begin to restart our journey. I will see to the young maiden."

"Can he stay with me?" Qrueinen says pointing towards Letete.

"No young maiden, he and his brother have other more pressing duties; I will gladly attend you for the moment."

Letete looks on and nods trepidatiously as he and his brother begin to walk towards the front of the camp.

"Can you believe her, she called me a creature. I would never hurt anybody, especially a girl." Lucas says.

"Yeah, I know, but you have been kinda hard on her. That's not like you." Letete responds.

"I'm telling you Letete it's something not exactly right about her. Even Thaddeus said the same thing. He is not fully comfortable with her as well. Just be careful and be on guard, that's all I am saying." Lucas says sternly to his brother.

The morning comes swiftly with the rising of the sun over the tree line. The two brothers mend their fences between each other and quickly go about getting the band of warriors together. Thaddeus sits with the young girl who seems to be doing much better after a quick morning meal with him and some of the others that are gathered. He still can't quite make himself feel fully comfortable with her story. None the less, he motions to Drash'Ur's Father to watch her as he places her on the wagon so that she does not have to walk on the sprained leg. She looks at Thaddeus in a peculiar manner. He stares at her, pondering the scale of her appearance and her ocular anomalies. He joins Letete and Lucas with the others at the front of the caravan. Letete motions to the generals and captains to resume their patrol. He also motions to Drash'Ur he sounds his trump signaling the continuation of their journey. As the day ages and the sun meanders to its apex, Letete atop Fire Sky, finds himself again in the company of Thaddeus his general.

"Thaddeus, do you have a moment? I would like to talk to you."

"Of course, Letete the Elder, you always have my ear. What is your query?"

"I was just wondering about our new friend, Qrueinen. What do you think of her? I talked with my Brother about her and he does not trust her. I, on the other hand, feel sorry for her. I mean, she really has been through a lot. I even hurt her myself. What do you think?

"Yes general, there are questions that I have about our quest. She seems to be a tragic victim of the one that we seek to vanquish. But I also agree with your brother. There is something strange about her, but maybe it's the magnitude of what she has experienced that makes her seem so strange. It could be the oddity of her birthmark. It could also be the fact that you have taken a fancy to the young maiden. She is quite fetching isn't she General?"

"I uh, want do you mean? I don't see her like that. I mean I do see her...uh I what do you mean?" Letete responds sheepishly.

"He means that you have a thing for your new girlfriend over there!" A voice chimes in from above as Lucas lands effortlessly near where his brother is standing.

"Girlfriend, what do you mean? She is just a girl that needed or needs our help."

"Seems to me that she only wants one person's help and that is you!" Lucas retorts.

At that moment in the distance, Letete catches a glimpse of Qrueinen who is making her way to where they are standing.

"See, here comes your girlfriend now!"

"She is not my girlfriend and stop saying that! I thought that we were passed this!"

"We are passed this or her! I just want you to be careful! Think about what I said. Maybe you should ask Neuma Ru what he thinks you should do."

"He would want us to help others. Isn't that what we are doing or have been doing since we have been here? I can't understand why you are acting like this. She is just a girl! A girl that needs our help!" Letete retorts.

At that moment Qrueinen arrives at the spot where the Generals are standing.

"Excuse me gentleman, pardon my interruption but I would like to have a word with you all. I have remembered a danger that I encountered when I was taken captive and then set free for sport by one of the beasts. While I was fleeing the beast, I remember coming across another threat. It was a number of serpents that dwelled in these parts." Qrueinen said ominously.

"Serpents?" Letete responds.

"Snakes? We are not afraid of snakes. We defeated a large dragon, the Ash Breather. What are a few snakes to us?" Lucas retorts back.

"Yes, little one, I know that you are all mighty warriors, but these are not your usual tiny serpents, they are large and dangerous. Large enough to devour a horse and there was more than one of them."

Lightning Sky and Fire Sky bristle at the horse remark.

"If that is the case "Roo", how did you escape the beasts?" Lucas asks sternly.

"I don't really know. I remember being pursued by the large serpents then all I remember after that is falling. I came to again only to find myself again being pursued by the large beast that I mentioned before. I know that you don't trust me, but I want you to know about the beast so that you will not be caught unaware."

Letete motions to his brother who was sure to reply sarcastically.

"We will take your warning as advice. Thaddeus, Lucas, everyone, we must be on high alert. We will not lose anyone with Neuma Ru's help on this quest!"

The others nod and respond in agreement. In the near distance, Trilleon listens intensely. He sees this as an opportunity to finally roust the two young generals and shame them before his fellow villagers.

"I will see to it that those serpents find their way to this place to finally show those two as the cowards that they are."

He goes to the supply wagon and takes a ladle full of animal fat and ties it securely within a tanned skin. He secures it to his belt under his cloak. Once secure, Trilleon reaches out to the gathered captains and generals to make his plea heard.

"Generals forgive me for the intrusion into your convocation, but I humbly ask you to hear my petition. I could not help but overhear your discussion concerning the serpents in this region. Maybe we should take an early respite and break camp here in this valley clearing before heading further towards the forest there on the horizon. We could send a small team of warriors to reconnoiter the area to ferret out any potential beast that could harm the larger group. If we break camp early, we would have the advantage still of a high afternoon sun, a late afternoon sun, but still a few hours before darkness would settle upon us."

Thaddeus motions to dismiss the notion but Letete holds up a hand to recognize it.

"Yes, maybe that is a good idea Trilleon. We will take a small band of us to go and make sure the way is clear. Lucas are you in?"

"You know I am! I always ready for a good fight! Besides, I don't like snakes, serpents or what other names they may have. I want to bruise their heads!"

Letete laughs at his brother's response.

"You sound like one of Dad's sermons. All right then! It is settled! To arms!"

Letete gathers Thaddeus, Drash'Ur, Doldren, and Ranke to be a part of a team to go forward and check the area for the serpents that were mentioned by Qrueinen. Lucas takes the lead for Drash'Ur and Thaddeus while Letete takes the lead for the remaining two.

"Lucas, have Lightning Sky to fly above and ahead along with Fire Sky. I have an idea on how we could use Aquis. We will take to the clearing by foot. In this enhanced armor, we can cover the ground quickly."

Letete motions to his brother to set up another rotating guard to protect the area while they are gone. Lucas returns in minutes with the report that the guard is posted at their positions and on standing ready. The small group of captains and generals start their way towards the wooded horizon. Fire Sky, Lightning Sky along with Aquis take to the air just above and ahead of the small band of warriors. But unknown to the band and the larger group behind them, there is a figure atop a dark horse that has taken to a ridge just to the west of the camp. The figure had a head start on the group of warriors. It is Trilleon. He is winded but determined to undermine the efforts of the two brothers and their band. He presses the horse around and through the forest surrounding the valley. He reaches into a pouch that hangs from a cord on his side and pulls out a short wooden stick that has swaddled cloths and twine attached to its end. It is covered thickly in what appears to be the animal fat that was taken from the stores before. He sloughs the viscous concoction onto tree limbs and trunks.

"I will have my revenge on those two aliens who have come to my world. I will show them as the cowards they are!" Trilleon belts out a threat.

He continues to smear the concoction everywhere that he can reach. He notices just how malodorous the oily paste is.

"This viscous jelly is vile and reeks! It will surely draw those serpent beasts towards the band."

He quickly empties the first bladder.

He reaches around his waist and pulls out another bladder. He places his wooden dowel into the second mixture of animal fat and begins his sabotage again. The Saboteur begins to navigate his way through a thicket. His footing is not as sure as he would like. He stumbles trying to pass around and under a low-hanging series of limbs and vines. Trying to right himself, he falls into a small ditch. During the fall, he tries to reach out for a broken branch and completely torques his descent. He face plants directly into the bladder that is stretched full of the nauseous fat and oil. It completely covers his entire face. He stands up and immediately notices a sensation of something warm running down the side of his face. He almost gags at the stench of the jelly-like paste. He tries to take one step and immediately grimaces in response. He instantly realizes that he has sprained his ankle and it is a bad sprain. He also realizes that he has cut the upper part of his brow. The cut is not too bad, or so he hopes but is bleeding quite a bit. His eyes are burning from the smelly concoction that is mingled with his blood.

"Mingled with my blood?"

He thinks to himself. With the blood and paste beginning to burn his eyes, he takes his cloak and wipes his face to rid himself of the caustic paste. His eyes are on fire as it were and his head throbs from the bleeding wound. He does not know just how bad the wound is, but he knows that it is nasty. He manages to get most of the viscous jelly off his face, but a stinging remnant is still in his eyes. He tries to take another step, but a sharp pain runs through his left ankle and seems to flow through its center. He stumbles again from the sharp piercing jolt and rolls again even further towards a deeper portion of the ditch. He feels something wet on his hands and his side.

"Water! It has to be water!" He exclaims.

There is a small amount of water that has gathered at the lowest part of the ditch. Trilleon tastes a small drop from a finger, then sips a little more of the liquid again to test it.

"It is sweet and cool!" He exclaims.

He cups both hands together and floods his face with the cool liquid. He manages to flush most of the animal fat from his eyes. His sight is still a little blurry, but it is much better than before. He can see but sees halos and clouds in his field of sight.

"Where am I? I fell quite a distance, didn't I? Dolt!" He says to himself.

"I have to get out of here and quickly."

He squints and rubs his eyes which are swollen and still a little blurry from the animal concoction. He manages to focus on his surroundings, the ditch, an embankment on the other side and something white and grayish that is set conspicuously at the top of the embankment on the other side of the ditch. He moves closer towards the strange looking thing that is reflecting a beam of light that pierces the tree canopy above. He crawls and grimaces with each moment of his sprained ankle. Once he arrives at the spot of the strange round object partially buried in the embankment, He rubs away some of the dirt then begins to remove some of the dirt with his hand. He pulls the round, strange item from the ground and immediately realizes what it is. He realizes that it is a skull or at least part of it. It appears that it was some sort of animal. He manages to climb and look over the embankment. What he sees sends cold waves up and down his spine. He sees bones scattered all about the area. What appears to be small pits or shallow holes scattered about with old skins of what appears to be the skins of some type of serpent.

"Oooh, my! By that which is all good! What have I gotten myself into? I was a fool, a trifling fool to come here! And for what?"

He scolds himself repeatedly.

"I must flee while I still have the chance!"

He tries to scurry back up the embankment, up the hill where he fell from. He stumbles to the ground due to a sharp wave of pain the runs like electricity through his ankle and leg. He rights himself up on one knee. He looks around the forest floor to see if he can find a broken limb that he could use as a tool that will help him. He sees a broken branch that resembles the letter y. He grabs the limb and immediately begins to use it start his ascension back up the hill from where he had fallen.

"I wonder what that horse is doing."

He his ankle and head pains him profusely. His anxiety begins to grow and ebb inside of him. Every single creek of a tree or a dead branch that falls to the forest floor sends cold chills through his spine and causes his head to ache even more. He finally reaches the top of the hill. He breathes a sigh of relief to see that the horse is still there grazing on a patch of grass that he has stumbled upon in a very small clearing. Trilleon quickly makes his way towards the grazing steed. He steadies her as he attempts to mount the horse and get back to the group. He begins to think of what he will tell them. They will surely notice his injuries and he is well beyond the camp's perimeter.

"I can't worry about that now! I will rejoice to just be able to get back to the protection of the group out of harm's way." He says to himself.

That thought angers him because it forces him to consider the fact that safety and protection follow the brothers whom he despises. The moment forces him to consider all his past actions towards the two young generals. Trilleon finally manages to mount the horse. As he mounts his horse, a gentle breeze reminds him again of his plan because the breeze bears the nauseating fumes of the paste mingled with his blood. The stench fills the area all around him or does it? He quickly realizes that the stench is coming from him. After falling face first into the fatty paste, the smell still permeates his body. He hears something in the distance beyond the tree line, below in the ditch where he found himself injured and covered in his own blood. His horse becomes startled and unruly.

"Whoa girl, steady you crazed beast!" He exclaims.

He steadies her again and pauses to focus his ears on a strange and foreign sound. He can hear the wind cascading through the leaves and branches. He can hear birds and other creatures of the forest. Then in an instance, the forest goes silent. Even the wind seems to stop its cascade through the leaves and branches. He turns his ear towards the ditch area. What he hears causes the hair on his neck to stand on edge. In a panic, he pulls and snaps on the reins of his horse and kicks hard into its sides. The horse instantly catapults itself into a full out gallop darting and weaving through the forest at a hurried speed. Trilleon has one thing on his mind and one thing only as he tucks his head low against the neck of his steed.

"I am beginning to wonder if this was a good idea!"

The band of generals and captains quickly cover the distance between the camp clearing and the forest line a couple of miles ahead. The three lead horses from the stables of Neuma Ru are flying just ahead and above the small band of generals and captains. All the warriors are in full armor with Letete and Lucas leading the way with their helmets and chest armor ablaze in a bluish green flame. The other captains are covering plenty of ground as well. Their armor is gleaming, and their chest plates are aflame as well. The exception is that of the two brothers their helmets are ablaze and glowing with a fiery flume. The flaming helmet of the two young generals signifies the level of their calling for their tasks. Lucas whistles for his horse who instantly lights beside him. He motions to his brother to get his attention.

"Hey Big Brother, I mean General, maybe you and I should take to our horses and quickly scan the outer edge of the forest line ahead. It would take only a few moments to go and return quickly to the band." Letete nods in agreement and motions to the band to stay put for a moment while they search ahead quickly via the air.

The band waits, and instantly the two brothers are aloft. Letete atop of his fiery steed and Lucas atop of his steed of lightning take the sky with a fury. The quickly scan the area and beyond into the forest line.

"I don't see anything out of place or strange as of yet that is." Letete states to his brother.

"I don't see anything either. I thought this might be a good idea to possibly scare off anything if it caught a look at us from the ground. Figured that it would make it safer for our captains below. We will make one more sweep around the forest edge to be sure!"

During the second sweep, Lucas nods at his brother.

"Hey Letete, do you see that over there towards the west? It looks like something is moving."

Letete looks towards the direction pointed out by his brother. He notices something moving and darting in and around trees and shrubs in the western portion of the forest.

"Yeah Lil bro, I see it. Let's check it out!"

The two warriors direct their magnificent beasts towards the area of the movement. In moments they are above what seems to be a man atop of a retreating horse. He is dashing away as if something is pursuing him. The two brothers look further towards the west.

"Hey, do you see anything Letete?"

"No, I don't Lucas…no wait! Look at the trees, they are shaking, and some are moving. It looks like a wave is moving towards that man on the horse. Lucas, fly back and get the others and meet me below. I will buy this guy some time until you come back."

"But you don't know what you're going up against and you can't-do this alone!"

"Don't plan on it! Now go!"

Lucas instantly, worried about his brother being alone, like lightning darts towards the general direction of where the captains are waiting. In the meantime, Letete nose dives his fiery steed towards a clearing in the forest below. Letete is already below the tree line with his horse Fire Sky. The otherworldly creature in great fashion and form, darts in and around trees at an unimaginable speed.

"Whooo Hooo!" Letete exclaims.

Fire Sky's fiery mane bristles in the wind. The fiery steed tucks and bends its wings in every direction causing it to navigate the massive trees with keen precision. Letete peers through his visor on his helmet, careful not to lift his head for concern of being knocked from the back of his flaming stallion. He can see the outline of a man on a horse. The natural horse that is carrying what appears to be a natural man is running true and swift, but the beast is still no match for Fire Sky. Letete motions to Fire Sky and pulls hard on the reigns of his horse. It instantly acknowledges the order of its master and increases its speed as if that would be even possible. But accelerate the steed does. Letete pulls on the left side of the horse's rein, and it flanks left sharply missing every branch that is its path.

Letete flanks the man on the horse and in seconds heads the rider off appearing in fiery glory before him. The apparition of the winged, fiery beast with its fiery rider startles the natural horse and causes it to rear up on its hind legs. This move by Letete, of course, throws the other rider for a horrible torque that is suddenly broken by the hard forest floor.

"Owwwwwww! You crazed barbarian! You could have killed me! Why would you do such a thing?" Trilleon belts out his dislike of being startled and thrown from his horse.

But within his mind and heart, he is glad to see the young warrior.

"Trilleon, is that you what are you doing here?" Letete asks of the fallen rider.

At that question, Trilleon has no response. He turns to hear the trees being shaken and displaced. Something in its movement is displacing the very ground of the forest floor.

"There is something coming for me there towards the west. I was fleeing from whatever it is before you caused my horse to dislodge me from its back."

Letete looks toward the west and can see something moving rapidly in their direction. He screams a one-word command to Trilleon.

"Ruuun!"

He turns his head, flipping down his visor, and is off again at an incredible speed towards the direction of the movement. Trilleon stands for a moment motionless as he sees the young elder warrior take off in the direction of the oncoming threat.

"By the Snarksen! He is fearless! All because of me, he may heading into harm's way."

For the first time, Trilleon feels remorseful for his actions towards the two warriors. He turns towards the direction of his horse only to see that the creature has long abandoned him. He begins to run towards the direction of the clearing. A few moments later, Letete atop of Fire Sky just below the tree line, is hovering just ahead of the disturbances in the forest.

"Fire Sky, do you see what I see?" Letete asks his horse.

Fire Sky responds in kind with a whiney and a shrill. Letete can see the heads of large snake-like creatures headed with sure speed towards the direction of the clearing. They are long as a school bus with heads the size of a boulder. They are large and ominous a dark bluish green and black hue that seems almost iridescent. Letete notices that some of the larger serpents have large yellow curved horns on their heads.

"Those must be the males. Bull serpents! That is so weird and cool at the same time. Wow, Lucas will love to see these things.

I can hear him now. "Take that you scaly snake freaks!"

I better get back to the clearing and help Trilleon along the way." Letete says to himself.

At that moment, one of the large serpents catches sight of Letete hovering above. It coils itself like a spring, rears its head and releases a hissing roar exposing multiple rows of razor-like teeth. It uncoils itself and springs up like a bottle rocket at Letete and Fire Sky.

"Whooa! Look out, incoming!" Letete says to his horse.

In quick otherworldly response Letete's fiery steed tucks its wings and nose dives towards the springing beast. Fire Sky opens its mouth and releases a deluge of flame and energy directly into the face of the encroaching serpentine missile. As the steed descends releasing its fiery discharge, Letete unsheaths his sword which is now glowing and aflame. Fire Sky alters its trajectory and spirals over and around the serpent whose head is now engulfed in flames. Letete, as his horse corkscrews under and over the beast, scores it with his sword from the base of its neck, around its underbelly and near the rear dorsal of the beast. It hits the forest floor with a thunderous concussive thud. It extinguishes the flames on the forest floor while hissing and writhing in pain.

"Whooo Hoooo! That was awesome! Letete exclaims.

He sends a thought to Aquis who is there in an instance. He signals to the horse to extinguish the flames below. It swoops down releasing a deluge of water in a tight focused stream. It rolls a few of the serpents from the impact of the stream.

"Ride Fire Sky, ride Aquis!" Letete says.

The trio dash quickly in the direction of where Trilleon was last seen. The serpents are not far behind. Letete sees Lucas atop Lightning Sky headed towards him with great speed.

"Letete, are you okay?"

"Yes, I am fine, have to explain later. We have to get to Trilleon to help him in the forest below."

"Trilleon? What is he doing here?"

"That is another story as well, but we don't have time! We have to get to Trilleon and fast! Follow me!"

The four dash towards the direction of where Trilleon was last seen, with Letete and Fire Sky leading the way. Letete swoops down again on the back of Fire Sky followed closely by his brother and Aquis flying on his wing.

"Yeeeahhh!" Lucas exclaims.

"Yeah Luc, I know! Cool right!"

"You know it! It's like the scene from one of our favorite sci-fi movies!"

At that statement, both boys chuckle and laugh. Letete pulls hard on the reins of his horse and Fire Sky accelerates to a breakneck speed. Lucas follows suit. All three horses with amazing agility and aerial acrobatics torque in and around tree and bush. Letete pulls back on the reigns of Fire Sky who opens his wings like sail and gently lights upon the ground where Letete last saw Trilleon. Lucas follows suit.

"Where is he? He could not have gotten that far without his horse."

"I see footprints on the ground! They seem to head in that direction towards the clearing. Uh oh! Look over there!"

At that moment both heroes see a swath of bushes, saplings and displaced earth leaning in the same direction.

"It looks like something is following him! A serpent!"

Letete exclaims.

"Move!" Lucas replies.

Immediately, they all fly in the direction towards the clearing.

Trilleon is now becoming more nervous with each passing moment. He hears someone, or something headed towards him. He panics and starts to double back away from the sound. He flanks back reversing his course. In doing so, he begins to panic and runs head first into a low hanging limb. It clips him, and he falls backward hitting the forest floor hard. The fall is hard and knocks the wind out of him for a moment. He sits up for a moment to clear his head and get his bearing.

"That was fool hearty Trilleon. You are a real imbecile Trilleon. You really got yourself into a fine pickle this day!" He says to himself.

He begins to think about his wife and his little girl. The thought brings a smile to his face, but he becomes saddened as well because he thinks that his preoccupation with shaming the young heroes may cause him to never see his family again. He stands up and straightens himself at that thought.

"I will see them both again!"

He takes a couple of steps and realizes that he aggravated his ankle injury again. He stumbles again and cascades down into a small ditch. He is in more pain than before. His face is covered in mud and sand. His head and ankle are now in more pain than before. He uses his tunic to wipe away as much of the dirt and mud from his face. His vision is blurred but it seems that there is something large that is just above where he has fallen. He struggles again to clear his vision of the sand and mud. He looks up again from where he is standing. What he sees causes him to wish that his vision was still impaired. He swallows hard to grasp what air he can to breathe, but it feels like he cannot take in another breath of air. He sees a large, horned head of a serpent with orange eyes and scales that look like tiny plates of armor looking down on him with an extreme focus. It inherently sticks out a forked tongue tasting the air all around picking up the scent of animal fat and... blood. Trilleon manages to finally let out a scream, a scream like he has never uttered before. Then suddenly there is silence.

Letete, Lucas and the horses all race towards the clearing. They notice something moving in the lower tree line and moving fast. It's Thaddeus along with the others. Letete and Lucas land in front of the band.

"Did you see Trilleon or anything else?" Letete asks.

"Trilleon? Why would he be here?"

"Long story. Has anyone seen him or anything out of the ordinary?"

Everyone replies that they have not seen or heard anything out of the ordinary. Then suddenly there is a scream. It sounds like that of a man. It is a horrible shrill of a scream.

"Let's move!" Letete shouts.

They all rush towards the direction of the sound. Letete and Lucas have bird's eye view of what the source of the sound is. They see a large horned serpent moving swiftly in the opposite direction of the other serpents still racing towards the clearing. Some of them, once passed by the serpent stop, sniff the air and then turn in the same direction. Lucas looks closer at the rear of the serpent; he sees that the serpent tail is coiled. It appears to be carrying something in its coiled tail. They swoop down to get a closer look. What they see sends them into immediate action. It's Trilleon. He is in the coiled grasps of the serpent's tail.

"Take him!" Letete shouts a command!

They dart past other serpents that are following behind the listless Trilleon. They snap and bite at the coiled prisoner in their kindred's grasp. Some of the serpents turn and coil hissing and spitting as the band of warriors close in on the ophidian assailants. They spring up towards Letete and Lucas with mouths agape. They instantly part in mid-flight leaving Aquis in the middle who is nose diving with a flume of water and ice streaming from its mouth. It instantly freezes one of the springing serpents in mid-air. It falls to the ground shattering into several pieces like a glass figurine on a marble floor.

"Whooo! That was close! Did you know that he could do that?" Lucas shouts to his brother.

"No, I did not! We must catch that serpent before he escapes with Trilleon! Wait, look there!"

In the distance before them, they can see several other serpents headed in the direction of the clearing.

"We have to end this now! Lucas, I have a plan!"

Letete maneuvers his horse through trees and focuses his will in the direction of the serpent and his seized prisoner. He motions to Lucas to approach as Fire Sky hovers in the air.

"Lucas! I will take the head, and you will take the tail! You got it?"

"Got it, let's do this!"

Letete pulls hard on the reigns of Fire Sky who instinctively has already begun the pursuit of the fleeing serpent. Lucas is on his right flank flying as his wingman. They accelerate to an unbelievable speed. Serpents below do not have time to react because of the blurring speed at which the boys are moving. They quickly catch up with the fleeing serpent that is still carrying the motionless Trilleon in its tails grasp.

"If that thing has hurt him I promise he will pay!" Letete thinks to himself.

"Lucas, now!"

Letete maneuvers his horse just behind the head of the serpent while his brother is positioned strategically towards the rear. He sends a thought to his brother who in sync dismounts into a full torque forward flip unsheathing his flaming sword while grasping it with both hands. He stabs the blade into the tip of the serpent's tail, pinning it to the forest floor. Letete, simultaneously sticking the end of his dismount, extends his shield and strikes the serpent in a downward sloping two-handed blow to the head of the screeching beast.

"Whoooo boy! That's going to leave a bruise!" Lucas exclaims.

Letete plants his feet firmly on the forest floor standing just in front of the stunned serpent. It shakes off the blow and focuses on Letete. It begins to talk in some strange tongue, a language that Letete not Lucas can understand.

"What in the world, the freak can speak?" Lucas exclaims.

"You dare sstrike me and maim me like ssome quarried pray childling?" The serpent says in some strange serpent accent. The serpentine beast rears its massive head, coils back its long neck and strikes at Letete with its mouth agape and menacing. Letete in quick fashion holds up his shield to block the strike of the beast that is surely trying to devour him. The creature with its mouth agape has locked its massive jaws around and over the uplifted shield of Letete. Lucas screams at the action of the beast and starts to remove his sword from the tail of the beast. Letete shouts a command to his brother instructing him to stand where he is. Letete grabs the shield more tightly and secures it in his grip. He looks directly into the eyes of the beast and utters these words.

"My faith is bigger than your bite creature. Care to see?"

At that moment, Letete's shield begins to enlarge inside of the mouth of the gaping beast. It begins to gag and grasp for relief from its predicament. Letete firmly takes his shield and torques it towards the left as hard as could. This turns to the head of the serpent towards the forest floor exposing its underside. At the identical moment, Letete sends a message mentally to his brother who moves swiftly like a cheetah along the back of the beast. He snatches out the sword that was pinning the beast's tail to the forest floor. He runs up and along the back of the serpent towards its head. He leaps to the front of the serpent's body near where his brother has his head torqued and twisted. His mouth is stretched wide almost to rip at the seam of its jaw.

"If you want your head to remain connected to your body I suggest that you do not move snake!"

Lucas utters a threat as he places his extended fiery blade next to base of the beast head. Letete catapults over the top of his shield and utters a simple sentence.

"Let him go nooowww!"

The beast fully understanding the threat and aware of its precarious predicament uncoils his tail and releases the listless Trilleon. Lucas utters another threat to the beast before he darts to where Trilleon is laying in a slump on the ground.

"If he is not breathing serpent, I will return to make sure that you will share in the same inability to breathe!"

Letete, now standing on the side of the head of the beast with his shield still stretched in its mouth, can see other serpents headed in their direction. He knows that he needs more time to make sure that Trilleon is ok and to leave the area safely. He motions to Fire Sky, Lightning Sky and Aquis to move in closer. He sends a thought to the winged, equine trio to give them cover from above. As soon as the trio above receive the command, they, move into action. They swoop down and begin a defensive strategy. Aquis opens his mouth and a stream of ice and energy flow from its mouth. He completely and swiftly encircles the band below within a high wall of solid ice. "Coooool!" Lucas and Letete shout.

"Literally!"

A thought they both here from the icy, winged horse.

"Good! That will buy us some time. Lucas how is Trilleon?"

"He is not moving! You better hope he is ok beast, or I will run you through!" Lucas belts out a threat.

Lucas motions to Aquis and sends a thought. The horse nods and immediately hovers over Lucas and Trilleon lying motionless on the ground. Lucas moves quickly a few feet away anticipating what was next. Aquis release a quick concentrated stream of water towards face of Trilleon. He rolls over and gags, coughing up water from his mouth. He jumps to his feet and screams at the winged animal.

"Injury and harm to me! What are you doing? Are you trying to drown me beast?"

"He's okay!" Lucas retorts while chuckling.

"Good news!"

"Trilleon, we shall be leaving soon. Are you okay to ride?"

"Yes general! Anywhere but here will be an improvement. I think one of my ribs is broken but that is acceptable to the alternative."

Letete nods in agreement. At that moment, a large serpent catapults itself over the melting icy wall. It is headed directly towards Letete. In a quick instance, a fireball hits the serpent squarely in its open, heavily fanged mouth knocking it backward with definite force into a dead trunk of a tree. Wooden splinters shatter into the air. Letete looks up and sees Fire Sky hovering above him, ready to send another blast if necessary.

"Good shot girl!"

He looks down at the beast that he is standing above and asks him a question.

"If I release you will you promise not to attack us?"

The beast, now wide-eyed and in great discomfort nods its large scaled head in agreement. Letete jumps down from the head of the serpent and grabs the stirrup inside of his shield. It slowly shrinks back to its original size. He removes it from the beast mouth. The serpent rights itself and shakes its massive head trying to gather itself. It focuses keenly on Trilleon who is seated nearby on a stump next to Lucas.

"Remember our agreement serpent!" Letete says ominously to the scaly beast.

"Why did you attack me strange, shiny creature? What concern is it of yours if we dine on that smelly prey that sits there like an inviting morsel to savour and devour."

Lucas receives a thought from his brother and they both lift the visors on their helmets.

"It is impossible! You are even smaller morsels to devour! How is it that you are so powerful? And why did you torment my clan with the aroma of that smelly one seated on the stump?" The serpent says with a strange visage in his eye.

"Hey watch it leather belt! If you say morsel one more time, I am going to clean your clock!" Lucas says while extending his fiery sword.

"Yes serpent, I agree. My brother and I will take great offense to your statement. And what do you mean taunt you? We did no such thing! We were warned about your presence and we came to investigate only to see...wait! I saw Trilleon. You never explained to me Trilleon as to why you were here in the first place! I think it is time to hear your story. Speak!" Letete says.

Trilleon finally admits to his reason for appearing in the woods out of sorts, the reason for the smelly aroma of animal fat and his larcenous plan to discredit the two brothers as cowards.

"So that's why you are all the way out here smelling like a snake burger? Not so smart are you Trilleon? As for being cowards, do you still feel the same now?" Lucas asks.

"No, I do not. I never actually believed that you were cowards. Not only are you not cowards, you are conquerors for he that sent you. And I am a mere jealous fool. I ask for your forgiveness for I am genuinely sorry and ashamed. I put myself at risk of never seeing my family again and for what? What?" Trilleon says as he begins to shed a tear.

"I don't know, you put us at risk and we still have to leave this place and drag you along as well. Still quite a few serpents out there." Lucas says.

Letete motions to his brother to go easy on Trilleon. He responds to Trilleon's plea.

"Trilleon, my brother and I will accept your apology and offer you forgiveness. Our father teaches us that we are to forgive often when asked to forgive and without expectation even if the request to forgive never comes."

Trilleon stands and reaches out a hand to Letete who in turn shakes it in acknowledgement.

"That's great, but we still have the matter of the serpents all around us. What about them?" Lucas asks.

The serpent within the ice wall with them responds.

"You will have nothing to fear from us. I will instruct my clan in this matter and we will return to the hollow from where we came. But be aware, the next time we see one another, this treaty will not be in effect. You can pass through without incident from us." Letete nods in agreement.

He motions to the three horses hovering overhead. Fire Sky and Lightning Sky, light near them while keeping watchful eyes on the serpent. Letete and Lucas quickly mount on the backs of their winged steeds. Letete motions to Trilleon to climb onto the back of his horse.

"Hold on!" Letete says to Trilleon.

Lucas, atop Lightning Sky darts toward the clearing to meet the others while Letete hovers above the entrapped serpent below. He sends a thought to his horse who quickly responds. Fire Sky release a short-concentrated stream of fire and energy from its mouth blasting an opening in the ice wall left by Aquis.

"Excellent shot Fire Sky!" Letete says to his fiery steed.

The serpent begins to exit to newly created opening in the icy wall. It pauses for a moment to stare at its opponent. Letete looks at the beast and does not utter a word. He pulls down his visor and with one motion, he and Fire Sky depart in a fiery flash. The serpent slithers through the opening back towards the hollow from where it came. It pauses for a moment and lifts its massive head. The horns on its head begins to glow and ebb. Serpents by the dozens begin to head back towards the hollow. Just to the left of the beast, something materializes. It is large and shadowy. The serpent bows to the shadowy beast. It is the dragon called Doubt.

"The master's plan is carried out as you have commanded general." The serpentine beast says.

"Good! Tannim will be pleased to hear of this report. You have served us well." The shadowy apparition fades out in a wisp of smoke and vapor.

Letete catches up with the others at the edge of the forest clearing.

"The serpents have left the area. I guess leather belt kept his word after all." Lucas says to his brother as he lights near where they are positioned.

"Yes, I guess that he did. We should probably get back to the others before it gets any later. It is almost completely dark now and the band will probably be concerned." Letete says. Lucas looks at Thaddeus and the others who in turn cannot hide their thoughts which are etched onto their brows.

"Letete, we were talking about everything and well... we think that we need to ask Qrueinen about her story of the snakes and other stuff as well. It just doesn't seem to add up." Lucas says with concern. "What! Are you still talking about that? I thought we were past that!"

"No, we are not past that and you seem to be the only one who can't see that there is something odd about her stories!"

"We will not discuss this any further!" Letete bristles and with a hard pull of Fire Sky's reigns, he is off and away back towards the gathered band.

"This is not over man! We will talk about this when I catch up with you!" Lucas shouts as he takes off in pursuit of his fuming brother. About an hour later when all the men who went on patrol to search for the serpents return back to the camp Letete and Lucas continue their heated dispute.

"Letete, you have to listen to us! It's not just me who has questions about the girl and her story. What is wrong with you?"

"There is nothing wrong with me! I just think that I am right! She has done nothing to harm us in any way. She even told us about the snakes before they could be a threat to us all. Can't you see how this was a great help to us?" Letete responds in an agitated fashion.

At the moment, Qrueinen is seen running through the camp in the direction of the small band of patrolmen.

"You were successful, weren't you? I just want know that you were successful!" She says excitedly. She runs directly to Letete and hugs him almost displacing him from his footing.

"Whooaa!" Letete exclaims bearing a sheepish grin on his face.

Lucas looks on with a scowl on his face as the girl who is the source of his distrust and unease hugs his brother tightly around his neck.

"Yes, we were successful. Your warning gave us what was needed to find the beasts and deal with them."

"Actually, it was the actions of someone who was jealous of us and not too bright or should I say their actions were not that bright. No offense Trilleon." Lucas responds in a terse fashion.

"None taken general. I deserved that, and I am humbled enough to accept your words. I am just truly happy to have survived my own schemes and yes stubborn stupidity. I long to see my family again after this journey."

"So, it was not her words that warned us but her words that lead to even searching for the snakes in the first place! They would have never known that we were passing nearby!" Lucas says with cutting sarcasm to his big brother.

"No, I wanted to warn you about the beasts and nothing else! Why do you not trust me? I mean you all no harm!" Qrueinen says with a saddened tone.

"I believe her and that should be enough. I was placed in charge here!" Letete responds.

"Ooohhh you make me so angry sometimes! Why won't you listen to us, to me? I am your brother! Your little brother! You are supposed to listen to me because we are family! I watch your back, you watch mine! Dad always tells us that. And you, you!" Lucas stares down the young girl.

"I have my eye on you! You better not be telling us a made-up story about who you are! General big brother, I will take the east side of the camp. Good night!"

Lucas, visibly angry, mounts his winged horse and catapults into the evening sky. Letete, Thaddeus, and the others look on.

SEVENTEEN

A Loss of Faith

Thaddeus moves closer to where the saddened Letete is standing still gazing into the evening sky. He motions for the girl to go with his two sons to get something to eat for the evening.

"Young General, please do not fight with your brother. You must show a strong front so that the warriors will not lose heart and faint in battle. He is not the only one that has some concerns about our young guest General." Thaddeus says.

Letete looks back into the face of Thaddeus to register his thoughts. Thaddeus places a concerned hand on his shoulder.

"Yes, okay. I see everyone's point, but do you believe that she is a threat? I mean, she gave us a warning that was shown to be true. If she was a threat, then why give us a warning?"

Thaddeus looks at the young general with sympathy and answers his query.

"That is a genuine question and merely adds to the pyre of questions her presence poises" Thaddeus responds.

At that moment, Qrueinen can be seen walking briskly towards Thaddeus and Letete. She is accompanied by Doldren and Ranke who are trying to keep up with her. "For a young maiden, she walks briskly," Doldren says.

She moves towards the direction of Thaddeus and Letete. She asks for their forgiveness and pleads with them to have an audience.

"General, captain, I would ask for an audience to make a plea."

As she finishes her plea, she begins to sob uncontrollably and falls at the feet of Thaddeus and Letete.

"I am so, so sorry! I do not desire to be a burden to anyone. If you can give me provisions, I will be on my way in the morn. I will leave this camp as so not to be a hindrance and a burden to this band." She says as she begins to weep again.

Letete and Thaddeus both kneel to pick up the young weeping maiden. She stands to her feet sobbing. Letete tries to console her and reassure her.

"You can't travel on your own. It's not safe for you being alone. And why do you think that you are a burden?"

"I know that the old man and the others don't trust me. I know that your brother really does not trust me!" Qrueinen responds still weeping.

"Thaddeus, look at her. Let's take this time to speak to her and see if we can't get to the end of this matter!"

The gathering of young and old begin to question the young maiden. She begins to tell them her story again in even greater detail. She also sobs and weeps uncontrollably when retelling them the story of her captivity and how the dragon played a horrible and terrible game of cat and mouse with her.

"I don't know what happened that lead to my release or my good fortune of still being in the land of the living, but I am grateful that I still have breath! Will you begrudge me the good fortune of having lived?" She asks the gathering of young and old.

Letete, Thaddeus and the others all listening intently, stare at the young maiden for what feels like an eternity. Then Thaddeus brakes his silence.

"Young maiden, oh fortunate young maiden! I do not begrudge you your good fortune, and for one, I am glad that you are among the living. I offer you my sincere apology and furthermore, I will not question you or your story. I pledge to help you get back to your people." The other warriors all nod in agreement as well as Letete, the Elder who responds directly to her.

"As well as I. I promise to help you as well!" A voice says from above. It is Lucas who materializes out of thin air on the back of Lightning Sky along with Drash'Ur.

"Whooa! How did you do that! Were you there the entire time?" Letete asks his brother excitedly.

"No, not exactly. I was on my way here to check on you guys. Drash'Ur decided to come with me. As we were about land, I spoke to Lightning Sky and told her circle above. During my thought command, she responded and said to me "Watch this young general!" I watched as she instantly began to disappear, head first, then her wings then us! I did hear enough to say something."

"Uh Oh! What could that be?" Letete says with a guarded tone.

Lucas dismounts Lightning Sky along with Drash'Ur and walks over to where a teary-eyed Qrueinen is standing.

"I am sorry Roo! I am protective of my big brother. I too will help you get back to your people. That is my pledge."

Qrueinen looks on silently at the little warrior and with a quick motion runs and embraces Lucas. The others and all looking on begin to cheer. Letete reaches out a hand to his little brother.

"I sorry too Letete, I could have handled the situation a little better. We both have to remember the reason why we are here, and that is to bring freedom to this land. That is our quest!"

The crowd cheers even louder at that statement made by the smaller general. Letete nods his head in agreement.

"Agreed Lucas!"

All the other warriors all respond in like fashion in unison. "Agreed!"

Letete raises a hand to get the attention of the cheering band.

"Now then, we shall eat and get a good night's rest. We will rise early tomorrow and start again towards the domain of the dragon!"

With that, the band cheers again and disperses. Letete, Lucas, and Thaddeus begin to walk together. Thaddeus again instructs his two sons to see to the needs of Qrueinen. He then turns to walk a little distance with the two Generals.

"Gentlemen, I am glad that the two of you have mended your fences. It is a boost to the moral of the band of warriors. Generals, do you think that we are closer to our destination? Have you heard anything from Neuma Ru?"

"It has been some time since I have heard him speak directly but I constantly feel his presence. I believe that we are getting closer because of the trials that are increasing. What do you think Lucas?"

"Yes, I agree. I want to get there and carry out the task that Neuma Ru has given us all."

"Letete, I am sorry again about "Roo" and what I said. I mean… I… uh, well you know what I mean."

Letete places a hand on the shoulder of his little brother and reassures him.

"No need, it's good to have someone to watch your back. Thanks, Lucas."

The trio speaks as to what the next move will be. They nod and agree. Soon their little convocation is over, and they begin to head towards the center of the camp where a large fire is already ablaze, and most of the camp has already settled in.

Letete sees Qrueinen seated with the band eating. She is doing something for the first time since being in the camp. She is smiling.

She seems a little more relaxed. She actually laughs at one of Doldren's silly stories. A story told at the expense of Ranke who does not seem too amused. Letete and Lucas look at each other and smile. Lucas breaks the silence of the awkward moment by speaking to his big brother.

"Hey, why don't you go sit near your new "girlfriend," you know that you want to."

Letete bristles and replies bluntly.

"Will you stop that? She is not my "girlfriend" as you put it. She is just someone that needs our help that's all!"

Lucas smirks and then releases a large chuckle.

"Hey, don't be so sensitive, I was only kidding, but you should go and sit near her. She seems to feel safe for the moment. That's all that I was saying."

"Yeah, you are right, not about the girlfriend thing but she does seem to feel a little safer and calm. Hey why don't we both go and sit with everyone. We can share stories from home."

Drash'Ur hears the two talking and replies.

"Will you promise to tell us more about those "Chezey Buggers" as you call them?"

The two brothers laugh out loud. Lucas replies to Drash'Ur's mishandling of the name.

"It's "Cheese Burgers" Drash'Ur, not "Chezey Buggers". Come on, I will tell you more of the stories from my world!"

Letete, Lucas and Drash'Ur join the group seated near the campfire. They talk of their world back home and the serpents they met while rescuing Trilleon in the forest. As the evening wanes on, the band settles in for the evening. The next morning, Trilleon, Drash'Ur's father and the others that help support the warriors are up at dawn. They have prepared an early meal for the group.

"This is a morning of victory and triumph! You will need your fill of a hearty meal! Come now! Rise and eat!" Drash'Ur's father says.

Trilleon takes a metal pot and strikes it several times to announce the arrival of the morning meal.

"I see that you are getting into the spirit of things Trilleon." Trilleon nods and he places the pot back on the wagon.

"Yes sir, I am in a humble state of the heart and I plan on making amends for my offenses."

"Oh, come now, we are well past those sort of pretences. You can call me Sim'drash'Ur. My friends call me Sim'."

Sim reaches out his leathery hand to Trilleon and shakes it vigorously.

"Yes, Sir, I mean Sim', I would like that. It is good to have a friend. Circumstances have accumulated and lead me to this conclusion. It is important to focus on the points of light that matter. Family and friends. I cannot wait to see them again, but in the meantime, I will relish in the company of friends."

"Good then it is an accord! We will be able to tell of great adventure, write a memoir of our experiences!"

"I pray that you will not be too unkind when you write of the wretch of man that I am."

"I don't think that you are a wretch of man Trilleon, I think you show great potential. You made a mistake and corrected it. My parents always tell me and my brother that potential is measured by how we correct our mistakes." Letete responds as he approaches the wagon with his brother and the others.

"Thank young general, you are gracious and kind, all of you are. I plan on making up for my past follies."

Letete and Lucas agree and reassure Trilleon.

"Now that is settled, let's break bread!"

The gathered band give thanks for the bounty and eat before beginning their quest again.

The band covers a great distance this day. As they are traveling the valley, it begins to narrow to a point on the horizon. A dense gathering of trees like arbor sentinels stands tall and ominous at the edge of the dark forest. The trail begins to descend towards the basin of the ridge. Small, murky, ponds of stagnated water can be seen dotting the changing landscape. Large moss columns can be seen hanging from mishappened tree limbs like green specters in the darkened forest. As the sun descends, the green columns of moss hanging from the twisting tree branches cast long eerie shadows across the darkening scape. As the band moves closer to the edge of the marshy forest, they look on into the dark foreboding forest.

"Are we going in there? It looks like a set of a horror movie!" Lucas exclaims.

Letete dismounts his steed and gives Lucas a sideways look showing his disdain for the question of his statement.

"Hey don't say that kinda stuff Lucas! Remember, we set the standard! If we look even a little off our game, the rest who follow us will lose faith. We do not have to be afraid right?" Letete responds to his brother by thought.

"Uh, no of course not! I'm not a scared of nothin'! Just caught me by surprise that's all. I mean you got to admit, the place looks like a reject from a Scooby Doo cartoon. That's all I'm sayin'!"

"Well, we don't want to disappoint the Dragon Master and the rest of his creeps! We must play the role "of those meddling kids!" Letete responds with a chuckle shared by his brother.

"Warriors, I feel that we are getting closer to the realm of the Dragons. We will dismount and send the horses of flight to cover us from above. Because of the density of the forest, we cannot maneuver the horses or even the wagons through that swamp. We will make a small base camp here! We will need a few volunteers to stay behind and protect our supplies and those who support us. The remaining will gather portable supplies and follow us through the forest. I believe at the edge of this forest is the beginning of our journey to the lair. Who will volunteer to lead the remnant that will stay behind? Four are needed. The remaining supporters will be equipped with armor as well for additional support."

Four brave warriors come forth quickly. Drash'Ur's father, Sim Drash'Ur, comes forward when summoned along with the others. They all accept and believe and are instantly endowed with sword and armor from head to toe.

"You will be given an important task. To hold this ground until we return to support you if needed."

Letete looks around and sees Trilleon leaning on one of the wagons holding his head down seemingly unnoticed. Letete looks at Lucas and they both nod in agreement.

"Trilleon, please come forward!"

Trilleon looks up startled by the request, the beckoning that echoes through the camp. He comes quickly and slides to a stop in front of the two young generals and the captains.

"Yes, yes, uh General! You called me?"

"Yes Trilleon, I called for you. Thaddeus, come forward and present the opportunity to our newest warrior."

Trilleon looks astonished and frozen in place at the words of Letete, the Elder. His mouth is agape, and his widened eyes appear as if they could split at their seams. He manages to utter a muttered word in response.

"You would like to make me a warrior? But I, I mean, I am a traitor."

Letete and Lucas look on with sympathy along with the others.

"But are you sorry for what you have done?" Lucas asks.

"Why yes my young general! I am truly sorry and broken about what I have done. I will do anything to stand behind you all in your quest."

At that moment, Sim Drash'Ur steps forward in his new armor and places a sympathetic hand on the shoulder of Trilleon.

"He speaks the truth; he shared his brokenness with me and his repentance. I feel that his heart is ripe for renewal." Sim Drash'Ur exclaims.

"Yes, my old friend Sim, I believe this as well. Trilleon it is the purpose of the will of the one who we represent to forgive you and to make you new, to reform you even, for our cause. We all forgive you as well and hold no ill will towards you. Will you serve him?" Thaddeus responds.

"Yes, my friend, yes I will." Trilleon says with no hesitation.

"Then it is settled!"

Thaddeus unsheathes his glowing flaming sword and places it on each shoulder of a now kneeling Trilleon. The greenish-blue flame drapes Trilleon like tattered cloth. It swirls all about and around his legs and head. Trilleon stands up with eyes wide and mouth agape and tears streaming down his dusty face. Armor erupts from the crown of his head and cascades down past his neck and envelops his entire body. He stands for a moment with both eyes clinched tight. Then he opens his eyes and looks at his armor-clad outstretched hands. He looks at his legs and feet. Then instantly a fiery sword materializes in his right hand. He looks at his sword and the armor and then the two brothers.

"Whooo Hoooo! I feel so alive and free!" Trilleon exclaims as he jumps nearly 10 feet into the evening sky.

He notices that his armor is slightly different than the others.

"Look at my armor, it is slightly different in color. It has a shimmering golden hue. What is this strange color?" He asks.

"It is the color of courage and forgiveness! You are truly a new man!" Trilleon laughs aloud and then releases a sound that is akin to almost that of a lion.

"I will serve you with every fiber of my being. I will fight to protect those in need and stand by the side of the warriors of faith. I have become a new person this day for the old has passed away." Trilleon responds as the warriors erupt into cheers.

"Good, Good Trilleon. You will stay with the remnant here and protect the camp. You will be one of the captains along with Sim Drash'Ur. The others form three groups about seven wide to ten men deep. Eighty of you will form a circle around the larger group. You will be on the lookout for any threat. And if a threat is seen or heard, you will all join the larger group and stand your ground. All Captains will be a part of the surrounding group. Lucas you will be with me along with Thaddeus. The others will divide into three with each positioned with the outer group. One on the east, the west and the north. The men in each quadrant will be the responsibility of each Captain. Doldren, I have a favor to ask of you. I will need you to leave your horse here with the others. It will not be good to take her into the dense forest marsh. Besides, she will be an asset for the others who are staying behind. Do I have your blessing Sir?" Letete asks Doldren.

Doldren looks down visibly shaken by the request but regroups himself and steals himself to reply.

"Yes General, I understand. These are dire times."

Doldren takes the reins of his horse and strokes the hair of her mane as he speaks to her and assures her.

"Laurel, I am going to leave for a short while. I will leave you in good hands. You will stay with Sim Drash'Ur and the others. You will help with support ok? Look at you with your beautiful armor and flaming horn. You will be fine. I pity anything that comes against you." Doldren says as Laurel replies with a whiney.

Sim Drash'Ur who is standing nearby comes to where Doldren and Laurel are standing.

"I will take good care of her Doldren. She knows me, and we get along well. I often give her treats of sweet sap apples which are her favorite. I have some on store in the wagon. I will guard her well." Sim Drash'Ur exclaims.

"Yes Sir, I know that you will. Until I return, take care warriors."

He turns to head quickly to where the others are lining up. Letete realizes that someone is missing from the band. It is Qrueinen.

She is not with the group.

"Has anyone seen Qrueinen? I don't see her anywhere. I was hoping that she could act as a scout since she did manage to escape the Dragon's Lair."

The gathered all reply that they have not seen her. One of the warriors gets the attention of Letete and the others.

"Generals! Captains! I found something that you may want to see. Follow me!"

They follow the warrior to one of the wagons located on the far side of the caravan.

"Items and crumbs can be seen on the ground along with a set of footprints that head out towards the dense dark forest." Thaddeus says.

Letete looks at Thaddeus with a look of concern and unbelief.

"Why would she head off into the forest by herself?" Letete asks.

"Wait, I see something! There! It looks like another set of footprints there at the edge of the clearing. There are broken limbs and branches. It looks like there was a struggle." Drash'Ur says peering with his keen eyes.

"Something must have taken her but how could that have happened without anyone being aware of a commotion?" Letete exclaims.

Letete turns quickly and places a hand on the shoulder of his younger brother. He looks at him with stern look.

"We have got to find her! Are you with me General?"

"Of course, I am! I want a crack at whatever could have done this and right under our noses! Let's find her!"

Letete motions to the militia that is lined up and ready for orders. He motions to Drash'Ur to blow his trump to signal everyone to move out. The winged horses take to the sky above and head off just ahead of the gathered band. Each of the equine luminaries brighten the evening sky like torchieres floating above. There light casts long, eerie shadows on the forest floor below. But their presence in the sky adds an additional scope of ease for the group because the darkened forest is not as dark because of their presence above. Coupling that with the illumination of all of the warriors below, vision is increased significantly in the otherwise ominous darkened canopy forest.

"We will find her young general. Be assured. Whatever has taken her could not have gotten very far." Thaddeus says to a concerned Letete.

"I believe that we will find them as well. Thaddeus, do you know anything about this region, this forest at all?"

"No Letete the Elder. I have no knowledge of this place at all! No legend or folklore to add to this place. It is a dire facade that casts a dark shadow in every direction. But we will prevail none the less! Agreed?"

"Agreed!"

The additional outer support of captains works well to possibly ferret out any potential threat to the gathered band. If something is out there, it will not catch the entire collective off guard. Lucas, being short in stature notices that forest floor is becoming marsh-like and the water level is growing higher.

"Hey, this stuff is like coffee and it is getting higher! It is already at my knees and it is getting harder to walk thru. Good thing we have this armor on or it would be impossible to walk through."

The forest canopy begins to thicken as they venture further into the dense marsh jungle. To warriors are pressed together tightly, pushing through the miry, stagnate pools.

"I wonder where she could be. I hope that she is okay." Letete says aloud.

"There is no sign of her anywhere. I don't see any broken limb or branch throughout the forest. It is like she was spirited away of sorts." says Drash'Ur.

"We will find her! We will not stop until she is located." Lucas says in response.

Letete communicates with the winged horses above and asks if they see anything in the distance and above where they are. They reply that they see nothing.

"It is a strange thing indeed" Thaddeus says in reply.

The forest canopy above them in the distance gives way to an open night-time sky. The opening in the tree line is shaped like that of a crescent. Beyond the crescent tree line, the marsh extends and gives way to a strange sight and sound. There seems to be billows of luminous clouds on the horizon line. All the gathered band look on, puzzled by the strange scape that is before them. There is a faint scent of sulphur in the air. A north westerly breeze caries the sulphur scent as it bristles through the canopy tree line. Letete holds up his fiery sword to motion to the band to stop and be alert.

"Lucas, Thaddeus, come with me to investigate this weird swamps edge."

The trio move closer towards the cloudy billows. The horses above mirror and shadow their motion below. Their light gives a clearer panorama to the scape and its hidden conundrum. The marsh begins to deepen a couple of inches. And there is a sound, a loud sound like that of running water.

"It is a water fall! A strange fall in which the water becomes a mist of sorts." Thaddeus exclaims.

As it cascades over the rocky face, the water is changed to a mist from the heat of fire pits below. The current is not strong as one would think a fall would generate, it is slow and almost non-existent.

"This is too weird! Let's get a closer look!"

Lucas motions to his steed Lightning Sky who lights instantly beside him. He quickly mounts his horse and is airborne in seconds. He quickly loops and arcs over the edge and back again flying through a large amorphous steam bank.

"That is sooo weird! There are fire pits below filled with what looks like molten rock and lava. The water is changed before it can hit the rocky floor below!" Lucas exclaims.

"That is unusual! We must be nearing the lair of the Dragon Master." Letete motions to the warriors to move on his command. As they begin to maneuver, one of the warriors that is patrolling with the outer group of eighty notices something moving in the distance among the trees near the edge of the marsh. He is part of the patrol that Ranke is captain of.

"Captain Ranke, I thought I saw something moving in the distance there towards the east. Look, there! It is definitely something moving there in the shadows." The young warrior states.

Ranke moves to where the position of the warrior and peers into the dark forest. He as well can see something moving. He can see small glimmers of light reflecting off something in the distance. The glow of the horses above illuminates small patches below on the ink-like water below. Another warrior now to the west also notices something moving as well. Doldren can see something moving too. Drash'Ur with his keen sight can see some movement where he is located as well. He notices tall, dark, shadowy forms moving and around the large mishappened trees that are dotted throughout the strange dark swamp. He immediately grabs his horn and blows it in short blasts, seven in total. This was a signal to the entire band that an eminent threat was present. The generals leading the band along with the chief captain hear the horn blasts signalling an unknown threat. A threat that is encroaching upon their position under the cover of dark. Letete motions to his chief captain Thaddeus to begin the maneuvers. "Warriors Eighty, form the phalanx! The rest tortoise formation!" Thaddeus shouts the command. The warriors begin to pull in close with their hands on their swords ready to unsheath them if necessary. Letete yells out a command.

"Generals, Captains and Warriors stand your ground and let nothing pass! You are more than any terror that creeps in the night! Lucas, Thaddeus! Ready your swords! Outer patrol, ready your swords!" Letete belts out a command.

One by one like a cascade of greenish blue torchieres being ignited. Fiery luminous swords are drawn by the outer patrol, eighty strong and courageous men stand ready to face an unseen threat. Letete and Lucas set their visors on their helmets and instantly their helmets ignite with the same greenish-blue flame. The same fiery flare adorns their swords and chest plate. The winged horses encircle above watching keenly the theatre unfolding below.

"We are ready for whatever may come! Stand your ground men!" Thaddeus says. Letete responds in unison as they both share a thought.

"Bring It!"

At that moment, the water in every direction with exception towards the falls edge begins to ripple like a small tidal break that is headed for the warrior band. Something is moving quickly below the water's surface. The ripples grow larger and quicker and at a certain moment and distance completely stop. It feels like time has ceased and stood still on its point. The wind can be heard whistling through crooked trees and twisted branches. Then suddenly a large shadowy form emerges quickly from below the water's surface. It is dark, scaly and quick. It lunges and catapults itself towards the outer band of warriors standing ready at the western portion of the militia. It is where Ranke is standing as a captain. Instinctively, Ranke extends his sword and leaps in the direction of the descending creature. He strikes the creature on the left side of its head sending it torquing in a completely different direction than the direction of the militia. The creature shrieks in pain as the left side of its face is lacerated by Ranke's blade. It splashes and dives below the surface of the water and completely disappears.

"Good show son! Make sure to hold that line!" Thaddeus says to Ranke.

An instance later. Two other creatures emerge from the dark murky swamp catapulting themselves towards the militia. Then three more followed by four more. They are held back by the warriors, but some begin to worry. One of the warriors begins to panic. His panic is followed by fear. His fear draws the creatures towards him. They are not just scaly creatures like that of some indigenous reptile to the swamp, but they are Fear Mongers of the Ophidian clan. They feed on fear and they are drawn to it like a moth to a flame. Several creatures manage to swim below the surface of the water unnoticed and unseen by the patrolling warriors. Three of the large scaly lizards manage to spring out of the water and descend on the warriors below. Most of them hold the line raising their shields to deflect the beast while gouging bits of the large reptilian creatures with their swords. But one warrior begins to doubt. He darts from the ranks of the militia dropping his shield in the dark waters of the swamp. He runs through and breaks the outer patrols line.

"Nooo! Stand on the inside of the outer line." Ranke shouts.

But before he can finish his statement, the young man now in full panic throws down his sword. It momentarily splashes in the inky waters below before it then springs and levitates vertically just above the surface. As the man continues to run and scream, parts of his armor begin to fall from him. The Fear Mongers can smell his fear and quickly pounce on him dragging him screaming and flailing below the surface. Letete and Lucas see what has taken place and respond quickly.

"Hold the line! We have to stop this!" Letete shouts.

In a quick move, he catapults himself in the general direction of where the young man disappeared several yards away. Lucas is close behind. Letete, as he lands on the surface of the water strikes his sword on the surface which displaces it down to the muddy floor of the swamp below. Lightning laced with fire separate and part the water in the direction of where he last saw the young man who was taken. Several reptiles are enveloped in the energy blast and are thrown several feet in every direction along with mud, stone and vapor.

"Whooooaaa! That has to sting somethin' bad!" Lucas exclaims releasing a childish chuckle.

The young man can be seen sprawled on the floor of the swamp below. The water begins to return to where it was displaced from.

"Go now! Get him and bring him back!" Letete shouts to his younger brother Lucas and Thaddeus.

"With pleasure!"

He and Thaddeus leap effortlessly, covering the distance in one leaping bound. Lucas upon lighting on the ground from his leap encounters two of the Ophidian clan who are in a rage from the sword strike of his brother. They begin a frenzied attack run in the direction of Thaddeus and Lucas.

"Get him back to the ranks, they are mine!" Lucas shouts.

In cat-like movement Lucas meets the charging reptilian duo with flips and torques that end in sword strikes that instantly disable the towering lizards.

"That's going to leave a mark!" Lucas says with a chuckle.

He manages to reunite with Thaddeus as they both manage to bring the captured soldier back to the band of warriors. Ranke motions to the inner testudo of warriors to take the startled and drained soldier back behind the militia's line. One of the warriors reaches down into the murky water to pick up the warriors shield which can be seen glowing, just submerged in the ink-colored waters.

"Here warrior, you will need your shield this night!" The warrior nods his head and rights himself.

He holds out his hand towards the still levitating sword which returns to him instantly.

"Are you ok warrior? Are you fit to fight?" Letete asks the wearied warrior.

"Yes, yes I am. I won't drop my shield again. Thank you for saving me generals."

"Remember, no one left behind and never lose your faith!" Lucas retorts.

At that moment, Drash'Ur blows his horn again signaling another round was about to start.

"They are coming in again! Steady yourselves!" He cries.

All of the warriors turn and ready themselves for what is surely to be a hard-fought battle. The horses above begin to hover a little closer to be prepared to offer cover fire for the warriors below. Letete and Lucas stand with sword ready, drawn and fiery. Letete begins to repeat a phrase from a scripture that his father used to read to him and his brother every night.

"Thou shalt not be afraid for the terror by night..." Letete says aloud.

"Nor for the pestilence that walketh in darkness!" Lucas continues.

"Ready yourselves men and stay your fears and congregate on courage!" Thaddeus shouts.

Drash'Ur releases a long shrill of a trumpet blast louder than he has ever blown before. It echoes throughout the night time sky rolling through the moors and trees.

"Give them your swords!" Letete shouts just as the murky water rolls towards the clan from every direction.

Then at a distance just before the encircled warriors, the Fear Mongers leap from their watery confines and pounce on the out band of warriors. The Mongers are a part of the Ophidian clan of the reptilian creatures loyal to the beast called Tannim. The chosen eighty are quick in their response. They are decisive with each lightning clad blow to the attacking reptilian marauders. Fear which fed the Mongers earlier ceases to be a food to feast on for the creatures are overwhelmed by the magnitude of the response. The power and nimbleness of the warriors is like nothing the Fear Mongers have ever faced. Ophidian clan are seen being tossed to and fro as they release blood curdling screams from the pain of fiery swords strikes.

"Advance the second movements!" Captain Thaddeus shouts.

The planning and training of the warriors seem to have paid off as a second smaller band moves in a concentric formation to support the outer eighty. The additional formation of just thirty warriors moves into position just to the right of the original eighty warriors who were standing their ground against the initial surge.

"Take back the ground and drive them into the forest!" Captain Thaddeus shouts.

The original eighty warriors begin to push back the attack Ophidian clan deeper and deeper, away from the group. The thirty now stand at the ready just behind the first wave to finish off anything that manages to get past the first hedge.

"Well done warriors of Rose Shar'on!" Letete shouts.

Letete motions to Lucas carry out the next maneuver. Lucas nods in agreement and whistles for his horse Lightning Sky. His steed lights just before him and Lucas in one singular motion mounts his winged companion.

"Ride Lightning Sky!" He Shouts.

The other winged horses are still flying patrol just above the fray below. Lucas flies low and fast in between the warriors eighty and the supporting band of warriors just behind them about thirty yards or so. Anything that managed to get past the first two hedges are immediately dealt with by Lucas and Lightning Sky. The inner core of gathered Soldiers are still in the tortoise formation. To two outer rings are still holding their own as planned with Lucas and the winged horses giving cover from above. At that moment, there can be seen another wave of Ophidians approaching from the distance with bow and arrow. Letete signals to his brother and each captain of the outer ring to fall in closer and pull back. The circle of warrior collapses on itself and forms a tight phalanx of both the eighty and the thirty. Lucas and the winged steeds fly to higher altitude to move beyond any potential range.

Then it happens with no signal or warning. The arrows are lit, and fiery darts are rained down upon the warriors. They fall in close and link their shields which expand because of the incoming darts. Not one warrior is injured by the incoming projectiles. At that moment, Lucas pulls hard on the reigns of his steed Lightning Sky and nose dives with extreme speed towards the line of Ophidians with arrows. Lightning Sky releases an incredible charge of lightning from its mouth and eyes. The resulting arc of energy rips through the swamps surface and displaces the line of lizards in every direction. But following close behind is Fire Sky and Aquis. Fire Sky ignites the floor below then is up like a flash followed by Aquis who instantly freezes the water below creating a wall of ice around the entire band of warriors. The Warriors all stand and cheer! They momentarily break rank and celebrate what seems to be a sure victory. Lucas hovers with his horse and the others just above the band towards the rear. He turns to see his brother facing him with his fiery sword thrust into the air cheering with Thaddeus and the others.

Then suddenly, Lucas notices a small petit figure standing behind Thaddeus and Letete about twenty yards or more near the edge of the strange waterfall. Illuminated clouds of steam and smoke are the backdrop for the strange theatre that is beginning to take place. Letete sees the look on his brothers face and sense what he is thinking. He turns quickly to see that it is Qrueinen standing precariously near the falls edge. He immediately calls out to her. "Qrueinen! Don't move!" He shouts.

Lucas sensing something that is not quite right about the theatre that is unfolding instinctively pulls hard on the reigns of his winged steed. As he begins to accelerate towards his brother who is running towards the girl, Lucas notices something strange about the amorphous columns of steams and smoke just beyond the falls edge. It appears that the clouds are beginning to glow brighter and brighter with each passing second. Then suddenly it can be seen! A large flume of fire pierces the cloud of steam and smoke. It is heading directly at Letete.

"Look out!" Lucas screams but the flume completely envelops his brother.

It flows over and around him even reaching to the first line of warriors who instinctively raise their shields. As the fire dissipates, Lucas is relieved to see his brother crouched low and on one knee with his shield extended and expanded to give him complete cover from the fiery deluge. He peers back towards Qrueinen who now crouched low on the falls edge and screaming in terror. What appears next completely shocks and surprises the warriors and the two young generals. A large talon can be seen emerging from the steam and smoke laden cloud. It grabs Qrueinen who screams even louder than before. As the talon grabs the young girl, the full image of the attacking beast is seen breaking the bank of the cloud.

"Oh nooo! It can't be!" Letete exclaims.

It is the Ash Breather. He chuckles fiendishly and disappears into the midst with the girl screaming in terror. Letete's anger swells inside of him. He covers the distance as quick as a falling star and catapults himself into the air hurling with his sword drawn overhead hoping to land a blow directly across the top of the beast's skull. "Noooo! Letete!" Lucas shouts.

He pulls and torques hard on the reigns and increases his speed. He sees just to his left a winged fiery comet hurl past him at incredible speed. He sees his brother miss the target that turns and flies off out range. Lucas sees him fall just below the fall's edge disappearing out of sight followed by the winged comet of a horse called Fire Sky. Lucas's horse clears the edge and tucks its wings and plummets over the edge into an almost opaque mist.

"Come on big bro! I hope you made it! Letete! Letete! Can you hear my thoughts?" Lucas says to his brother with no response.

As his horse is in a complete nose dive over the edge of the cliff, Lucas can see whisps and billows rush by him giving him momentary glimpses of the floor below. Then suddenly he sees it! What his heart had hoped for beyond all hope! Fire Sky managed to catch the falling warrior before he hit the rocky floor below.

"Whooooo Hooooo! Yes! Good catch Fire!" Lucas exclaims as his horse levels off and is on the same trajectory as his speeding brother just ahead of him.

"Letete, are you okay? Man, you really freaked me out!" Lucas exclaims.

"Yes, yes I am! Did you see him! The Breather is back and he has Qrueinen!" Letete exclaims.

"Yes, I did! We will get her back and if he harms on hair on her head, I will make him pay!" Lucas retorts.

It is a matter of seconds before Lucas has managed to catch up with his brother. They both watch as the Ash Breather lands just below on the rocky canyon floor below. It is filled with fire pits and reaks of sulfur and ash. Stalagmites dot the canyon floor like that of teeth of some ravenous beast. The Beast lands on one of the larger structures with girl grasped in one claw. The brothers hover just in front of the beast. Letete wastes no time in issuing a threat.

"Ash Breather! Release her now or will run you through with my sword!"

The Breather chuckles and holds the now listless girl over a jagged ridge of sharp stony structures.

"Oh, really now fleshie! Do you want her to fall to her death on the rocks below? If that is your wish, then I will grant it!" The Breather says mockingly feigning to release the girl to her demise.

"Nooo! Don't drop her!" Letete says.

"Oh, come now hero, which is it? Release her, don't release her I really wish you would make up your mind!" The Ash Breather says mockingly with a fiendish chuckle.

"You see fleshie, you thought this was over! But truly it is the beginning. The beginning of your end!"

"If you harm her, if anything happens to her lizard, I will destroy you!" Lucas retorts.

"Yes, you! I have not forgotten you, little one. I have a score to settle with you!" The Ash Breather says ominously holding up a maimed claw that was dealt to him by the youngest brother.

"ENOUGH OF YOUR TALK! BREATHER! Release her gently to the floor below and we will spare your hide for maybe a moment!" Letete exclaims.

"Arrogant, arrogant worm! How dare you talk to me with such insolence! I am Ash Breather!"

The Beast retorts as he hurls a large flume of fire towards the two heroes. They manage to deflect the fiery deluge with their shields. Once the deluge is past, they lower their shields to see the Breather further away in a cleared area that is not as congested with the stone structures that dart the canyon below. They notice that the Breather has momentarily placed the girl on the canyon floor. Even though it is an area that is a little clearer than the rest, Letete can see that it will not be enough room to navigate with both horses on the canyon floor.

"Already ahead of you big brother."

Lucas dismounts and slides in a spiral down one of the stone pillars protruding from the canyon floor. Letete follows suit. They both motion to their steeds to hover above and to cover them. The Ash Breather reaches again for the girl with one of its talons and clinches it together picking up the listless form of the girl.

"Do you think she is alright Letete?" Lucas asks as he positions himself near a tall, stalagmite structure.

"I hope so. If something happens to her, it will be my fault!"

"Before you try anything heroic, I have an ultimatum to propose. Drop your weapons or the girl is no more!"

"We will not! We will do no such thing!"

"Hey, wait a minute Lucas, wait. We need to save the girl. We need to save Qrueinen!"

"Hey, don't speak out loud, the creature can hear you. I know that she needs saving but use your head. If we drop our weapons, we will have no way to help her!"

"Drop your weapons and send those creatures above away or the girl will be destroyed."

"No Breather! We do not trust you!" Lucas says.

"Wait, if we promise to do what you ask, will you release her?" Letete asks the Breather.

"What are you doing? Don't trust him! He wants to destroy us all. We should never give in to his demands." Lucas now says to his brother audibly.

The Breather can sense their conflict.

"Elder fleshie, surely the younger does not care for the girl as you do. Send him away as well and you and I can come to an accord to save the girl!"

Letete looks at his brother in a strange manner.

"No! No! No! Don't even think about it! I am not going to leave you here with that thing with no weapons! He is lying! Dad said that we should always be there for each other! I won't allow it!"

He instantly catapults himself towards the direction of the Ash Breather who is caught unaware. Lucas hurls a charge of fire and lightning towards the direction of the beast while Lightning Sky above matches his attack.

"Nooooo! I said stand down! I am the general and that is a command! Lightning Sky, Fire Sky! Fall back now!" Letete shouts.

The Ash Breather raises three of its remaining talons in a threatening manner.

"I will take my talons and run her through! Relinquish your weapons now!" The Breather threatens.

"Okay! Okay. Just don't hurt her!" Letete responds.

"No Letete, don't do this!"

Lucas watches helplessly as his brother lays down his sword and shield. He begins to feel something that he has not felt in sometime since coming to this alien world...fear.

"Now you little hero, discard your weapons!"

Lucas reluctantly lays down his sword next to his brothers. He clinches to his shield tightly holding it to his chest.

"Drop your shield now!"

Lucas reluctantly drops his shield letting it fall hard on the rocky canyon floor. The Ash Breather looks on with anticipation.

"Yes, that is a grand move fleshie. Now rid us of the company of those revolting flies above. Bid them to leave now!"

Letete motions to the winged steeds to leave. They both leave reluctantly and fly away to turn and hover just far away enough to still see their masters.

"Now I have you both! If it were not for my master, I would destroy you now! Ophidian clan take them!" The breather threatens.

"Wait what about the girl? You said you would spare her! Is she okay! Let me see her beast!"

"Yes, hero, I did say that. I will keep to our agreement. Here is your precious girl that you hold so dear!" The Ash Breather says with disdain as he tosses the girl in the direction of the two warriors.

Letete manages to catch her before she can hit the hard canyon floor. She is limp and not responding. Letete attempts waken her to see if she is harmed. Lucas stands nearby looking on and watching as the numbers of the Ophidian clan begin to swell.

"Qrueinen! Qrueinen! Are you okay? Answer me! If he has harmed you, I will make him pay!" Letete threatens.

She begins to stir and move. She places one hand on the cheek of Letete and begins to speak.

"Oh foolish, foolish boy! I am fine! It is you who needs saving now!"

She releases a hideous hissing sound and strikes Letete knocking him to the canyon floor. He stands quickly with the assistance of Lucas standing near him. They are both startled at what transpires next.

The girl Qrueinen sheds the form of a young maiden girl and morphs into the form of the serpentine dragon know as Slither!

"Nooooo! What have you done with Qrueinen?" Letete screams.

The serpentine dragon laughs and responds.

"My dear boy, I am Qrueinen! That is one of my names in your tongue. I am so moved that you have such a care for me!" The beast sarcastically replies.

"Take them to the master!"

Letete falls to his knees in a slump and simply cries for a moment then is silent. He looks up to see his brother in a panic strike several of the approaching Ophidians. There are so many of them. It seems to be a never-ending stream, Ophidian clan come from every side. He thinks of his friend whom he has lost and feels despair followed by...fear. His armor begins to drop from different parts of his body like leaves from a dying tree, piece by piece. Lucas the younger witnesses his Elder brother's sorrowful predicament and the same begins to happen to him. Fear begins to grip him and feels as real as any eminent grasps of the beasts that are encroaching upon him. His actions begin to show just how fear can affect those of younger years. He cries out his brother's name as he sees the Ophidian clan carry him off into the night. He tries to muster a retreat. He runs and attempts to hide behind a stone structure hoping to elude his pursuers. But they are unrelenting. Now sobbing, in a moment of panic and weakness, Lucas utters that certain phrase.

"Trumpet the adventure! Trumpet the adventure! Trumpet the adventure!"

And instantly, he disappears in a flash of light and smoke from sight.

EPILOGUE

*...but the Spirit of God was moving over the
surface of the water.*
Genesis 1:2

*But you will receive power when the Holy Spirit
has come upon you, and you will be my witnesses
in Jerusalem, and in all Judea and Samaria, and to
the farthest parts of the earth."*
Acts 1:8

Beginning in the Book of Genesis, Old Testament and New, God revealed His Spirit to mankind. He rested His Holy Spirit (Ruach Ha'Kodesh) on those that believed in Him in the Old Testament and resided His Spirit (Pneuma) inside the hearts of men that believed and trusted Him in the New Testament. He offers those that believe in Him, through Christ, His power and counsel through the Spirit.

These things have I spoken unto you, while *yet* abiding with you. But the Comforter, *even* the Holy Spirit, whom the Father will send in my name, he shall teach you all things, and bring to your remembrance all that I said unto you. Peace I leave with you; my peace I give unto you: not as the world giveth, give I unto you. Let not your heart be troubled, neither let it be fearful.
John 14:25-27

An Elder Brother torn between duty to a cause to help those less fortunate, his faith and the comfort of safety. The younger who desires to help but feels fear in the face of unsurmountable odds. What will be the fate of the two young heroes? And what of the menacing clans of Ophidians and the core of dragons lead by the dark and ominous Dragon Master called Tannim? Will the villagers survive the next wave of terror before the next Gibbous? How will the gathered band of warriors survive the onslaught without their young gifted generals?

To find out what happens next, read the upcoming Book Two of the Knights of the Rushing Wind Series.

Trumpet the Adventure!

Made in United States
North Haven, CT
18 February 2023

32782510R00118